BAG MEN

praise for **BAG MEN**

"*Bag Men* is terrific. The hard-knocks, hard-boiled world of Boston in 1965 is brilliantly re-created.... This book is pure pleasure."
—Scott Turow

"[A] crackerjack crime sizzler...An exhilarating page-turner."
—*San Francisco Chronicle*

"Cinematically sharp sequences, dead-on dialogue, poignant and painful insights, lean prose, vivid imagery, jaw-dropping surprises."
—*The Wall Street Journal*

"[A] terse, engrossing debut, which earns high marks for its original setting and plot."   —*Publishers Weekly*

"[Costello] subtly re-creates the Boston of three decades past, populates it with completely believable, vividly real characters, and provides a clever but plausible plot. This excellent thriller will have readers eagerly awaiting [his] next effort. Highly recommended."
—*Booklist*

mark costello

BAG MEN

a harvest book / harcourt, inc.

orlando / austin / new york / san diego / toronto / london

This is a work of fiction. A few small liberties have been taken with the
geography of Boston and certain dates in 1965. The rest is one big liberty.

www.HarcourtBooks.com

First published by W. W. Norton & Company in 1997

Library of Congress Cataloging-in-Publication Data
Available upon request
ISBN 0-15-602821-2

Text set in Transit 521 BT

Printed in the United States of America
First Harvest edition 2002

C E G I K J H F D B

for henry

1965

1

Ray Dunn parked his car behind the morgue truck, locked the doors, and trudged through flying snow. He counted three Buicks from Homicide, six blue-and-whites from the airport police, and Crime Scene's unmarked van.

A small man huddled by the chain-link fence, steering an umbrella into the wind. He wore a blue belted ski parka, orange mittens, a hat with flaps, and buckle-across galoshes.

"You Pringle?" Ray asked him.

Pringle nodded glumly, as if stuck with it. "You the DA?"

"Assistant DA. What seems to be the problem?"

"The problem? The problem is the dead man lying on my runway." Pringle's glasses fogged as he talked.

"What about him?"

"Look around you," Pringle said. "What do you see?"

Visibility was nil. "Not much," Ray said.

"*Snow* is what you see—a foot on the ground and more on the way. Up north and inland, it's even worse. We're the only civilian airport open above New Haven."

Ray was a diplomat. "Really?"

"Really. Airliners land *into* the wind, friend, which is presently fifteen knots, north-northeast, at the tower"—Pringle pointed over his shoulder—"but shifting to the south." Blinded by eyeglass fog, he shot a mittened hand southward, straight out. Ray ducked.

"If the wind keeps shifting, Five South-A will be the only usable runway at the only open airport in this part of the United States. There are twenty-one flights, a few thousand souls, waiting to land over our heads. They're running out of fuel at eight thousand feet."

"So land them," Ray said. "No one's stopping you."

"*He's* stopping me!" A knot of gawkers a few car lengths up stared at Pringle, who was windmilling with his free hand and bouncing the umbrella for emphasis.

Ray tried not to get poked in the eye. "He who?"

"The dead man!"

"Move him then," Ray said, stepping back from the dangerous Pringle.

"I tried. Some men from the morgue—not nice men, either—say nobody but them can move a corpse. A union thing."

"Teamsters," Ray sighed. "Let *them* move him."

"They won't, and I tried everything, including bribery. They took my money and laughed at me. I wrote their names down." He patted his pockets. "Something should be done about them."

"Why won't the morgue guys move the corpse?"

"They say the police have to sign for it first."

"Why won't the police sign for it?"

"They will, they *all* will, that's the problem. The Boston police and the airport cops started arguing about whose body it was. That was two hours ago."

Finally, Ray understood: BPD Homicide owned all murders in the city limits, but Massport Police was sovereign on Port property, Boston or not, and both departments claimed the case.

Ray walked to the gap in the fence, Pringle at his heels. Stringers from the *Globe* and *Record-American* waited by a trash can for anything that smacked of news. They passed a bottle back and forth, grumpy and uncomfortable. A detective guarded a hole in the fence, keeping them at bay.

Ray waved hello. "Happy New Year."

"Well, if it isn't the henchman, Mr. Dunn. About fucking time," the guy from the *Record-American* cracked.

"Any truth to the rumor that your narcs roughed up those three Negro kids outside the Sheraton on Christmas Eve?" the *Globe* asked, passing the bottle.

"Yeah," the *Record-American* said. "You ever gonna investigate what happened to those kids?"

Ray waved goodbye. He stepped through the slit in the fence, gathering the tails of his gray overcoat so as not to catch them on the clipped chain-link. As he did, his fedora was brushed off his head. The *Record-American* snatched it up and held it hostage.

"Give us a quote on the corpse at least," he said. "We're a pair of starving birds over here."

The detective seized the hat from the reporter's hands, knocking it to the snow again. Pringle, jostled, stepped on it.

The detective picked the hat up and passed it to Ray through the hole in the fence. Ray punched the galosh print out of the crown.

"You want a quote?" he asked the stringers, fitting the misshapen hat on his head with dignity.

"And a picture," the *Globe* said.

"You can get a picture when we come down the hill with the body. Here's your quote." Ray's voice went suddenly sonorous. "Just after dawn, officers of the Massachusetts Port Authority Police found the body of a male." This was the civil service speaking.

The stringers' pencils raced across their pads.

"While the identity of the decedent is not yet established—"

"Murder?" the *Record-American* asked.

"What color?" the *Globe* added, pencil in the air.

Their editors would need to know. Slain Caucasians went on page two. Everything else was space-as-available.

"Likely murder," Ray said. "Definitely white. Where the hell was I?"

"'Identity...decedent...not yet established,'" the *Record-American* cribbed from his pad.

"—however," Ray continued in his other voice, "detectives from Massport and the Boston Police Department are cooperating in a joint investigation—"

As he said this, a Massport lieutenant pushed the Homicide lieutenant into the snow up the hill, shouting, *"That corpse is yours over my dead body!"*

The *Record-American* stringer whistled. "Christ, what a quote."

Ray said, "Use that and I'll yank your creds." He could make good on the threat, and the stringers knew it. Ray was the DA's Mr. Fixit. He leaked lurid scoops to the helpful tabloids and sent pesky columnists to a colder place than this. It was one of many hats Ray wore under his fedora.

Ray left Pringle skulking at the fence with the *Globe* and *Record-American*. He hiked up a small rise to where the corpse lay. One runway over, a silver-bottomed jet dropped from the fog, appearing all at once, ghostly and majestic, its sound catching up to it a moment later. The jet sledded in for a rough landing, vanishing down the runway, throttling turboprops muffled in the snow.

Two teamsters from the morgue stood together, hands in armpits, watching the cops lock horns.

"Happy New Year, Guvinah," the teamsters sassed.

"The guy from the airport wants your heads," Ray said.

"Who, Pringle? He's our pal," one of the teamsters said.

"He likes to hand out money," the other said.

"And we just met him," the first man observed. "Nice hat, by the way."

"The corpse is *mine*," the Homicide lieutenant shouted, brushing snow off his ass, jaw to jaw with his Massport counterpart. The cops were about to brawl, eight or nine guys from Boston Homicide, all in plainclothes, versus a dozen blue uniforms from Massport.

Ray ignored them. Crime Scene technicians snapped pictures from fifty different angles of what was a fairly simple thing: one dead man in a fur-lined raincoat, name unknown. Port patrolmen walked grids, looking for Clues, like in the movies. The black asphalt runway, thirty yards across, was quickly snowing over.

The corpse lay under an Army-green tarp in the middle of a large circle of trampled slush, bloody in the middle, muddy toward the perimeter. The slush was littered with cigarette butts, canisters of film, gum foils, and crushed Styrofoam cups.

Ray dropped to his haunches and folded the tarp back. The corpse wore suede desert boots and tan corduroy pants. The left hand lay palm-up in pink snow. The right hand was across the corpse's chest. Blood from fist-sized head wounds had soaked the raincoat and frozen it stiff. The dead man looked like a professor of anthropology at a small college in Vermont, except for his face, which could have been anything.

"I'm thinking robbery-gone-wrong," a hovering Massport patrolman said to Ray, as if asked. "Prolly a hooker."

"Hooker?" Ray said. "Where do you get that?"

The patrolman squatted next to Ray and parted the stiff raincoat, revealing a gray crew-neck sweater and white turtleneck, which the Crime Scene men had scissored down the front. Under the turtleneck was a wraparound linen vest, also cut open by the cops. The patrolman peeled the vest away. Inside, where the vest met the skin, were a dozen rows of rough steel studs. The chest of the dead man was dotted with scars—new, old, and ancient—in the pattern of the studs.

"He was some kind of sex freak," the patrolman conjectured. "Pain is pleasure, pseudo-masochism, that type. Hires a gal for some kink, but the fun gets out of hand. She pulls a knife. They struggle and she cuts him. She panics, brains him, and clips his wallet and watch as an afterthought. Seen enough?"

"What knife? What cuts?"

The patrolman let the vest fall closed and pushed the corpse's sleeve up, exposing hashmark slashes on the inside of the forearm.

One looked recent. The rest didn't. Another plane boomed in next door, gear down.

Ray cadged a thermos top of coffee from one of the morgue drivers and tried to put everything he knew together in his head: professor arrives with one of last night's flights, or is here to meet a passenger, or to catch a plane himself, or none of the above. There was no blood leading back to the slit in the fence, so the beating happened here. Signs of robbery were present: the missing wallet, watch, and suitcase. But one big thing didn't fit: rob-murders were generally businesslike; whoever killed the professor lingered here to beat his face off. Whoever killed him hated him.

Ray called the cops into a huddle. "Enough's enough," he said. "I want a canvas of the whole airport. Massport, handle that. Talk to everybody—and check the trash cans between here and the front gate. See if whoever took this guy's wallet threw it away. I need to report to the DA tonight, so get back to me by dark. I'll follow the body to the autopsy. Call me there with something good."

Ray buttonholed the teamsters and snatched their paper-work, scrawling a big R.D. across the bottom. The two morgue-men tucked the tarp around the corpse. Each grabbed an end and struggled toward the hole in the fence. Ray led the way, coattails dramatic in the wind, looking like a general at Stalingrad. The stringers, snapping pictures, were in heaven.

The duty ME for January 1 was Herr Doktor Gunther Lubash. Big and ruddy, pushing eighty, Lubash was basically deaf. He played Strauss waltzes ultraloud as he sectioned corpses. If the mood was right—and when wasn't it?—he hummed along.

An assistant stripped the airport man, removing the strange studded vest last of all. As the corpse was prepared, Lubash donned a vinyl apron, put a record on a battered phonograph, and turned the volume up.

"Called 'Danube Maidens,'" Lubash shouted. "Nice, ya?"

Ray gave the deaf coroner a thumbs-up and said, "Dreadful." He leaned against the cold tile wall, cracked his neck, and popped in a stick of gum.

Lubash stepped up with two gloved hands in the air, maestro-like. He inspected the corpse, top to bottom, humming all the way. Nothing between any of the toes, soles of the feet normal. He traced the muscles of each leg to the base of the scrotum, and pushed aside the testicles for a peek at the anus. The assistant fed a hose down the dead man's throat and pumped his stomach into a jar. Ray thought he saw cashew bits swirling in the clouds of bile. Next up, "The Blue Danube."

Ray said, "Check out the defensive wounds on the forearm."

Lubash gave a cheery nod, no idea what Ray said.

"*Defensives*," Ray shouted, making slicing motions up the inside of his own arm.

Lubash examined the fresh and healed incisions on the inner arm, then ran his glove tips over the dotlike scars patterning the chest. He made Ray and the assistant flip the corpse on its stomach, uncovering another lattice of scars across the back. Lubash spent a long time on the dead man's back, from the top of the buttocks to what was left of the skull. The assistant rolled the corpse over. Lubash went at the chest with a surgical saw.

The Strauss, the saw, and the off-key crooning drove Ray to a pay phone in the corridor. He dialed the Massport Police and got an update.

The airport cops had found a few good witnesses. An International Arrivals skycap had seen a white man in a tan raincoat rushing through the terminal at about nine o'clock the night before. The man stumbled over a miniature Christmas tree, nearly broke his neck, but kept right on going out the last door on the southern end of the terminal, a hundred yards from the stretch of runway where the body was later found. Others saw a second man go out the door just after the man in the raincoat. Ray jotted the pursuer's description on an index card: male white, stocky, young, in a black knit cap and a blue peacoat.

Ray chomped gum. "What else?"

A wallet had been found by the side of an access road on the outskirts of Logan. The wallet was empty except for a driver's license in the name of George D. Sedgewick, 48 Montvale Ave., Stoneham. TWA said a G. Sedgewick had landed the night before with the seven-thirty from Rome via London. The blizzard had stacked planes halfway to Halifax, so the Rome-London-Logan had come in an hour late. Add fifteen minutes for passport control and five for luggage, and George Sedgewick would be in the terminal more or less when witnesses saw the man in the raincoat.

There was more. Boston Homicide had sent a unit out to Stoneham to see if George Sedgewick had made it home from Rome the night before. 48 Montvale was otherwise known as the Church of Mary Queen of Angels, Roman Catholic.

The cops spoke to the housekeeper who answered the door at the rectory, a Mrs. Zimquist. The housekeeper confirmed that George Sedgewick owned a tan raincoat, desert boots, and a gray crew-neck sweater, and hadn't arrived from the airport the night before. Mrs. Zimquist also told them something else: George Sedgewick was a priest.

"Who else knows the dead man's a priest?" Ray asked the Port lieutenant.

"Just me and my guys and the BPD. That's it, I think."

"Make sure," Ray said. "No leaks, you get me? It's important."

Ray hung up as Lubash stepped out of the autopsy theater. Lubash pulled a flask from his back pants pocket and took a drink.

"I'm going to see the DA," Ray yelled. "What do I tell him?"

Lubash smacked his lips, exhaling schnapps fumes. "Cause of death is massive blunt trauma. Manner of death is multiple blows to the cranium."

"We're thinking he's a sex freak," Ray said. "What with that S&M undershirt and all."

The assistant pushed the gurney past them, wheels squeaking all the way to cold storage.

Lubash laughed and took another swig. "The 'sex freak undershirt,' the thing with studs? Is called *scapular*. I have not seen one since I was a young doctor working countryside in Austria, but I am sure. Scapular is worn by religious people who have sins. The pain from the studs"—Lubash laced his fingers across his own barrel chest—"is supposed to purify. Every time you move, it cuts. Every time it cuts, you remember the bad thing you did. The 'defensive wounds' on forearm? These have almost no serration."

"Meaning?"

"Self-inflicted," Lubash said. "Some are over and over: man cut himself, heal, cut himself again. They call it scourging."

"So he's not a sex freak?"

"Maybe man like unusual sex, and maybe this is why he thinks he must wear scapular. Maybe he did something else in his past he feels bad about."

Ray's head swam. "Like what?"

The coroner polished off the schnapps and shrugged. "That's *your* job."

2

Ray Dunn rang the doorbell of the Honorable Johnny Cahill, District Attorney for the County of Suffolk. The doorbell was vintage Johnny: a six-gong chime—the fight song of the Boston College Eagles.

The DA opened the door. He wore a silk brocade gown over striped pajamas. "Jesus Christ, get in," he said. "It's cold as hell tonight."

Ray knocked the snow from his shoes and stepped into the DA's foyer. Johnny's manse was done in the faux-baronial splendor favored by successful Irish-American men of Johnny's generation. A fieldstone fireplace in the study burned logs for heat and imported peat for ambience. Above the fireplace was an elaborate coat of arms for the Clan Cahill or Cawill or Cael—they sold them to Americans in the Dublin airport duty-free shops. The walls of the study were crowded with antique maps of Eire and framed pictures of the DA with everyone that mattered: Mayors Curley, Hynes, and Collins, a line of governors, the Cardinal, Ted Williams, and, in a central place of honor, Johnny C. with old Joe Kennedy at a Friendly Sons of St. Pat's dance, flush-faced, years ago.

The study was linked by French doors to a heated indoor pool. Ray heard splashing and a woman's squeals, and knew that Eddie Cahill, the DA's playboy son, was home. Ray and Eddie Cahill had been classmates at BC Law. Eddie was clever and lazy. He had been an assistant DA in his father's office for a few months after graduation, until he found that crime victims, as a group, got on his nerves. He'd quit and built a lucrative practice chasing ambulances, but in his personal life he was almost monumentally careless.

Ray had rescued Eddie Cahill from a lot of bad publicity as a favor to Eddie's all-powerful father. When Ray was a young DA, Johnny Cahill dispatched him to Miami to snuff a vehicular assault beef and get Eddie out of the Dade County Jail. Later a girlfriend of Eddie's killed herself with pills, and the DA sent Ray to ransack her apartment and find her diary. Ray asked his boss if he wanted the diary brought back so the DA could read about his libertine son, but Johnny was very clear: "*Burn it,*" he said.

Then there was the abortionist in Fall River, who got an envelope of money from Ray, and a loan shark in East Boston, who got money and a warning. "Go near the DA's kid and I'll be back with an arrest warrant," Ray told him. A few years back, Ray found himself dragging Eddie out of a blackmail trap. A local tinhorn had some pictures of Eddie with a teenage girl. Ray showed up, seized the pictures and the negatives, sent the grifter to prison for parole violations, and gave the girl a bus ticket to Los Angeles after convincing her she was pretty enough for the movies.

Whenever Eddie Cahill got himself jammed up, Ray bailed him out. Whenever Ray did one of these "jobs," he grew closer to Johnny.

"You think my father really cares about you?" Eddie asked as Ray drove him home after some escapade. "He doesn't," Eddie said. "You're an errand boy to him. The minute you ask him for something—something you really want—he'll chuck you out. You hate me, don't you?"

"Actually, Eddie, I couldn't care less."

"Of course you hate me. You hate me because I've got something you want badly, and I don't even *deserve* it."

"What would that be?"

"My father's love," Eddie said.

Ray had joined the District Attorney's office in 1957, and rose through the ranks. He was promoted to deputy chief of trials in '59, counsel in '62, first assistant DA in '64. As first assistant, he ran the office day-to-day and oversaw the investigative units— Vice, Rackets, Homicide, and Narco. He also personally handled Johnny's "special projects," like the bloody clubbing of a Catholic priest with sins on his conscience and scars on his chest. Ray was thirty-three and on the fast track.

Johnny handed him three fingers of Bushmills in a Wexford crystal tumbler as Ray shed his overcoat.

"How was Logan?" Johnny asked, returning to the fire.

Ray placed his tumbler on the coffee table. Johnny always poured Ray whiskey, though Ray didn't drink. "The cops got themselves into a jurisdictional pretzel," Ray said. I worked it out."

"That's the boy. Papers show?"

"A couple of stringers, *Globe* and *Record-American*. They asked about the Negro kids."

"You say anything?"

"No."

"They know anything?"

"No."

Johnny nodded. "Don't give me that look."

"What look?"

"The long face. You don't approve?"

"Those Negro kids were from the Howard University Glee Club," Ray said. "They were scheduled to sing for the governor's wife at the Sheraton. The narcs roughed them up for no good reason."

"They were muggers," Johnny said.

Ray shook his head. "Glee Club, all three. Checked it out myself. The cops are lying to us, boss."

Johnny made a mock-horror face, like Buster Keaton seeing a ghost. *Lying? To us?* Then he looked bored. "You going soft?"

Ray was stung. "Just facing facts. The truth will come out eventually. About Operation Pressure Point, I mean, and the deal with Hanratty and the state rep. The whole truth."

Johnny got comfortable in the wing chair. "I've crushed bigger scandals in my jammies, kid."

"It's not the fifties anymore. Times are changing."

Johnny stirred the fire with a poker. He was worried, Ray could tell. Behind the old DA, in the poolhouse, Eddie and the girl played a form of water polo.

"We have a name for the airport corpse," Ray said. "George D. Sedgewick. He's a Catholic priest out in Stoneham."

Johnny pursed his lips. "My, my. He somebody?"

Meaning was Father George Sedgewick someone they should worry about, someone who could injure Johnny or his friends. Ray had whitewashed embarrassing priests for Johnny before—this was another specialty. There was the priest who ran the orphanage and spanked the boys bare-assed. There was the boozehound pastor who embezzled bingo money and blew it on his "niece."

"Don't know yet," Ray said. "Sedgewick died wearing a scapular—a vest of studs designed to hurt him every move he made. The cops think the scapular was part of a kinky sex game, and they want to start looking at hookers."

"Sounds like a priest with a skeleton in his closet," Johnny observed. He sipped Bushmills through a thin, connoisseurial smile. Church scandals were Johnny's candy. Whenever Ray tamped them down, the DA earned favors from Richard Cardinal Cushing, who was, when all was said and done, the biggest bastard in Boston.

"I hope none of this leaks out," Johnny said.

"I've got everyone in line."

Johnny smiled. "I'm sure you do. Do we buy the hooker theory?"

"We don't," Ray said. "Witnesses in the terminal saw a stocky male in a black knit hat following Sedgewick after his Rome flight landed. I think that's our guy."

Johnny warmed. "The priest did him dirt, somewhere, somehow, and the stocky fellow killed him for revenge. That explains the scapular and it motivates the killer." Johnny certainly hoped so. He could earn some chits from the Cardinal for covering it up.

The pool doors opened and Eddie Cahill paraded past wrapped in a towel, arm around a brunette, who pulled off a flowered bathing cap.

"*Raymond*," Eddie sneered.

"Have you met Eddie's fiancée?" Johnny Cahill said to Ray, who rose. Her name was Yvonne, and Eddie Cahill said he'd met her in Palm Beach, where she was a cocktail waitress. She was certainly tan. Ray noticed a white line where her wedding band belonged. Ray figured he'd be bribing her lawyer by Easter.

"Did you tell him yet?" Eddie asked his father.

"Tell me what?" Ray asked the DA.

"Get upstairs, you two," Johnny said to the swimmers. "It's cold as hell down here." Eddie and the cocktail waitress scurried out.

Johnny stoked the peaty coals. "She's a helluva girl," he said.

"She's married and you know it. Tell me what?"

Johnny stared at the knot in the belt of his bathrobe. "I been the DA for twenty-four years. It's time to go. Like you said, Ray, everything's changing."

Retire. Johnny shunned the word. He slapped his knees, coming to the point. "The politicians will ask you to stand for DA in November. And why not? You've run the shop the last few years. Might as well have the title to go with the headaches—that's what they'll tell you. But listen, Ray: don't do it. It's not in your best interests. I want you to stay on. Help my successor. Nobody knows the mechanics like you. And then, in a few years, I'll get you something good, a judgeship maybe, or a slot in my law firm."

Far back in Ray's brain, a bell went off. "Your successor? You have someone in mind?"

"Eddie," Cahill said. He talked fast, shifting into shameless hard sell. "Eddie's had his problems, I admit. You know better than anyone. But he's a talented lawyer and he's done a lot of growing up the past few years. He's human and he's made mistakes—"

"Mistakes?" Ray felt a head of anger rise. "We call them *felonies.*"

Johnny struck back hard. "And you've committed felonies to get Eddie out of trouble, haven't you? Breaking into that poor girl's apartment, paying all those little gratuities, threatening Eddie's shylocks with indictment. It's all quite *improper,* wouldn't you say?"

Johnny draped a hand on Ray's shoulder, softening the blow. "It stinks, I know. You're angry. You're disappointed. Of course you are. But you've been more than an aide to me, Ray. You've been like family. And that's why I feel I can ask you to make this sacrifice for my family—for *our* family."

Ray was stumbling out of the study, hat on, coat off, before he knew exactly what was happening. As he crossed the DA's snowy lawn, he heard Johnny at the stoop calling his name.

Ray dropped his car keys in the snow and stooped to find them. Johnny gave up yelling and went inside, closing the door and shutting off the front walk light, leaving the first assistant DA on his hands and knees.

3

Ray's wife was picking up the living room when he straggled home.

"Remember me?" Ray said.

Mary-Pat Dunn had an empty wineglass in her hand. "Remember dinner? It was four hours ago."

Ray hung his things in the hall closet. A picture about Tangier was open on the floor, along with a copy of *Life* and some record albums, in and out of sleeves. Joan Baez revolved in the corner, waiting for the needle. They had moved to this house a year before, when Ray became first assistant, but the place still looked empty. It was all the rage in Sweden, apparently—something called "minimalism." Ray figured Mary-Pat was too busy with her causes to shop for chairs.

He sat on the couch and she joined him, folding her legs under her butt. She wore the latest fashions for pretty Catholic wives: brown rayon stretch pants and matching slippers, white cotton blouse with puff sleeves, a tiny gold-plated crucifix at her throat.

"You get your man?" she asked.

"My man?"

"The murder at the airport. I heard it on the news. Priest found bludgeoned. You get the bad guy?"

"They said a priest?"

"Found bludgeoned," she confirmed.

Ray yanked his tie loose. The leaks were starting already.

She read his face. "Was it bad?"

"Fairly bad. The priest was wearing a scapular when he died.

It's like a wraparound vest lined with rough metal studs. Sinners wore them a hundred years ago."

"How gruesome," she said, getting up from the couch and slipping Joan Baez back in her cardboard sleeve.

Ray saw a second wineglass under the coffee table. "Company come?"

"The Hunger Group was over."

The Hunger Group was Mary-Pat's new passion—a circle of activists who met to discuss malnutrition in the ghetto. Their guru was a man named Win Babcock, bright light of the local left. Babcock drank wine and loved Joan Baez. Lately, so did Mary-Pat.

"Doesn't *look* like the Hunger Group was here," Ray said. They usually ate like pigs and left a mess.

"Win stayed behind and helped clean up."

And sat on the carpet, because that's where his glass is, and you sat with him, because nobody sits on the carpet alone.

She shut off the hi-fi. "What's wrong?"

Ray lay out on the couch. "Johnny Cahill is retiring."

"Good," she said, with venom. Whenever Ray came home late, he told his wife everything he had done that day, from beginning to end, as if confessing. She heard about his honest work and about the bad things too—the bribed abortionists and burned diaries, the black-bag jobs for Johnny C., the scandals throttled in the cradle. Ray couldn't bear the thought of her loving someone else, even if the someone else was just himself cleaned up. He had no feel for honesty; he knew he was telling the truth only when she recoiled. Anything short of that might be sugarcoated. It was hell on Mary-Pat, of course, and she blamed Johnny Cahill.

"Is it cancer?" she asked. "In the colon, I hope."

"He wants to anoint his son as the next DA. He wants me to stay on as Eddie's first assistant."

"Quit," she said. "Run against them. Beat them all, Ray. *You* should be the DA. God knows you've earned it."

They had covered this ground many times; Ray could have the conversation in his head and save her the trouble. Ray didn't have the money or the stomach to take on Cahill's machine. He'd point out that Cahill had a dump truck full of dirt on Ray and on Ray's father, the famous cop and dead bag man, Tim Dunn. She would retort that Win Babcock said *this,* and Win Babcock said *that,* the voters want change, the machine's a dinosaur, and anything is possible—

"You *have* to stand up to Cahill," she said. "Jesus, be a man. You're afraid of them—"

"Do you have any idea what running against Johnny means?"

"Yes, Ray, I read the paper. Books, sometimes, too."

"It means that our lives will go under the microscope. Johnny will sling mud—at me and at my da. They'll go back to the old days if they have to."

"I see," she said. *The microscope. The mud. The old days.* The conversation always left them where they started, trapped by the past, trapped by each other. Win Babcock never made her feel this way.

"The boys asleep?" Ray asked.

He saw her nod on her way upstairs.

Ray lay on the couch until he was sure that she was asleep, then went into the kitchen, made a chicken sandwich, and climbed the stairs as softly as he could. His sons slept together in the back bedroom. Ray Jr. was eight. Timmy was seven. Baby Stephen, in a tall crib by the door, was their Christmas present from a year ago. Ray stood in the doorway and chewed.

Ray Dunn was the product of a certain time and place: Boston, the Depression, and the war. His three sons, with their toy astronauts and Montessori schoolbooks, were strangers to him.

Ray was born in a cold-water tenement on D Street, Telegraph Heights. When he was older than the baby, but not as old as Timmy and Ray Jr., he learned that the Communists in Spain were raping nuns, or so people said. Ray asked his mother where the Communists lived, and his mother got vague.

"They started in Russia," she said, "but now they're everywhere."

The only place Ray knew besides D Street was Ireland, from Da's stories of milking cows and feeling lucky that you had a cow, but Ray knew the Communists didn't live there because picture calendars from Ireland had rainbows all the time, like Paradise. Ray thought perhaps the Communists lived in this bad place called Roxbury. Ray's father went to Roxbury every morning and came back with stories that sounded like war. Uncle Gus Hanratty went with him, as did everybody's favorite drunkard, Jerry Drogheda. Sometimes they came back with cut knuckles or black toenails from kicking somebody hard.

"You should see the other guy," Gus Hanratty always said. "His *whole body's* black."

When Ray went to grade school, he saw a wall map. He realized Boston was a speck in one corner of the U.S.A., and Mother Ireland was puny. Russia, evil Russia, was ominously brown and three feet wide, so wide it fit its full name in black letters: THE UNION OF SOVIET SOCIALIST REPUBLICS. Russia made Ray shiver. What chance did Ireland, and D Street, and Ray, have against *that*?

Ray was a cop's kid. He thought everybody was. He thought all the men in Boston carried .38 revolvers in worn leather holsters. Da's gun smelled like holster, and his holster smelled like gun, and neither of them smelled like anything else. Ray thought all fathers got up at dawn, and put on woolen tunics with brass buttons that dug into your face when you hugged them, and met up with other men who dressed the same and had guns too. All kids had uncles like Gus Hanratty, who taught Ray and Ray's little brother secret code, which would surely foil the Communists when the Communists finally came: *EOT* meant End of Tour, when Da came home; *steady midnights* meant the months Ray never saw his father; a *beat* was a street, like Ray's own D street; a *sector* was a set of beats; a *precinct* was a *station*, and a station was a set of sectors. This was secret information, very, very serious, and Ray, the king of secrets, held it dear.

The only other place with things as serious was the Church. Ray sensed a deep connection between the cops and the Church: both had dark uniforms and special power, and both had secret code. The Church's code was called Latin, and the Church had *beats*, called *beatitudes*. The Church had stations too, called Stations of the Cross. There were fourteen Stations of the Cross and nine stations of the Boston Police Department.

But the more Ray learned, the less he understood. Mother said that it was a sin to use tobacco or alcohol, but Ray often got up early and found his father on the kitchen floor, bottle of Power's by his head, Uncle Gus and Jerry Drogheda draped all over the parlor furniture. Mother came out from the bedroom in the back of the flat, cursed the stink of booze and Lucky Strikes and socks, and dumped a glass of water on Da's face. Da sat up fast, like a puppet, reaching instinctively for his gun, which was usually someplace improbable, like the freezer. Da would poke Uncle Gus and Jerry Drog, who would sit up fast too. Mother fried them eggs and ham steaks in a skillet.

Ray won a scholarship to Xavier Prep when he was twelve, and started going crosstown by trolley every day. He saw slums from the elevated tracks. Roxbury went on forever, and looked nothing like D Street. It was smoky, and confusing, half torn-down, and this, somehow, embarrassed Ray, who buried his face in schoolbooks until the trolley crossed back to what he considered Boston. Ray saw that Roxbury cops hung out in small gangs around patrol cars, like men around a campfire, swapping laughs and counting money. Later, his da would come home from a midnight tour out of the Roxbury station, with black toenails or a sprained wrist, and say the sector was a madhouse.

"On the go all day, didn't have a chance to take a meal," he'd say. Mother would get a ham steak sizzling, her solution to everything. Ray would think: I was in Roxbury today too, and to me it just looked sad.

Everyone else seemed to get along fine. Biff was Ray's little brother. Like all the other kids around, Biff rooted for the Red Sox and the Allies, in that order. After Pearl Harbor, the Russians were good. After VJ Day, the Russians were bad. Ray tried not to notice that this made no sense.

Da was transferred twice or three times, Ray lost count. In '46, when Ray was fourteen, Tim Dunn wound up back in Roxbury with Jerry Drog and Uncle Gus, who was now Da's boss, and a whole new crew of rookie partners.

Da got quieter as he got older. He and Ma spoke less and less, and then not at all. Ray knew that something was wrong with his father, and he knew it had to do with his job and with money. When Ray went from Xavier Prep to Boston College in the fall of '50, Da paid for his whole freshman year up front, in cash. The same thing happened every September.

Then came the morning that Ray would never forget, when everything went wrong: a quiet Saturday in April '55. Biff was fifteen, a budding hoodlum who parted his hair with Kiwi XTRA Sheen cordovan brown shoe polish, enjoyed smut on the sly, and smoked Lucky Strikes. He preferred radio *Dragnet* to TV *Dragnet*, saw crusading cop Glenn Ford's wife get blown up by Lee Marvin sixty-two times in *The Big Heat*, memorized Mike Hammer's comebacks from *Kiss Me Deadly* when it doubled with *Chicago Syndicate* at the F Street Loews. Ray was twenty-three, living at home, a first-year law student at BC. Ray's mother had been after Da to beat the carpets, and at the breakfast table that Saturday morning, she handed her husband a baseball bat.

"Beat the carpets," she said.

Da took the bat from his wife, stood it against his chair, and went back to the sports page. Ma snatched the paper away from him.

"Start with the rug in the parlor," she said.

Da gestured at the sports page. "It's spring training," he said, as if the Sox couldn't make a move without him.

"Spring cleaning," she said, and cleared his plate.

Biff, in a shiny Elvis pompadour, licked his teeth and laughed.

Spring cleaning. Biff and Ray moved the couch and rocker and end tables from the parlor to the kitchen. Da helped them roll the carpet up, maneuver it out the front door of the flat and down the narrow tenement stairs to the stoop. They hung the heavy, ugly rug over an iron fence, and Da took a swing into the carpet, dead center. A puff of dust leaped up.

Ray remembered every detail: Harriet Dunn leaving for the grocer, buttoning her housecoat and tying a flowered scarf over her gray hair, squeezing past Ray and Biff, who hogged the stoop. Men in sport shirts washed their cars or fixed busted chairs and warped doors with their sons, suds and hosewater carrying wood shavings down the steep hill, where the Harbor sparkled blue. Da was soft in the gut and starting to sweat. He stripped down to a white T-shirt, laying his wristwatch, wallet, and bulky service .38 on the sidewalk between Ray's feet. Ray pulled his father's things closer as Tim swung the bat into the hanging rug.

"Let me," Biff said, hopping down the stool. Tim handed him the bat, and Biff hit the rug. *Thud.*

Biff looked up the street and stiffened. Ray followed his eyes and saw two men approaching. They wore black raincoats, collars turned up.

"Hey, Da," Biff said. "Look at me. I'm knockin' homers." He beat the carpet.

"I see you," Tim Dunn said, relaxed and smiling, his back to the men. Shafts of dust hung in the sun. Biff had a nice flat swing. *Thud. Thud.*

Da turned just then. The men in the raincoats were a car length away.

"Timothy James Dunn," one of them said. The other took a step closer, cuffs open in his right hand. He said, "FBI."

Upstairs in the flat, the phone started ringing.

Ray went to his father's side. They almost touched. Behind him Ray heard Biff drop the bat to the sidewalk.

"Go inside," Tim said to his sons.

"Get out of here," Biff shouted. He was at the stoop pointing his father's gun at the man with the cuffs. Biff had a mad look on his face and his bony finger on the trigger. The .38 was big-framed, old-style, and heavy. Biff aimed at the FBI agents with both hands. The phone upstairs kept ringing.

"Biff," Tim said, "put it *down.*"

Ray stepped in front of the agent with the handcuffs. Now Biff was pointing the pistol at Ray's chest.

"You heard Da," Ray said.

Tim took the gun from Biff and handed it, butt first, to the FBI agents. They cuffed Da from behind, Da looking at Ray and Biff as the agents patted him down. Da's lips moved. What was he saying? *Don't look* or *Go upstairs* or *Find your Ma.*

The phone rang and rang. The ringing followed Ray up D Street, when he ran to find his mother after the agents put Da in a car and pulled away. Biff ran after them, waving a bat. *"You lousy fucking FBI cocksuckers!"*

The phone was still ringing in Ray's ears when he and Biff

found their mother at the butcher's on the avenue, Ray and Biff babbling to her at the same time:

Ray: "Da's been arrested—"

Biff: *"Fucking lousy fucking fuck—"*

Ray heard the ringing as they sat in the flat until dark waiting for word from Vinnie Sullivan, their lawyer. When the call finally came, Harriet Dunn said, "Yes?" and "Yes," and then hung up.

"They gave him bail," she told her sons. "Da's coming home."

Biff exploded. *"Lousy bastards, Jesus Christ—"*

And Ray just heard the ringing in his head. He snuck out and bought a late-edition newspaper. Da had made page one: SIX NABBED IN PD SCANDAL. The feds said a bookmaker named Ed Weiss had paid Lieutenant Hanratty four hundred dollars a week, with Tim Dunn and Jerry Drogheda and three other cops as "bag men."

That's what the papers said: *bag men.*

Ray figured the FBI would try to trace where the bribes went. He envisioned a subpoena on the BC bursar, who would tell the world that Patrolman Timothy Dunn had bought his son a Jesuit education with money from a bookie. But Da had a stroke before his trial, and the subpoena never came. Ray scraped through law school with grants and loans and half a dozen part-time jobs. When he met a girl he liked, it took a month to get a night free and ask her out. Her name was Mary-Pat McCallion. Her father owned the biggest Chrysler dealership in Massachusetts, and her brother, Chipper, played hockey for Harvard.

They fell in love fast. People did that back then. After a couple of dates, she wanted Ray to have dinner at her parents' "place"—that's what she called it. Ray put her off with transparent excuses. She thought he had another girl and stopped returning calls. Ray gave in and explained the real reason he didn't want to meet her family.

"My father was Tim Dunn," Ray confessed. They were fighting in the doorway of her apartment. Ray was in his last year of law school.

"I'm sick of your excuses," she said, still too mad to let him in.

"He was the cop in the papers, the one that got arrested for bribery. The *Globe* called him a 'bag man.' He had a stroke and died before the trial, so nothing was ever proved, but still, that's who he is, or was, or whatever. Okay?"

"What's that got to do with you?"

"I'm his son," Ray said. Wasn't it obvious? Your da hung all over you, his good and his bad. You made a life in the hide of his reputation, until your sons inherited the mess.

She laughed. "Do you believe in horoscopes too, or just destiny?"

It slowly dawned on Ray that she meant it. It amazed him then. It amazed him now.

He went out to Dover, met her father and mother and brother, and no one even asked who his "people" were. Instead, they talked about movie stars and Ivy hockey and the latest line of Chryslers. Suddenly, Ray was free.

They got married at a lavish high mass outside Wellesley. Ray's side of the wedding mostly got lost on the drive out from Boston.

The reception was at a country club. A dance band played Ink Spots and Sinatra. Ray's cousins stampeded the lounge, which was lined with leather-bound volumes on fly fishing. They drank every drop of beer in sight, and stared at the walls in horror. *What kind of people put books in a bar? It's like selling shots at the library.* It seemed barbaric to them, disrespectful to the books and the booze.

Ray's little brother, Biff, then seventeen, got drunk and introduced himself to waiters, thinking they were with the bride. Ray's mother sat on the dais, wholly mortified. Toward the end, in a nod to the Boston crowd, the band did a waltz-time "Danny Boy," which was the insult Ray's cousins had been waiting for. They left in a caravan right about then and got lost on the way back to Boston.

After graduation, Ray started looking for a job. He had plenty of interviews—his in-laws saw to that. He went sailing with a law partner who had roomed with Mary-Pat's father at Colby. He went golfing with the president of the company that insured the Chrysler dealership. Ray was top of his class at BC Law, and he knew how to act around middle-aged men: sober, eager, pliant.

Mary-Pat had fallen in love with a handsome three-bedroom tudor near Jamaica Pond in West Roxbury. Her parents were fronting the down payment, and Ray could pay the mortgage with his salary at a downtown firm. But by then Ray had already called his father's pal Gus Hanratty, and asked if he knew anybody in the DA's Office. The betrayal of Mary-Pat was under way. Johnny Cahill had hired his new prosecutors for the year, but Hanratty cashed in favors galore and got Ray a meeting with Cahill himself.

A defining moment—high summer, 1957: Johnny Cahill in his sordid glory, Ray in a seersucker suit from Filene's Basement.

"You married a girl with bucks," Cahill said. "You got jobs out the ass—swank ones, too. Yet you want to work for me. That it?"

Ray felt ill. "Yes," he said.

"You're Tim Dunn's boy. D Street in the Heights." Cahill talked five minutes straight about D Street. He knew the pot-holes, the parish, the pols, and the precinct, knew Silent Tim Dunn and Gus Hanratty, Manny Manning and Jerry Drog, knew everyone and everything, Ray knew—or so it seemed. An awe-some performance, even for Johnny, who was then in his prime.

"You want kicks, that it?" Cahill asked. "See a little of the seamy side? Play at cops and robbers?"

"It's not a game," Ray said. Both of them thought of Tim Dunn, who had been both cop and robber.

Cahill nodded, point taken. "So, why? What the hell are you about, Ray Dunn?"

Ray wanted to see the world for itself. He wanted to see power naked. He wanted to see how bad it was. The truth was something like that. But Ray didn't owe Johnny Cahill the truth.

"Just hire me," Ray said.

"Got some spunk, do we?" Cahill smiled. "See you after Labor Day, kid. Now scram. I got a city to run."

That afternoon, Ray met his bride in a Howard Johnson's on Route 9 to tour her dream house. She was at the counter, doing lipstick in the reflection of a polished napkin holder, looking like Audrey Hepburn on a manhunt. Ray grabbed her from behind and she drove him to Jamaica Pond.

The real estate agent walked them through three bedrooms, kitchen, den, and breakfast nook, a finished basement with a washer-dryer combo, and a garage under the screened-in porch. The agent saved the backyard as a deal-clincher—a small but perfect lawn, sloping gently down to pine woods.

Ray sent the agent on his way and wandered along the treeline. He could hear the whine of cars on the Jamaicaway, but only faintly. He was just inside the Boston boundary. Beyond these trees was everywhere else. Mary-Pat watched him closely.

He walked back to her and said, "We can't afford it, Mary-Pat."

"Why not?"

"Because I'm not taking any of those jobs your da lined up."

"Why not?"

"Because I'm going to work for the district attorney."

She sat on the grass in a heap. Ray checked for dog shit, then sat down next to her.

She said, "Explain it to me, Ray."

"The DAs help people, Mary-Pat. They protect the innocent and serve the public. It's my dream." This was the first big lie of their marriage and also the last.

"That's beautiful," she said, and hugged him on the lawn. They went back inside the house, made love in the breakfast nook, then said goodbye to all of it. In September, he got married all over again—this time to Johnny Cahill.

Ray finished his sandwich and checked the boys. Ray Jr. moaned softly. Timmy, on the next bed, snored. The baby coughed, and Ray turned him on his side. Down the hall, Mary-Pat was long asleep.

Ray roamed the house, checking little things for flaws: the furnace sounded sooty, several doors weren't plumb, and the kitchen clock was three minutes slow. He switched the back porch light on and off to see if it worked. Outside, the snow was thinning.

This house was the seventh place he and Mary-Pat had lived in eight years together. First they tried Dover, with Mary-Pat's parents, but Ray's commute to the courthouse downtown was impossible. Then they tried D Street, with Ray's mother, but Ray's mother was impossible.

They rented a studio on Beacon Hill, and Ray started walking to work. Mary-Pat taught delinquents how to paint. When Ray worked late, she went alone to lectures by French Marxist priests. She was the kind of burning, do-good liberal turned out by Catholic colleges in the 1950s, and she thought their tiny apartment and Ray's job with the DA were grand adventures. She told everyone that her husband was a prosecutor, a crusader for justice. They moved again—a one-bedroom in Back Bay—and Mary-Pat got pregnant.

After Ray Jr. was born, Biff Dunn passed the police exam. Ray didn't want his brother on the force, and he and Biff stopped speaking for a while.

Mary-Pat asked her husband why. "Just let him join," she said.

"You followed your dream, why not let him follow his?" They were pushing Ray Jr. through Boston Common.

There were many safe answers to her question, but all of them were bullshit, and Ray had resolved not to bullshit her anymore. Her faith in Ray broke Ray's heart, so he let her in on the truth.

"I don't want Biff to become a cop because a lot of cops are crooked," he said. "They don't set out to be crooked, they just get sucked in. That's what happened to Da. That's what will happen to Biff."

"Biff says your father was innocent. Biff says that the tragedy was that he died before he could be exonerated."

"Biff's a fool."

"If cops are so crooked, why do you work with them?" She was baffled: how could Ray be a crusader if his cops were corrupt?

Ray stopped the baby carriage. "Do you really think I go out and do justice all day long? I don't. I help keep a lid on this city. That's what you married: a lid."

He turned on Mary-Pat. "Why are you crying?"

She wiped her face. "Because I'm pregnant again."

The birth of Timmy forced a move to the top floor of a drafty triple-decker in Hyde Park. Mary-Pat threw a housewarming party in November of '58, though they only had a floor, not a whole house, and it wasn't warm, even with the gas on high. Her brother, Chipper, brought a case of champagne and a Harvard classmate named Win Babcock.

Ray's people dropped by too. Biff was a rookie patrolman by then, and his date was, likely as not, a whore. They trooped up the wooden stairs with some goons from Narcotics.

The party was strangely edgy. Ray's mother came and left, apparently afraid that Mary-Pat's mother would show up. Ray Jr., who was one, clattered through the kitchen in a walker. Timmy, the baby, got passed around, and a platter of ham-and-cheese heroes was consumed by the cops. Johnny Cahill sent a note and flowers. A *dozen roses*, he wrote, *and all my best*. Mary-Pat counted the roses and found only eleven. When Chipper and Babcock popped corks in the kitchen, a narc in the front room half-pulled his gun.

After the party, Ray and his wife did dishes. Mary-Pat asked Ray why his family didn't like her family.

"We're nice," she said, handing Ray some wet forks. "Chipper mingled. His friend was nice too."

Ray took the forks in a towel. "Harvard boys," Ray observed.

"It's not like we're Cabots or Lodges," she said, giving him a plate. "Dad had business success, but we're Irish too."

Ray wiped the plate. "Nobody minds that the Cabots have money. That's what the Cabots are for. But if the Irish start going to Harvard, it's a reproach to the Irish who don't."

"That's a very twisted attitude."

"Welcome to Boston," Ray shrugged.

"That man who played with the baby for an hour—who was he?"

Ray racked some plates. "Manny Manning, a sergeant in the Narcotics Division. Probably the best street cop in Boston."

"He's very good with children."

"He'd better be—he's got six or seven of his own."

"Your brother follows him around like a puppy."

"After Da died, Biff was pretty wild. Manny kind of took him in."

"Is Manny crooked?"

"No," Ray said. "And his men aren't crooked either. Manny sees to that."

She pulled the last bowl from the water and turned it upside down. "Why don't you like Manny Manning, then?"

Ray took the dripping bowl. "Who says I don't?"

"You act funny around him—curt, sort of. It's like you're mad at him. He knows it, too."

"Manny was my father's partner toward the end of Da's career. When Da got indicted, the rest of his squad got indicted too. All except for Manny."

"Maybe he was the one good apple."

"Maybe."

"Do you blame Manny for what happened?"

Ray thought for a moment. "No."

She reached into the dishwater and yanked the stopper from the drain. "Do you forgive him?"

The drain sucked. "No," Ray said.

They left the drafty triple-decker when Timmy and Ray Jr. were walking. There were too many stairs in the place, Mary-Pat said, so she rented them a house with no stairs, none, except for two front steps. The house had been a junior officers' billet on the marshy grounds of the Weymouth Naval Air Station, and it was amazingly flat. The boys' backyard was also flat, and a mile square, but it was said to be full of unexploded ordinance. The move was a temporary thing, two or three months, just until Ray could work up the nerve to demand a raise from Johnny Cahill so they could buy a house.

"A *real* house, with no bombs in the yard," Mary-Pat said. "Like normal people."

Two months became two years. Mary-Pat claimed that Ray actually *liked* the house on the old bomb range, and she was almost right. He didn't care about the house, but he liked the life he had there. Ray would come home late, like tonight, and find Mary-Pat drinking alone. He'd tell her what he had done, and she would take it all in. Sometimes the phone rang after they had gone to bed, an emergency downtown. Sometimes detectives would show up in their driveway, a war party, and ask to see Ray.

Manny and his men were frequent late-night visitors. Manny was all obsessive narc, always working. When Manny came by, Ray knew something good was afoot—Manny needed a search warrant, or a rat sprung from jail, or buy money for an undercover sting, or maybe a quick-hit wiretap. Mary-Pat would let them in and put on a pot of coffee as Ray threw on clothes. Ray would come out in a sweater and slacks and Mary-Pat would go to bed without a word.

"Can we talk?" Manny would ask. "Someplace private?"

The flat house had thin walls. There was nowhere private. So Manny and Ray and whichever other narc was there, Shecky Bliss or Nat Butterman or Paddy Hicks, would go out to Manny's car and talk shop as the sun came up. They were good years to Ray.

Mary-Pat hated the place. Ray Jr. was in second grade and Timmy was a year behind, and she was pregnant yet again.

Ray went to Johnny Cahill and said that he owed his wife a house, and threatened, respectfully, to quit. Johnny gave him a small bonus and a big raise, and Mary-Pat moved them to this place, which was on the block they had looked at back in '57.

She made new rules for the new house. Johnny Cahill would never set foot here. Cops would not appear in the driveway at four in the morning, except maybe Manny, who was Mary-Pat's pet. Finally, Ray would be home on time at least twice a month so that they could entertain.

"Like normal people," she said.

Their first dinner party at the new house was an eclectic affair. Chipper McCallion, Mary-Pat's brother, came in from Dover with his wife and with good old Win Babcock. Mary-Pat invited the neighbors, an Italian computer programmer and his Japanese wife, and, to add some grit, Manny and Ray's brother, Biff. Mary-Pat served cheese fondue, a smorgasbord of herring, salmon, and Swedish meatballs, and a bowl of something she called "guacamole."

Chipper and Win were fascinated with police work, as if Manny and Biff were gentlemen huntsmen. The Italian thought mainframe databases could greatly aid police work and asked Biff how often he used a computer in his job.

Biff had a mouthful of guacamole. He looked at Manny helplessly.

"We're pretty primitive," Manny said.

Mary-Pat went around the table and asked everyone what they thought of the nuclear test-ban treaty. Win Babcock, the great liberal, was strongly in favor. The Italian supplied the obligatory European perspective. Chipper wasn't so sure.

"Can we afford to trust the Russians? That's the question," Chipper opined.

"Can we afford *not* to?" Win Babcock thrust, and everybody tittered, except for Ray and the cops, who found the whole thing a strain. Babcock patted Chipper's hand and said, "You raise a very valid issue."

Ray watched Babcock work Chipper, who now ran the Chrysler dealership and was worth about a million. Chipper pumped money into worthy causes, with Babcock as his condescending Rasputin. Every few minutes Babcock mentioned that a *number* of people were *begging* him to run for Congress, and Ray, who made a living reading motives, knew that Babcock was going to spend Chipper's money when he ran.

Babcock's flattery towered. The fondue was *tremendous*, the meatballs *thrilling*. He let on that he had been in love with Mary-Pat since his frosh year at Dunster House. Babcock was one of those impoverished Brahmins who somehow took the best vacations. He'd been a Fulbright in Morocco and got arrested in Mississippi. He knew the sort of people Mary-Pat yearned to know. The poet Robert Lowell was some kind of distant cousin, and Babcock called Leonard Bernstein "Lennie."

"What's Bernstein really like?" she asked.

"Tremendous," Babcock said.

When the guests were filing out, the Italian kissed Mary-Pat's hand. Babcock, next in the *arrivederci* line, kissed her hand and held it. Manny, seeing this, shot Ray a look as if to say, *Gimme the nod and Win won't make it home.*

Win Babcock was coming over a lot these days, once a month for dinner, sometimes with Chipper or the Hunger Group and sometimes—perhaps—alone. He filled Mary-Pat's dinner parties, and her head, with great talk.

He said that by 1975 we wouldn't recognize the United States. By then, we'd all go to work on monorails speaking Esperanto, and the races would be equal. Poverty would be cured, and, with it, crime. Guys like Ray and Manny would be obsolete. Guys like Win Babcock would be senators and famous.

The snow finally stopped an hour before dawn. Ray went upstairs to bed, and found Mary-Pat awake. He got undressed and swooped to kiss her.

She pushed him back. "Are you going to use the Thing?" The Thing was Mary-Pat's latest and raciest sexual innovation—a latex rubber sheath that fit over the penis and prevented pregnancy.

Ray started to whine.

She got up on her elbows. "I've had all the children I'm going to have. There's a population crisis going on. Win Babcock says..."

Ray burrowed under the covers. He resurfaced with a great idea. "We could use the rhythm method."

She jeered. "The rhythm method is a trick designed to get me pregnant. Wear a condom or do without. Those are your choices, buster."

"But it's been more than a year since we..." Ray slurred it: "...made love."

"Boo-hoo," she said. "What time is it?"

"Six-thirty."

You've been pacing. It woke me up."

"Sorry."

She fell back in the sheets. "That's okay. I was having a bad dream. I was pregnant—the first pregnant woman ever. Everybody was terrified because they'd never seen a woman get that big that fast. Everyone thought I was dying, or turning into some kind of monster."

"Let's have Chipper over to dinner," Ray said. "Let's get some of your political people together."

Mary-Pat jumped out of bed. "You're gonna do it? You're gonna take on Johnny Cahill?"

Ray didn't say yes or no. He said, "I was thinking of the old house, the Weymouth place."

"With the bombs. Do you miss it?"

"I miss those days. I went to work and came home. I had you and the boys and nothing else. It was stable."

"It was stifling."

Ray said, "I never thought so."

"You've never gotten over your da, have you? One minute he's a cop, next minute he's a crook, and the minute after that he has a stroke and dies. Ever since then, you've wanted bedrock."

"Don't you?"

"Bedrock's a lie, Ray. We can't go back, and we can't stay still, not when everything's changing around us. I think that's really why you hate condoms—because they're *new* to you."

"I hate them because I can't feel you when I'm inside you."

"Well—" she kissed him lightly on the cheek—"*adjust.*"

4

Sergeant Manny Manning worked the slums alone, in plainclothes and an unmarked Chevy. Nothing moved in Manny's sector except the junkies, who crawled out of ratholes to bang on doors or rattle grated storefronts. They stood in the streets and yelled up at third-floor apartments, begging for dope. It was almost three on a frigid afternoon, and the junk spots had been closed since the blizzard hit. The addicts, getting desperate, looked like ghosts.

A woman named Marcy Fay and a man called Old Bob limped up to Manny's car. Marcy hooked by the buses in Park Square, real name Mary Kathleen Fay. She'd added the c to "Mary" for business reasons: banging a hooker named for the Virgin made decent Boston johns uneasy.

"S'up," Manny said, rolling down his window.

"We need help," Marcy said. "What day is it?"

"Sunday," Manny said.

"Been three days," she said. "Nearly four. I think my husband's dying."

Marcy Fay and Old Bob stayed in a Salvation Army dorm on Sheridan Street in a cluster of blocks named after Civil War greats. Sherman, Stanton, and Grant were over there too. Marcy used to live on Hooker, which was good for a laugh, but Hooker Street was flattened, along with a quarter of the neighborhood, paving the way for urban renewal. Bob had once been a surgeon— at least that's what Marcy claimed. Marcy hooked for him, and scored for him, and almost always spoke for him. He had a kind, triangular face, and looked about seventy. He nodded at Manny to confirm that he was dying.

"So score," Manny told them.

"We checked all the spots," Marcy said. "Nobody got."

"You try Clarence's?" Manny asked.

"He don't got," she said.

"The Cubans?"

"Skunked."

"Yin's?"

She coughed. "Tried him."

"Roller rink?"

"Roller rink? You sent them clowns to jail five years ago. Fuck, where's your head at?"

"Has it been five years?"

"Think I'm making crap up just to keep this useless conversation *going*?" She stamped her feet. "The spots don't got because they can't get from the middlemen, because the middlemen can't get from the source, because the source don't play in the snow. Anything else I can explain for your dumb ass?"

"Yeah. The electoral college. How does it work, and why?"

"G'head. Make jokes. Bob's dying"—she lowered her voice— "and I don't feel so hot."

She leaned into Manny's car. "*You* got dope," she said. "You got that big Narco evidence vault. You could help us out." She winked at Manny's crotch. "And I could help you out. Be like old times."

She was confusing him with another cop, Jerry Drogheda, who'd taken a piece of Marcy once a week when Truman was in office. She had been something of a camp follower back then.

"I can help you out in other ways," Marcy was saying. "Be your informant. Dope for dope."

"I'm all ears," Manny said.

"Well," Marcy said, "you know them black kids you stomped outside the Sheraton on Christmas Eve? Turns out you got the wrong kids."

"That wasn't me," Manny said. "Don't waste my fucking time."

"*Touchy, touchy.* How 'bout this: Bennie Anastasia. He's heavy. Sells morph, pills, hash oil, Mary J, and some freaky shit you never heard of. Shit the beatniks take."

"You ever take this beatnik shit?"

"We don't experiment with drugs," she sniffed. "We stay with what we know."

Marcy was the fifth or sixth street source to tell Manny that new drugs were coming out. He chalked it up to addict claptrap.

"Does Bennie still sell H?" he asked. "Or is that just too humdrum for him?"

"He middlemans."

"So go to him. Bet he's got."

"*Tried* that," Marcy said. "Bennie don't got either." She coughed and shivered. Bob leaned on the car, cramping.

Manny gave her five bucks. "For soup," he said.

Manny pulled away from the curb and poked around the slum at three miles an hour, chained tires grinding through the snow. Skags here and there recognized the Chevy and tried to flag him over for their own little evidence-locker pitches, but Manny kept moving.

He scanned the blizzard-bound streets and thought, *I'm old.* He was, in fact, forty-two—a Boston cop half his life. He'd joined the force in '45, after seeing the world with the Army Airborne, and nearly dying a dozen times. He came home with a Silver Star and a French wife named Dorothée. They Bostonized her name to Dot, and Manny went on steady midnights out of the Roxbury station.

The rest of the cops who joined with Manny after the war

were new vets too. Tough Tony Nollo, from the Sixth Marines, partnered up with Frank Hicks, another Iwo Jima jarhead. Vin Phelan was fresh from the Airborne, like Manny. All the vets were hard beyond their years and in a funny kind of hurry. Nollo and Hicks conquered Japan; they weren't about to take lip on the corner of Mass Ave and Shawmut. Manny's sergeant on Roxbury patrol was Gus Hanratty. Manny started working with an old-timer, Timmy Dunn, and Vin Phelan partnered up with old Jerry Drogheda. They were like a mule team: Phelan and Jerry Drog, Nollo and Hicks, Manny and Tim Dunn, with Sergeant Gus holding the traces.

They broke a lot of heads that first year back. One night, Manny was cornered in an alley by six hoods and a nasty mob on the sidewalk. Manny was a goner, plain and simple, except Tim Dunn arrived with Sergeant Gus, Hicks and Nollo on their heels. The four cops waded into the mob—they had to nightstick fifty assholes just to get the chance to knock the hoodlums off of Manny. Gus Hanratty was a fucking *lion* in the streets—toughest beat cop Manny ever saw.

He owed these men his life, so when Jerry Drog came to him and asked his help running bag from the local bookies, what was Manny gonna say?

Manny just walked out of the precinct and climbed into a squad car. Jerry followed and slid behind the wheel. It was snowing that night too—almost as hard as today. They made a string of stops, like a paper route, getting envelopes at each. Jerry knew the way. The last man they saw was Beany Ed Weiss, the bookie king of Roxbury. Ed said, "Merry Christmas," as he bribed them.

Other cops came and went over the years, maybe a dozen total. Most of them took their share and moved on, except for Patrolman Shecky Bliss, who spent a year on the midnight tour in '53. Shecky was an old-timer, and Jerry Drogheda, who knew him from before the war, approached him just after Shecky came on board. Manny went along to meet the new man.

Jerry Drog laid it out for Shecky in the precinct showers and said his cut would be twenty bucks a week. "Easy money," Jerry said. "Everybody's in. Call it combat pay for working in this shithole."

Shecky put his hands up like he was being robbed. "No thanks," he said. "Nice to meet ya, Manning."

Shecky's steering clear of the bag-man thing made Nollo and Hicks uneasy. They talked about doing "something" to him, but the other old-timers—Tim Dunn and Jerry Drog—ruled that out.

"Shecky don't take dough, that's his business," Jerry Drog said. "But he ain't a rat. He'll live and let live. I vouch for the guy."

Lieutenant Hanratty solved the Shecky problem by getting him made a detective and having him sent to East Boston. When Shecky left, he shook hands all around and wished everybody luck.

For a decade, Manny's life was midnight to dawn batting cleanup in the ghetto with a shifting crew of guys; home in time to help Dot get the girls off to school. Manny could braid hair, pin a kilt, and iron cotton blouses on the kitchen table. When his daughters were on the bus, Manny cracked a beer and dug the money from his socks, tens folded over once, a flat pad. He gave the pad to Dot, who hid it in a coffee can and spent it on the girls. Dot never asked where the money came from, not then, and not later when the newspapers broke the story that the Boston office of the FBI was investigating cops for bribery.

The day the feds arrested all of Manny's friends, Dot shook him awake. "You'll protect my girls?" she demanded in her heavy accent.

Manny should have let her have it. He should have told her: I'm doing what I got to do. Every time you thought I was fishing, I was really in the basement of the U.S. Post Office downtown spilling my guts to the Department of Justice. The hickies on my chest are from where they ripped the wires off me after every day of taping. The feds think I'm a bag man trying to clear my conscience, and for all I know they might be right. I've ratted every man I ever loved. This is what I've done to protect your girls.

He told Dot none of this. He didn't know where to begin. What was "bag men" in French? *Les hommes du sac*—something like that. The men of the sack. Yeah, right. Instead, Manny hid in his pillows, and one by one his buddies met their fates:

Tim Dunn had a stroke and never spoke or moved again. Charges were dismissed and Tim wound up diapered in a nursing home, hanging on for a year.

Jerry Drogheda copped a nice deal, a plea to bribe solicitation, and testified against Hanratty, Hicks, Nollo, and Phelan. He served nine months in Lewisburg, and was paroled to the California desert, where he drank himself to death.

The remaining four stood trial in October 1955. The feds had plenty of weapons. Jerry Drog was the government's star witness. He was on the stand for a week. Beany Ed Weiss, the bookie king of Roxbury, was a cooperator too, and Hanratty's phone had been tapped. The cops looked dead in the water, until Hanratty took the stand in full-dress blue, medals running into his armpits, and boldly told the jury that he had taken money from Ed Weiss as part of an investigation of bribery.

"I was just about to arrest Mr. Weiss myself when the FBI arrested me," Hanratty said. Imagine that.

It was the dumbest fucking defense anybody ever heard. The stenographer suppressed a giggle. But Boston was a town that loved its cops, and the jury bought it, sort of. Hanratty was acquitted. The others got hammered:

Patrolman Vincent Phelan, seven years.

Patrolman Anthony Nollo, nine years.

Patrolman Francis X. Hicks, nine years.

Manny's name was never mentioned. The feds kept him out of it because they had agreed to. The cops kept him out of it because that's how cops are: *semper fi*, simply *fi*. The feds had targeted the worst offenders, and the fact that Manny was left out got chalked up to his good luck. Other guys were left out, too, and the prevailing wisdom seemed to be that the rat had been the only guy who said no thanks, Detective Shecky Bliss. Shecky was a pariah for a while, and Manny let him take the heat.

After the trial, Gus Hanratty threw a victory bash at Jimmy's Harborside and insisted that Manny attend.

Gus threw an arm around Manny's neck and gave him a half-headlock hug. "We're the survivors, Manny."

Manny pretended to hug him back, but really pushed him off. Gus gripped the bar rail, drunk off his ass and wearing a tux for some goddamn reason. He looked like he might break into song.

"I make lieutenant next week," Gus confided. "I'm promised a captaincy year after next. I'm getting a new command, Narcotics."

Manny registered this information dully. He had always wondered how high the graft went. Hanratty's promotion meant that just as Manny and Tim and the others had kicked up to Gus, so too Gus had kicked up to the chiefs.

Hanratty asked him, "What do you think?"

"Of what?"

"Of coming to Narco, fathead. Me, personally? Couldn't give a fuck about catching drug dealers. But you? Bet you'd actually *like* it. I'll need a good sergeant to make some cases." Hanratty had a sugar-daddy grin, and a handshake the size of Alaska.

"I won't steal for you, Gus."

Hanratty waved this off.

"I mean it," Manny said. "You want trophies for your wall? Clean stats, good cases? I'll make 'em. You want a bag man? Look elsewhere."

Hanratty's grin went cold. "Is that it?"

"One more condition: let me pick my senior detective."

"You got a name in mind?"

Manny nodded.

Hanratty grabbed somebody else's vodka highball from the bar and threw it back. He looked sideways at Manny. "And what I do is my own business?"

"Your own business," Manny said.

They shook on it. Hanratty didn't ask who Manny planned to draft as his right-hand man—and a good thing too: the name Manny had in mind was Detective Shecky Bliss.

Manny parked in an alley and had a smoke. He wouldn't have minded a coffee, black, but the avenue was shuttered.

Manny watched some white scarecrow get his car stuck in the snow. The scarecrow gunned his engine, and his tires whined on the ice. Manny watched him try to dig his rear wheels free with his bare hands, and figured him for a suburban addict downtown to hook up. The scarecrow saw Manny and came over. Manny rolled down his window and blew out steam and smoke.

"Hey there" the guy called.

Manny showed his shield. "I'm gonna take a ride," Manny told him. "Don't be here when I get back."

"B-b-but my car is stuck—"

"Then walk," Manny said. He made the junkie jump aside when he pulled out of the alley.

Manny started thinking that the blizzard was a godsend, a once-in-a-lifetime chance to study a world emptied of everything except addicts out to score.

Manny was always dealing drugs in his head, and he did it now, as he drove. The importer gets a pound of heroin from overseas and cuts it with quinine, milk sugar, laxative, junk. He sells the load to three rival brokers, who junk it down again. Now the pound is nearly two pounds, sixty-forty pure. The brokers know ten Bennie Anastasias who mix it down to forty-sixty and pump it out to spots around the town: Clarence's, the Cubans, Yin's, the roller rink, except forget the roller rink. The spots cut the powder too, then sell to Marcy Fay and a thousand others like her. When Marcy gets her nickel bag it's only ten percent real, until she buries it in her bloodstream, and then it's one part per million. Injection is the great, and last, dilution.

Somewhere in this pyramid of nonstop junking-down was Manny. He watched the streets, tailed the junkies, targeted the spots and, from the spots, worked up: to Bennie A., to Bennie's broker, to the broker's source, with the promise, at the top, of untouched purity. Manny had never seen that kind of purity, but he knew it must exist because he saw it hit the neighborhoods.

He loved the life. He had turned down many career-path transfers because all of them led back to patrol. Working a beat, you could handle a triple murder, then a fender-bender, then a kid selling fireworks, and spend five hours typing up the arrest. There was no quest on patrol, no core problem. You handled whatever, and it handled you.

Patrol was dangerous, for sure, but even the dangers were mishmash. You could get shot, but that was rare. You could get stomped by a brawler who didn't feel like taking orders from some white jerk in a dumb blue suit, but your squad mates were always there to back you up. The real danger was your own boss or the old hands around the station house, who'd tell you that it's normal—absolutely normal—to get an envelope of money from the bookie in your sector. They'd tell you that it's normal to bring the money back to the precinct and whack it up in the locker room. You could get hurt—get cut—a million different ways working as a cop in uniform, and never know it until years later when you watch yourself call a guy a nigger in front of his kids just because you can, or until you hear the bookie king of Roxbury is cooperating with the feds. Patrol did to you what the dealers did to bags: diluted you and made you less, sold you after cutting you both ways.

Manny figured half the cops in Boston were corrupt. A few—like Hanratty—were grand thieves, running precincts like planta-tions. Many more were on the take off minor, lazy scams: fuck a hooker once a week, take a payoff once a month, then sham a line-of-duty whiplash and retire on three-quarters pay. There was a code of crookedness, and it was pretty strict. Gus Hanratty ex-plained it all when Manny was a rookie, another chapter in the Book of Gus.

"Some things only scumbags do," Hanratty said. He told Manny about the Four Nevers. Never lie to frame the innocent, because that meant a guilty guy went free. Never beat a cuffed man, because that meant you feared his hands. Never embarrass Internal Affairs, but never help them either.

If you had asked Jerry Drog how the bag-man thing got started, Jerry would've said he did it for Tim Dunn, and Tim would've said he did it for Manny, and Manny always thought he was doing it for them.

Try explaining *that* to the fucking FBI. Manny tried. The agents asked him how he could sell his honor for twenty dollars a week. Manny told them that the money was nothing. It disap-peared into Manny's life the way Marcy's heroin disappeared into her bloodstream. Manny tried to tell them it wasn't about money.

"I did it for them," Manny told the feds during his first Q&A in the Post Office basement. "For Jerry and for Tim, for Nollo, Hicks, and Phelan. I couldn't let them go it alone."

"Why?" the feds asked.

"Because they did it for me. It was one more risk we shared, one more way of sharing. Do you see?"

Sure. Manny didn't get it until later. After everything went in the shitter, Manny went to Tim's room at the nursing home and

tried to explain how wrong all of them had been. Tim was cata-
tonic, which made it easier.

"You didn't do it for me," he told Tim. "I didn't do it for you.
We were working for Hanratty the whole time. He probably told
you I needed the money, and told Phelan you needed help. He got
Nollo to do it for Hicks and Hicks to do it for Jerry, and told Jerry
to ask me. We thought it was our thing. But who made out? Who
really made out? *Captain* Hanratty, that's who."

Manny checked to see the door was closed, swallowed hard,
and said, "I was an informant for the feds. I ratted you, Tim. So
help me Christ, I did. I ratted the others too."

He told Tim how it happened. "They jumped me. Four
agents. They took me to Post Office Square. They showed me all
the tapes and pictures and a sworn statement from Ed Weiss saying he owned us. There it was, on a table, you and me and all of
us, crooked fucking cops. They shamed me, Tim. It wasn't fear. I
wasn't scared of jail. But they showed me my own life. I couldn't
let my girls see that."

Search for purity in that whole mess and you'd be more
strung out than Marcy Fay.

In an hour it'd be dark, and tonight it would get down to zero.
Manny was starting to worry about Marcy Fay and Bob. Jonesing
junkies froze to death in doorways in weather like this. You get too
crampy to walk. You sit down, telling yourself it's just a rest, a
little rest—one last lie you tell yourself. Neighbor dogs find you
first.

He cruised every corner west of the elevated trains and asked
the junkies he ran across if they had seen Bob or Marcy. He
checked the Salvation Army dorm. He looked across the flat white
blur of Taylor Fields—empty lots, cleared tenements—and saw
two distant figures struggling against the wind. He worked his way
to the far side of the Fields. This took a while in the endless
Boston red lights and one-way streets.

He could see from their side-by-side tracks that Marcy and Old Bob were heading north and east, tramping overland toward Telegraph Heights, a former Irish stronghold going black from the harbor in. Marcy, who grew up in the Heights, probably hadn't been there in twenty years. Now, with her jones and Bob in tow, she was going *exploring?* Where was Marcy headed? What did she know?

He followed them a half mile up the avenue to the D Street Bridge, then over the saltwater channel. Manny watched as Marcy coaxed Old Bob up Broadway, a steep hill, cresting it at the traffic rotary. Bob could barely walk. Marcy could barely drag him.

Manny stayed well back, itched his salt-and-pepper crewcut, and puzzled. Marcy had held out on him. She knew a spot she hadn't tried, a spot she didn't think Narcotics knew about. Manny came around the Heights peninsula, Navy Ave to Gibraltar Street, and ran along the waterfront. There, like Oz, was Marcy's spot: the Gibraltar Street projects, three grim towers on the water.

Manny watched Marcy help a retching Bob into one of the towers. Manny figured he would let them score, pick them up afterward, and chauffeur them back to the South End. He'd trade the ride for the name of the mystery source inside the projects.

He waited with the motor running and smoked his last four Larks, cranking the heat, trolling the police bands and AM radio, until he got restless. He waded through a foot of snow to the projects. He checked every floor and stairwell, ending in the basement of the southernmost tower. He saw Marcy Fay snuggling with Bob behind the furnace, a cozy corner.

Marcy had died first, syringe still in the hollow of her elbow, just below a tied-off length of red-checked gingham. Bob had spent his last strength mashing her tits with his hands. A final feel-her-up? No, pulmonary massage for Marcy's dope-induced cardiac. Bob's medical training was wasted but not entirely forgotten.

Manny eased the spike from Marcy's arm. It was full of blood, her kickback cut off in midstroke.

The terror in Marcy's face was wax-museum, but vivid. She didn't deserve this. Nobody did.

Manny searched his two dead friends and found what he wanted down the front of Marcy's girdle: a waxen bag, one inch square, pinch of chocolate-brown powder inside. He wrapped the needle in the gingham and went outside to clear his head.

It was dark now. Manny opened his hand and examined Marcy's spare nickel bag under a streetlight. Manny put it to his nose and smelled it: it wasn't street heroin, but it wasn't rat poison either. He licked a pinkie and tasted: too rich. It was dope, but not like any dope Manny had ever seen.

A drug dealer had killed them. The dealer lived in these buildings, or on this street, walking distance anyhow. Manny had almost nothing to go on—but he was a narc's narc of the old school.

Snow was sticking to his coat; he shook it off. *You're out there,* Manny told the dealer. *I'm coming for you, are you ready for me?* The projects stood in floodlights.

Manny knew that he would find the dealer because he already had a piece of him. The strange little bag was in Manny's palm, under his thumb. Manny took his thumb off the bag and closed his fist.

5

On any other night, the bar would be mobbed, but with the blizzard just ending and the city shut down, only the losers were here.

Joe Mears sat in a corner booth by the fogged-up front window. He rubbed a hole in the window fog and checked the street. A taxi passed without stopping.

He heard gum pop and turned from the window. The barmaid was there, weight on one hip, cork-lined tray under her arm.

"Need another?" she asked.

Mears looked down at his untouched scotch. The ice had melted. A pile of bills sat by the glass. He pushed some ones at her.

"Don't come back," he said.

The bar was called the Onion, which was the third or fourth name it had gone under in the last couple of years. Mears hated the Onion, but he couldn't seem to stay away, probably because it was the first place he ever really knew when he arrived in Boston.

Mears came in one night to get warm. This was back when Kennedy was President and Mears was sleeping in boxcars in the Brighton freight yards just down the hill, and the Onion was called Chico's.

Chico's was wall-to-wall kids, thick smoke, and loud jabber. Chico himself was fat and forty and had a goatee. He said his life's work was introducing beatniks to Latin jazz. His real name was Wendell.

Mears couldn't afford a drink back then, but no one seemed to care. The bartender got Mears a beer, then drifted off to smoke a joint with guys setting up microphone stands in the corner. The bartender came back stoned and gave Mears somebody else's change. The jukebox died and the mikes went on with a burst of feedback. Then three kids read poems about mushroom clouds. It was October '63.

Mears went in to see Chico one afternoon before the place opened. Chico was eating pork chops, rice, and black beans at the bar.

"I know you," Chico said. "You been coming around."

"Yes," Mears said.

"You retarded or something?" Chico was referring to the ticks and twitches Mears had when his headaches came on.

"No," Mears said. He explained about the headaches.

Chico cut his chops. "You ought to see a doctor about that."

"Doctors gave me the headaches," Mears said. "I was institutionalized." He used the long word because he was here for a job and didn't want to seem retarded.

Mears said, "I need work."

Chico finished his lunch. "Where you from?" he asked.

Mears looked at his shoes.

"Last job?"

Mears said, "I'm not sure."

Chico chewed. "Hospitals, headaches, blankness. Lemme guess: electroshock. Where?"

Mears touched his temples.

"I mean, what hospital?"

"Up north," Mears said.

"I got mine at Riggs in '58. Jimmy Piersall was there too— unless I imagined it. Cured me of practicing law."

Chico looked at Mears. "How long you been like this, friend?"

"Since I got out. A few months."

"How much do you remember from before the treatments?"

Mears shook his head.

"Nothing?"

"Pretty much. If I see something I knew before, I can tell it's familiar. Like church. Church is familiar."

"The memory loss wears off."

Mears said, "I guess."

"You're from Boston," Chico said. "It's the accent."

Mears washed Chico's dishes all winter and made enough money to move into a hobo hotel downtown. He spent his days walking around Boston trying to recognize buildings, streets, signs, anything. He usually wound up in a big dark church someplace, and he was happy there. He joined the prayers, felt the Latin coming out of him, though he didn't know from where. When it got dark, he went to work.

In those days, Chico's was jumping and the cops raided it weekly. The hipsters thought the raids were a gas. Usually, Mears slid along the wall during the raids, ducked into the john, and squeezed out a window to the alley in back. From the alley he could hop a fence and roll down a steep dirt embankment into the freight yards, where he was safe. On cold nights, Mears would lie still and watch a solitary worker go from track to track with a flashlight, pouring oil on the switching gear. The worker would stoop and light the oil, and it would burn and keep the switches from freezing. On those nights, Mears would hide from the cops and watch twenty little orange fires in the distance.

Sometimes the cops were federal narcs—the USBN—who always singled out white girls with Negro dates and asked them what their parents would think. The girls would respond with pantomime yawns.

Other times it was precinct vice, who came in uniform, broke some chairs, emptied the cash register, and shook Chico down for free shots.

Once in a while, Boston narcs, showed up. They scared Mears

the most. They didn't hassle anybody or break anything. They just strode in, four at a time, wearing porkpie hats and trim gray suits. They would wade through the suddenly quiet crowd to one particular guy at one particular table. They always called him by his name, the guy they came for. The guy would stand up and the city narcs would cuff him, When the narcs led someone off like that, no one ever saw the guy again, and word would circulate a few months later that the guy was doing fifteen years at Walpole for heroin.

The beatniks went to Harvard Square to see the movie *Breathless* over and over just to study and copy what cool looked like. The boys would walk and smoke like Jean-Paul Belmondo and the girls got short haircuts and French bras like Jean Seberg's, and everybody rode scooters and talked about moving to Paris. To Mears, it all seemed an act. To him, the narcs were cool for real.

Mears first met Bennie Anastasia in the winter of '64. It was a busy night at Chico's and Mears was taking a break by the bar. Some BU kid was at the mike reading a poem about Martin Luther King in the Birmingham Jail. Two Negroes next to Mears started heckling the poet. One of them was small and dark. Mears learned his name later: Garrett Hays. The other was lanky and light-skinned. He was Bennie A.

Garrett shouted, "What the fuck you know 'bout Birmingham?"

The kid tried to finish his poem, but Garrett cupped his hands. "Shut the fuck up 'bout Birmingham!" Garrett was drunk.

The kid was rattled. He tried to tell Garrett that he was just "doing his thing," and that he was "hip to" Garrett, but Garrett mocked him brutally.

"You *hip* to me, *bro?*" Garrett was imitating a white person imitating a Negro, and it wasn't pretty. The whole place got edgy for real, instead of fake-edgy. The kid at the mike slunk away, and Mears never saw him in the club again.

Garrett and Bennie went back to their conversation. Mears,

impressed, started listening in. Garrett was demanding money from Bennie and Bennie was squirming.

Suddenly Garrett was looking at Mears. "You mind, Chuck?"

Mears said, "My name is Joe."

Garrett said, "Yeah. You mind?"

Garrett and Bennie went back to their conversation. They mentioned sums, dates, and weights—clipped phrases, but unmistakable. They were dealing, and Bennie was in the hole.

Garrett was looking at Mears again. "Chuck, what the fuck is the problem? We're trying to *talk* here."

"My name is Joe."

Garrett gave Bennie a weary look and Mears felt a knife prick just above his belt. Mears looked down at the knife and up at Garrett, who smiled.

Bennie said to Garrett, "I got to go."

"You won't stab me," Mears told Garret. "Not here. Not over this."

Garrett goosed the blade. "Yeah?"

Mears said, "You want product, right? Well, I can get anything you want."

Garrett took the knife away. "Dag, Joe, why didn't you say so? I nearly cut you. So, who you with? Feds or BPD?"

Mears said, "I'm for real."

Bennie said, "Garrett, I'm going."

Mears stayed deadpan. "I'm new to Boston. I don't know enough people to sell to the streets, but you two do. I can get product. I got a connection in a mental hospital."

Garrett loved it. "I *bet* you do."

Garrett followed Bennie through the crowd, laughing at Mears as he went out the door.

Mears trailed them to the sidewalk and up Cambridge Street. They got to Brighton Avenue and waited for the light. Bennie saw Mears first. He nudged Garrett, who turned.

Garrett said something to Bennie and started back toward Mears. His coat parted and his arms were wide, an open hug. Passing streetlights glinted off the knife in Garrett's right hand. Mears was ten feet from Garrett's waiting hug, and closing. Bennie was circling around to where Mears couldn't see him. Garrett stutter-stepped, right shoulder dipping slightly, knife hand slashing up and across. Mears blocked it with a flying elbow, his hand continuing through Garrett's arms to his windpipe. Garrett fell.

Bennie was slow and Mears was already pivoting. Bennie took an elbow in the middle of his face and rolled toward the trash cans.

Mears took the knife from the sidewalk and helped Garrett up. Garrett was coughing.

Strangely, Mears spoke now to Bennie—as if Garrett weren't there. He said, "I'll prove I'm not a narc or some kind of bullshitter. I'll prove I'm for real."

He stepped behind Garrett and hitched the blade under his chin. He backed Garrett down an alley. Bennie followed, wanting to help Garrett, afraid to make a move.

At the end of the alley, Mears stopped. He said to Bennie, "Would a cop do this?" He snapped his wrist and cut Garrett's throat.

Bennie didn't speak for a long time after that. Mears led him down Comm Ave to another bar, the Hi-Lite, which catered to a hard-core junkie crowd.

Mears kept talking all the way to the Hi-Lite and was talking when they found a booth deep in back. Bennie finally said, "Shut up. You just committed murder."

"I heard him at Chico's," Mears said. "He wasn't your friend. He was taking your money. What do you care?"

Bennie said, "Who *are* you?"

"I was locked up," Mears said.

"What were you in for?"

Mears turned bitter. "My own good," he said. "I got a guy who can get me drugs. Anything you need."

Bennie said, "Man."

Mears said, "Test me. Do a package. If I can't deliver, if I ain't for real, you can tell the cops what I done to Garrett."

And that was how it all got started, a long year ago.

The door to the bar swung open and Bennie came in. He didn't look happy.

"That synthetic shit was supposed to be *safe*," Bennie said. He was spilling as much coffee as he drank. He left his overcoat on and bunched a wet beret in his free hand.

Mears said, "What happened?"

Bennie put the cup down on the saucer with a clink. "People are getting sick."

"I told Caesar it was safe, but strong. He's got to cut it different, hundred-to-one. I told him." It was rare for Mears to sound defensive. "How much did he sell?"

"All of it."

Mears absorbed this. If Caesar had put an entire shipment on the streets, his dope was already in the hands and veins of hundreds of junkies by now. Some of them would have gotten it directly from Caesar's own organization. Others would have gotten it from middlemen, jobbers, and scalpers who bought bulk from Caesar. Same thing either way. It wasn't like a batch of bad cars; GM could simply recall cars. This was dope, and it was gone now. There was nothing to do but wait for the damage.

"Caesar's a clown," Mears said.

"If people die from this, the cops'll come down on us all."

"On Caesar," Mears corrected. "You want your package, or what?"

Bennie said, "I'm out." He slurped coffee and snuck a look at Mears, trying to read his face.

Bennie put down the cup. "I been in the middle too long."

"You mean the narcs?"

"The narcs, Caesar, the junkies, you. I'm everybody's middle-man for everything. It's too much. So I'm out."

"Nobody's ever *out*."

"I am."

"You still gotta live. You gotta eat."

Bennie put on his hat. "I'll move to Cambridge. It's a whole different scene over there. I'll sell the other shit, the shit we talked about." His voice made the last statement a question, almost. He was waiting for Mears to react.

"Yes," Mears said.

"But no more dope," Bennie said. "I ain't gonna be in the middle no more."

Bennie brought an envelope from his coat and slid it to Mears's glass. It was an even grand in tens and twenties.

Bennie stood up. "Call me when you get the other shit. I'll leave a number at the Hi-Lite."

Bennie was gone awhile before Mears put the envelope in his pocket. He was thinking that he had been careful. He had only sold to two customers, avoided the phones as much as he could, made his meets in well-scouted spots, and kept tabs on the narcs. He was careful to be careful, like a double wall between himself and the risks of this business. But Bennie was right: if junkies died, the cops might trace the dope from the streets to Caesar's network, maybe to Caesar himself, and just behind Caesar was Mears.

Two college girls came in and sat down. They ordered White Russians and talked about the good old days when this bar was really hip. Now it was just so *square*.

One girl said, "Let's go to Paris."

It dawned on Mears that the "good old days" they were talking about were last year.

He made a decision. It was time to leave Boston.

He went out to the street and walked down to the old Brighton freight yards. He hopped a fence to take a better look. On a cold night like this, the switches on the tracks would be burning.

6

Leaning on his car outside the Suffolk County Courthouse, Manny watched the Dunn boys come down Bowdoin Street. Ray wore his tweed overcoat and snap-brim hat, newspaper rolled under his arm. He carried a briefcase, cut a swath, and looked like what he was: a ball-busting company man. Biff bounced at his brother's elbow, punching the air to make a point. Biff had just joined Narcotics after seven years on patrol. He had applied to be a Narco undercover, and was by all accounts suited to the job. The promotion had nearly happened several times, but Ray, pulling strings, blocked it three years running.

"Too dangerous," Ray had said. "Biff's a boy."

Manny finally got his way by lobbying Mary-Pat, and Ray, outflanked, surrendered. Biff's transfer was in effect from the first of the year, and today he would meet the team.

Manny tossed his cigarette and stepped in front of the brothers Dunn. "S'up," he said.

"See the morning paper?" Ray asked Manny as they climbed the courthouse steps.

"Fuckin' Bruins," Manny said.

"See the *front* of the paper?" Ray asked. "Page A-4. The Negro kids from the Sheraton hired a lawyer. They're talking about a police brutality suit. They want to look at pictures of all the plainclothesmen on duty that night to pick out the three who beat them up."

Manny jammed his hands in his pockets. "I had nothing to do with that."

They went up to Ray's big office, next to the DA's. Manny started in about the death of Marcy Fay and Old Bob.

"I did a little checking over the weekend," Manny said. "There was a total of eight fatal overdoses in three days, all from dark-brown dope."

Ray buzzed reception for messages. "So?" he said, distracted.

"So I sent Marcy's stash to the lab. The dope came back strange: the chemists say she was killed by something called fentanyl, cut by common laxative."

"Fentanyl?" Biff asked. Ray glanced at Johnny Cahill's door, ignoring Biff and Manny.

"It's synthetic heroin," Manny explained. "But it's a hundred times as potent. This stuff's from a new source, Ray, and it's very, very dangerous. The guy selling it probably mixed it like it was heroin, and made the bags too pure."

Ray jumped at a banging in Johnny's suite, a cleaning lady rattling dustbins.

"We got eight dead junkies and a new killer dope," Manny said. "We got a plague on our hands."

Ray held up a Crime Scene picture of a white man in a raincoat with a head like a smashed melon. "See him? He's a Catholic priest. That means he's more important than eight damn junkies. Do what you got to do. I'll okay the expenses."

Manny saluted sarcastically and left the office. Biff hurried after him.

Ray buzzed his girl again. "Call Monsignor Martin Pasqua at the Archdiocese. Tell him I need to stop by—at his convenience."

Narco was housed in the basement of a precinct in Dorchester—a former bomb shelter decorated with pinups of girls sitting on cars, or just cars, and mug shots of Narco fugitives past and present. The seven metal desks against the walls had been stolen, one at a time, from fat-ass Robbery detectives upstairs, who never detected the culprits. The fluorescent lights were always lit.

Manny and Biff found the squad room empty except for Detective Shecky Bliss, who lay on the couch in his stockinged feet with a carton of steaming takeout gruel and the *Globe*. Shecky was gawky, bald, too old for his rank, and a self-proclaimed coward. He'd been wary when he went to work for Manny at Narco; he had known Manny as a steady-midnight bag man, after all. But Manny kept his nose clean and won Shecky's trust. The two men had been the soul of Narcotics for ten busy years.

"Hey, hump," Manny said to him. "Meet our new undercover."

Shecky sat up and shook Biff's hand. "I knew your da," Shecky said.

Biff grinned and took a chair.

Shecky folded the *Globe* in half and dropped it on Manny's desk. "Seen that?" he asked.

"Them kids," Manny said, pushing the paper aside.

Shecky picked it up and read aloud: "'The three youths were scheduled to sing at the governor's Holiday Gala that evening, a Howard University spokesmen confirms. They have claimed that they were abducted by three males carrying walkie-talkie-type radios and handcuffs, driven a quarter mile into the South End, where they were beaten. Suffolk County DA John Cahill said, through a spokesman, that no investigation is planned. The BPD has denied that the three assailants were police officers, but sources report that units from the Narcotics Division were conducting a secret operation in the area that night called Pressure Point...'"

Manny, at his desk, looked seasick. "Some secret," he said. "Skip the rest, huh, Sheck? Marcy Fay is dead."

Shecky took off his half-moon glasses. "How?"

"By the sword," Manny said.

Detectives Nat Butterman and Paddy Hicks arrived just then, car-pooling in from the GI Bill tract-bungalow hell both called home. The two detectives had just closed on side-by-side, mirror image starter ranches—three beds, a bath and a half, and loads of room to grow, on sixty-four-dollar-a-month mortgages arranged through Morty Moore the Mortgage Magician, whose radio slogan was *Sixty-four in '64*. Hicks and Butterman were virtually married. They did everything together: Korea, patrol, Narco, suburbia.

Shecky Bliss, a lifelong West Ender, hated the suburbs. He needled Butterman and Hicks, but mostly Butterman, nonstop.

"How's life?" Shecky insinuated. "Guess Morty the Mortgage Magician will have to raise his prices now that it's a new year and all."

"A buck," Butterman said, putting on a pot of coffee.

"Unless the Mortgage Magician changes his ads, by the year 2000 houses will be free," Shecky said.

"When the Commies win, sure," Butterman said, sitting at his desk. Butterman was president of Lawmen for Goldwater, Boston Chapter, now defunct. Shecky, the house liberal, still pined for Adlai Stevenson.

"I heard Butterman had to sign a paper to get into Happy Valley, or whatever your town is called," Shecky said.

"No Jews," Butterman confirmed. Coffee smell filled the basement.

"We told them Nat was German," Hicks bragged.

Shecky shook his head. "You're a big forgiver, Nahum."

"The name is Nat. So I signed the no-Jews thing, big deal. Everybody else signed it too—and signed a no-neeg thing, no spics, no chinks or Commies or antisocial beatnik lowlifes who sell drugs and don't mow their lawns, which means my kids *and* my investment are protected." Butterman poured coffee for everyone.

Detective Jay Scanlon drifted sleepily through the door. Scanlon was the new kid, big, blond, and, quite possibly, dumb—nobody was sure yet. He'd come over from patrol with a rep for slugging suspects. Manny smelled meanness and greed on Scanlon, and never let him work alone. Nobody said anything about the white plaster cast on his left wrist.

"Goldwater," Shecky said, "is a Nazi."

"Goldwater speaks the ugly truth," Butterman told his audience, Hicks. "I guess the truth makes Shecky uncomfortable."

"Don't tell me about uncomfortable," Shecky said, sucking the last of the gruel from the carton. "I ain't the one passing for German."

Butterman turned to Manny. "What do you say, boss?"

Manny hadn't voted in his life. The patrolmen's union made every member vote, and drove the cops from the precincts to the polls in leased school buses to support a preselected slate of Special Friends of the BPD. Manny always went along, slid into the voting booth, closed the curtain, and stood there looking at the names of all the losers whose big goal in life was becoming probate surrogate or Suffolk County sheriff or registrar of deeds. He noted the names on the ballot—Kelly, Quade, Shanley, McKay, like a Charlestown graveyard, and about as promising. Manny stood in the voting booth and killed five minutes, long enough to make it look good, thinking about bass fishing or what to eat for lunch or whether his pants fit, pulled the lever back, then collected his sawbuck from the delegate and got lost.

"I agree with Shecky," Manny said.

"You *always* agree with Shecky," Hicks and Butterman chorused. Jay Scanlon cleaned his boot sole with a penknife and stared Biff down. Biff sat in the corner and ignored him, or didn't notice.

The last narc through the door was Dave LeBlanc, Scanlon's partner and opposite. LeBlanc was a schoolteacher who had joined the cops to double his pay, a serene teetotaler and respected oddball. He advanced his day-a-page desk calendar to January 4, saw that the coffee was gone, and started another pot.

Manny rapped the blackboard with a knuckle. "A few things,"

he said. "First, the kid in the corner is Patrolman Biff Dunn, our new undercover."

Biff stood up.

"Make him welcome," Manny said. "Siddown, Biff."

Biff sat down.

"Next," Manny said, "is *this*." He held up Shecky's newspaper and pointed to the little story on A-4.

Butterman squinted at it. "The Bruins win?" He elbowed Paddy Hicks, who tried to elbow Jay Scanlon, who sat apart with the cast across his lap, looking put out.

"It's no joke," Manny said, staring at Butterman, Hicks, and Scanlon. "The kids have a lawyer. They figure the guys who jumped 'em are cops, on account of the radios and cuffs. They know about Operation Prussia Point. If they push, they might put the rest together, whatever the rest might be."

"We were told to clear the riffraff off the block," Butterman said. "How was we supposed to know they were from Harvard—"

"Howard," Shecky said.

"We barely touched them," Hicks complained.

"One of them has a broken nose and the other two have bruises," Shecky pointed out.

"And Scanlon over there sprained his wrist breaking that guy's nose," Butterman said. "It's a *bad* sprain, too. You don't hear Scanlon crying *citizens'* brutality do ya?"

Manny said, "Nat, shut up. I don't know what happened that night, and I don't want to know. The point is, *no more random ass-kickings.*"

"We ain't Avon ladies," Hicks grumbled.

Butterman nodded. "We got a job to do."

Scanlon tried to scratch inside the cast.

"So do your job," Manny said. "A doper, a known hood, some guy with a mouth on him—fine, handle it. But three choirboys on a stroll? No. Am I clear?"

Not very, the cops' faces said.

Manny sat down. "Speaking of your jobs, we got a double DOA from Friday, Marcy Kathleen Fay and her husband, known as Bob."

"RIP," Shecky said.

They were overdosers," Manny said. "On strong, brown dope laced with something called fentanyl, and they didn't die alone. Six other ODs were reported between Friday and Sunday. That's eight total so far—we'll find more corpses as the snow melts. The drugs are coming out of the Gibraltar projects. I want inside-out surveillance over there. I want to know who's selling fentanyl, and where they're getting it from. Finish your coffee, then hit the bricks. Anybody needs me or Shecky, we'll be seeing a friend."

Bennie Anastasia heard banging at the door. Through the peephole he saw Manny Manning, rounded by the fisheye lens, Shecky Bliss a yard behind him. Bennie looked at the boxes on his floor and mustered a quick lie. Moving? Me? No, all my shit's in boxes because I suddenly got bored with everything I own. I'm giving it to charity.

Manny kicked the door. Bennie let them in.

Bennie Anastasia was half Negro, half Greek, half Irish, and half Portuguese. His birthday was July 3, 1938, or '39, or '42—he got younger as his juvie hits piled up. Anastasia came out of Mattapan. He'd joined the Mummies, a local gang for light Hispanics and non-Irish whites, when he was thirteen. The Mummies sniffed glue, stole cars, rumbled with Negroes who started moving into Mattapan after the war, pulled the odd robbery, and faked retardation to get out of math class. Their trademark was a genuine Lon Chaney mummy walk which scared the hell out of their guidance counselors. The last time he was booked, Bennie had changed his race from "Other" to "Negro." Bennie was a four-time felon who couldn't go straight, and *five*-time felons got life without parole. So he serviced Narco as a paid informant, and Manny kept him out of handcuffs.

Now Manny stood in Bennie's flat and kicked an empty box across the floor. "Moving?"

Bennie kept his head. "Up the block. I got rent problems here."

Manny stepped in close. "Little bird says you're dealing heavy. Says you push H, but handle everything else too, including some freako drugs for the beatniks. That so?"

Manny's usual little-bird spiel. Bennie relaxed. "Junkies lie," he said. "You know that. I sell dope, just dope."

"To who?"

"Well, there's Ortwen, my little bebop bud. He takes ten or twenty nickels a week and sells to the cauc hepcats at the Onion and the Cambridge places. I know you know about me and Ortwen, because last time I was with him, I saw Butterman and Hicks on our ass, trying not to look official."

"Ortwen spot the tail?"

"He couldn't spot a tail on Mr. Ed," Bennie said.

"Ever hear of fentanyl?"

"Junkies're always talking pie-in-the-sky about some new drug," Bennie said. "Like it's gonna help."

"You know the Gibraltar Street projects?" Manny asked.

"That's where all the killer shit is coming from. Lotsa junkies'll be making the trek, you watch."

"Even though it killed Marcy Fay?" Shecky asked.

"*Because* it killed her," Bennie said. "Means they got some no-shit purity over there. It's your own fault. Everything was nice and stable in the South End. Junkies buy, get high, buy again. Then you came in with that Pressure Point bullshit and shook it all loose. Now folks are dying."

Manny lit a cigarette. "Who's behind the Gibraltar operation?"

"They say there's a black kid who manages the spot. There's also a Cuban, name of Angel. He's at Gilbraltar a lot too, but he's just a steady customer, they say. Angel took a drug collar over the summer, so you probably got his mug on file. He should be pretty easy to find, even for you."

"Watch your mouth," Manny said.

"Or else what? I ain't no glee club boy—"

"I had nothing to do with that," Manny told the whole room.

"Your guys did," Bennie said. "And everybody knows it. You try to play the stand-up Joe, the honest narc, all that shit, meantime your troops act like Klansmen. Can't have it both ways, pal—"

Manny grabbed Bennie's chin, tipped it up. "Call me *Sergeant.*"

Shecky had to turn away. He watched kids play chicken with snowplows outside, and preferred it. "Let's go," he said to Manny.

When the narcs, left. Bennie put on his last clean clothes: a white shirt under a black suit, cut almost zootishly, a black beret, and sharp-toed boots, also black. He scooped up cigarettes, loose bills, and a stiletto. The stiletto was a memento from a better, simpler era, when Bennie ran with the Mummies. The handle was black with an Egyptian eye in mother-of-pearl like the eye atop the pyramid on the back of a U.S. dollar bill.

Bennie closed his door quietly, leaving everything he owned behind.

7

There were two places where Ray Dunn allowed himself to be kept waiting. One was anywhere his boys were. The other was the Archdiocese of Boston. After an hour in a plush and purple hallway, Ray was admitted to the presence of Monsignor Martin Pasqua, chancellor of the Archdiocese, Cardinal Cushing's hatchet man.

Ray had dealt with Pasqua many times before. After Ray covered up the business with the spanking priest, Pasqua sent him a box of Cubans and a gracious note. When the embezzling pastor was delivered to the chancery with a blanket over his head, and the press none the wiser, Pasqua told the Cardinal to tell the DA to make Ray first assistant. Hatchet men love hatchet men.

Ray declined coffee, tea, and sherry. He felt jangly and nervy. He might say anything this morning. He might even tell the truth.

"I'm here about Father George Sedgewick," Ray said, as both men sat down.

"A horror," Pasqua sighed. "Do you have any leads?"

Ray told Pasqua what he had: a savage beating on a snowy runway and vague descriptions of a squat man in knit cap and peacoat stalking Sedgewick through the terminal.

Pasqua took it in. "How much do you know about George Wedgewick?" he asked.

"Only what you learn at an autopsy," Ray said.

Pasqua winced, but let the remark pass. "George was the best we had. A great and liberal preacher, a scholar, a scientist. We were in seminary together. George went to Harvard after ordination, and became a psychotherapist. He was way ahead of his time. He held every job a priest can hold—rich parishes, poor parishes, a chair of theology, Navy chaplain—and excelled at all of them. He was a saintly man, a model to us all."

"So you were friends," Ray said.

"Close friends."

"You ever take his confession? Don't look so shocked. Priests confess, right?"

"Yes, I took his confession."

"Anything out of the ordinary?"

"That is an outrageous and offensive question."

Deep inside, Ray was sick of Pasqua and himself, of hatchet men everywhere.

"Ever see a scapular?" he asked the chancellor. "I'm told they're not very liberal or modern. The coroner found scars on Father Sedgewick from self-inflicted wounds, years' worth. It's called scourging, and it, too, went out with the Inquisition. Something was on Sedgewick's conscience, eating him alive. So I'll ask again: was there anything out of the ordinary in Sedgewick's confessions?"

Pasqua was speechless. This was a new Ray Dunn.

"Whoever killed Sedgewick had a motive," Ray explained, backing down. "And something else: Sedgewick saw it coming. Sedgewick knew the killer and the killer knew him."

Pasqua wouldn't have it. "It was a mugging like any other. It was random, simply random."

"There were three Massport patrolmen in that terminal, Chancellor. Yet Sedgewick rushed right past them to get away from his pursuer. If Sedgewick knew he was about to get jumped, why didn't he flag a cop?"

Pasqua fled to the window.

"Why did Sedgewick go to Rome?" Ray asked his back.

"Business," Pasqua told the drapes.

"What business?"

"I have no idea."

"Then how do you know it was business?"

"He had many friends in Rome. He was fluent in Italian—"

"And a model to us all. Did you send him?"

Pasqua turned from the window. "George Sedgewick's death was a random tragedy. There's nothing else I can say to you."

A Massport detective was waiting for Ray at the courthouse with a new witness: the customs inspector who had checked Father Sedgewick and two bags through passport control on New Year's Eve. The inspector gave Ray a statement, which squared with the others. Sedgewick came in from Rome, met a white male in a knit cap by the glass doors, then took off.

"Did you see Sedgewick say anything to the man in the knit cap?" Ray asked.

"They had a word or two. Then Sedgewick scrammed."

"Running?" Ray asked.

"Like run-walking. Looking over his shoulder. His luggage was slowing him down. He dropped his little carry-on valise because it was getting tangled in his legs. Plowed over a Christmas tree, then disappeared out the far door, with the other guy after him. That's the last I saw of 'em."

"Sedgewick dropped the little bag?" Ray asked.

"It was slowing him down," the inspector said.

But not the bulkier suitcase, Ray thought.

The story was wrong, somehow. Ray took the inspector through the whole thing again. "You walked Sedgewick through customs?"

"Yup."

"Why?"

"He had them bags. I thought I'd be a nice guy."

"Why? Why did Sedgewick get the red-carpet treatment?"

"Well," the inspector said, as if Ray were being obtuse, "Sedgewick was a priest. Don't know about you, but *I* was raised to show 'em respect.

"But how did you know he was a priest? Sedgewick wasn't in habit that night."

"No," the inspector said, "but what the hell else is he going to be? Carrying the Blessed Sacrament and the priest suit in his luggage and all."

Ray went cold. "Carrying what?"

"Sacrament. Hosts. I told ya: I inspected his bags at customs. He came in from Rome with a priest suit folded up in his suitcase and a bunch of communion wafers—*thousands* of 'em in clear plastic bags. Jesus, what a sight! He had some fancy letter from the Cardinal saying if anybody but a priest touched them, we'd all go to hell."

For the second time in five hours, Ray found himself with Chancellor Martin Pasqua.

"You said it was urgent," Pasqua prompted irritably.

"Sedgewick came back from Rome with a suitcase full of Eucharist wafers," Ray said. "He also had a letter of authority signed by Richard Cardinal Cushing. You lied to me this morning. Why?"

Pasqua jerked forward and pulled open his top desk drawer. For a wild moment, Ray thought he was going for a pistol, but Pasqua's hand came out with a brass pillbox. He placed two pills on the end of his tongue and bit down.

"Water," he croaked.

Ray poured him a glass from a pitcher on a side table. Pasqua took it, slopping water all over his desk, and drank. His head fell back on his chair. He shut his eyes. Pasqua's breath returned.

"You've laundered the Church's linen before," he said. "You've kept her secrets well."

"And I'll keep this secret too, whatever it is. But the man who killed Sedgewick is an animal, and we can't let him walk around free. I have to know why Sedgewick was bringing Eucharist back from Rome."

Pasqua took a pamphlet from his desktop and held it up. It dripped on the rest of his papers. "This document is called *Sacrosanctum Concilium*, the latest bombshell encyclical from Vatican II," he said. "Issued by the Pope, this bull decrees mass in English by Palm Sunday. That's fourteen weeks away."

This was hardly a secret. "I don't understand," Ray said.

"It's not a very popular decree, Mr. Dunn. Some priests are talking openly of defiant Latin masses. The Cardinal is scared. I'm scared too. We have fourteen weeks to win the hearts of a million Boston Catholics violently opposed to change. We have fourteen weeks to undo sixteen centuries."

Ray got impatient. "What about Sedgewick?"

"George had been arguing for these reforms all his life. George was special. He went out into the world. He said science was full of miracles—polio vaccines, and computers, and men in orbit. He said the Church had to get in step with the times. Either that, or shrivel up and die. He convinced me, and he and I convinced Cardinal Cushing, and Cushing and a hundred others like him voted in a wave of reform at Vatican II."

"And the Eucharist in the suitcase at the airport?"

"George understood PR. He said the first English mass should be in Boston, because it was the most conservative Catholic city in America. So *start* in Boston, as a statement. Sedgewick wanted to bring the Pope here personally to celebrate the first English language mass, but that was impossible because the Holy Father is frail."

"And doesn't speak a word of English," Ray added.

"So we hit upon the next-best thing. We brought the Pope to the mass in another way. Sedgewick persuaded friends in the Vatican to allow us to bring in four thousand communion wafers consecrated as the Body of Jesus Christ by the hand of His Holiness Pope Paul VI in Vatican City three weeks ago. Under special arrangement with the Holy See, the papal sacrament was to be served to the faithful at a special mass at Holy Cross Cathedral, the first English-language mass on American soil."

Pasqua took some water. "Sedgewick left Boston on the day after Christmas, picked up four thousand Eucharist at the Vatican, and was bringing it back by hand. The suitcase was never out of his sight. We gave him a letter of transit to answer any questions the authorities might have. The letter explained that Eucharist has no monetary value and is exempt from import regulation—somewhat like a diplomatic pouch, I suppose. Because the wafers were already consecrated Eucharist, they were, under Roman Catholic law, the very flesh of God, and should not *under any circumstances* be touched by the hands of a nonpriest."

"Who knew about Sedgewick's mission—besides you and him?"

"The Cardinal, of course. Rome knew—"

"Anybody else on this side of the Atlantic?"

"No. We thought it was best. Sedgewick may have mentioned to his friends that he was going to Rome. He probably offered to bring things back—Italian coffee, Italian olive oil. He was that sort of man."

"But even if he told people he was going to Rome, his orders were to keep the Eucharist part a secret."

"That was our agreement, yes."

"The stocky man I mentioned this morning, is he familiar?"

"It's not much of a description," Pasqua said.

Ray rubbed his face. "What did Sedgewick confess to you?"

"I can't tell you," Pasqua said. "You know I can't."

"Did Sedgewick ever hurt anyone?"

"Of course he did. We all do."

"I mean hurt *bad*. Bad enough to make that person want to

kill him. There must be something—in the past, long ago, but something. What about the scapular, and the private little slashes Sedgewick gave himself each night?"

"He had no real enemies," Pasqua said. "It sounds impossible, but it's true. I can tell you, as George Sedgewick's confessor, that he was a saintly man."

Back at the courthouse, Ray knocked quietly on Johnny Cahill's door and waited for the yodelly *"Yay-uh"* Johnny always gave when he wanted you to enter. Johnny was behind his huge desk in slacks, shirt and tie, and a bright-red cardigan. He seemed especially jolly.

"You got home in one piece," he said. "Thank St. Christopher for that. The roads were awful, even this afternoon."

Ray knew that this was as close as Johnny would come to acknowledging that Ray had stormed out of Johnny's house when they were last together. If Ray didn't bring it up, Johnny would assume that Ray regretted the scene, and that he would do as he was told and serve whomever Johnny saw fit to make the next DA, even Eddie Cahill. That's what Johnny wanted—a loyal rearguard. Which was why Johnny even now was changing topics, from Ray's trip home, to the New Year's blizzard, to snow jobs as a whole.

"Boss," Ray said.

"Of course, snow was snow when I was young. No plows or snow tires, none of that—"

"*Boss.*"

Cahill beamed, benevolent and twinkly. "Yes, Ray?"

"I'll work for you. I'll work for your successor. But I won't work for your son. It's not because I hate him, or because I want the job myself. It's because he's unfit for any office, high or low."

Cahill's cheer went undented. "Well, of course, Ray, sure. That's fine. Anything else?"

Johnny wished him an especially booming good evening, which was how Ray knew that he was in trouble.

8

Father Sedgewick's housekeeper was emptying the box of Kleenex Ray kept on his desk.

Her name was Laura Zimquist, and she was not at all the priest's housekeeper type. She wore a stylish deep-blue serge suit and large sunglasses, had ash-blond hair to her shoulders and a good figure. The Homicide detectives wondered if she had been boffing the padre.

Ray patted her arm and said, "You knew him best. You answered his phone and opened his mail. Tell us about George Sedgewick."

"He saved my life," Laura Zimquist said, and burst into fresh tears. Ray had heard this before from other people. Homicide and Massport had compiled a fat folder of testimonials from all who knew the slain priest: he was brave, godly, gentle, brilliant, loving, and moral. Ray could find no hint of a dark side in Sedgewick, no unexplained trips or shady friends or funky bank accounts. A model to us all, Chancellor Martin Pasqua had said of the dead father. Except he cut himself, wore a scapular, and had at least one enemy, the murderer.

Laura Zimquist tried again. "My husband's name was Seth Zimquist. He was young and gifted, and he loved me. We had everything to live for. One day, two years ago, Seth walked into the woods and blew his brains out. He left a note, 'I hope this ends it.' Who ever heard of using the word 'hope' in a suicide note?" She was looking at Ray, but speaking to Seth.

She took off the sunglasses. Her eyes were violently blood-shot. "I stayed alone in a little apartment in Portsmouth, New Hampshire, and stared at the wall for a month. I'd probably still be there if it hadn't been for Father Sedgewick. He coaxed me down to Stoneham, put me to work around the church. I did everything—cooked, cleaned, shoveled sidewalks, answered phones. Father said, 'Keep busy,' and so I did. Seth and I were atheists, and I never believed in God. Sometimes I'd ask Father why Seth did it, why God let him do it."

Her voice took on a sleepy, chanting cadence as she spoke of Father Sedgewick. Her hands stopped mashing Kleenex. She seemed transfixed. She gave Ray the creeps.

"Father said we should never ask why people get sick, or go blind, or shoot themselves and leave absurd notes, because there's no answer. Things just happen, and we suffer, and the only defense is a day full of chores. Slowly, I guess I began to believe him." She caught herself wandering, and summed up. "Because of George Sedgewick, I'm alive."

"How did you meet him?" Ray asked, hoping for a short answer.

"He was the chaplain at the Navy base in Portsmouth when Seth and I came east in '58. Seth was just out of grad school in psych. We were newlyweds and Californians, and that first winter nearly killed us. Seth's work was secret, so there was nobody he could talk to about it. Father Sedgewick saw that we were struggling. He reached out to us."

"What kind of work did your husband do for the Navy?"

"Something experimental. I don't know the details. Seth studied ECT at Berkeley—electroconvulsive therapy."

"Shock treatment," Ray said.

"Seth hated that name. Whatever he was doing for the Navy was exciting. He'd lie awake at night and tell me that they were closing in on a breakthrough. 'We're making history,' he'd say. The men from the hospital used to joke about it. They called themselves the Manhattan Project—you know, after the ones who built the A-bomb."

"There were others working with him?" Ray asked.

"There was Lem Childs, a pharmacologist. Lem and Seth were codirectors of the project. When the patients got out of line, they had a man named Harlan Poole to handle the security. 'Head goon,' Seth called him. Father Sedgewick was the glue.

"Seth and Lem would argue the merits of electroshock, Seth's thing, versus the new drugs. That was Lem's baby—the drugs. They were working miracle cures in the Special Wing, I know that much. They often bragged to Father Sedgewick."

"What did they say when they bragged?"

"Oh, they talked about an admiral's wife, a frigid insomniac who felt as if she were choking. The wife spent a month in a locked ward. Seth said they returned her to her grateful hubby, sunny, productive, content. Another time, they treated a test pilot who was a kleptomaniac. Seth said after just two weeks of their experimental treatments the pilot was broken forever of the urge to steal. They were excited, and so was the Navy."

"Sedgewick left Portsmouth early and very suddenly," Ray said. "Do you know why?"

"Harlan Poole," she said. "First they said he was murdered, and we were all questioned by the state police. Then they said he was hit by a car. I guess we'll never know."

"When was this?" Ray asked.

"That summer," she said. "July 1963. After Harlan died, Seth and Lem Childs had a terrible falling-out. Seth wouldn't tell me what it was about, but it was bitter, and they never spoke again. A few weeks later, the Navy came in without warning and shut down the psych ward. Seth said they put the patients on a bus and the files on a truck, and drove them off in opposite directions. The Navy gave us twenty-four hours to get off the base."

"Did the Navy give a reason?"

"All Seth would say was that there had been a mistake. 'One mistake,' he kept saying. Because of one mistake, the whole project was scuttled."

"Whose mistake? Poole's?"

"I think Seth blamed it on Lem Childs. I think Lem blamed it on Seth. Father Sedgewick came by as we were packing up. He said he was leaving too—going back to a parish in Boston. He was worried about Seth, I think. They stood in the street and talked a long time, and then Father left. I begged Seth to take me back to California. I said, 'Let's leave Portsmouth and pretend we were never here.'"

"And—?" Ray pushed gently.

"Seth wouldn't go. He said he wouldn't let the Navy run us out of town. We moved into a one-bedroom place above a body shop, and Seth started talking about Harlan Poole all the time. He'd visit the place where they found Harlan's body, as if he was trying to get to the truth. He thought the Navy was spying on us. He put triple locks on all the doors and wouldn't let me out for groceries. He'd shout out the windows at passing cars, *I'm not afraid of you! I won't go away!* The police came once or twice and told him he was disturbing the neighbors."

"How long did this go on?"

"All fall. Then one day, Seth saw something, or someone, and everything changed."

"What did he see?"

"A man, I think. A man across the street from our apartment. Just a man. After that, Seth lost his anger. He didn't blame the Navy, or Lem Childs, or anyone. He just gave up, gave in, whatever. He sat all day long with his eyes on the street as if he was waiting for someone to come pick him up. Then he left for a few days. Later, I found out he had come down here to see Father Sedgewick. Father Sedgewick told me that at Seth's funeral."

Ray nudged her again. "And—?"

"And Seth came back to Portsmouth. He gave me a kiss, a long kiss." Laura Zimquist wiped the memory of the kiss from her mouth. "They found him later, in the woods...."

She went to pieces on Ray's shoulder. Ray was thinking: *Head Goon Poole dies in July of '63, then electroshock wizard Seth Zimquist a few months later. Father Sedgewick hurries home to Boston and lives another year and a half in a vest of pain, until death catches him on Runway Five South-A.* Laura blew her nose.

Ray showed her three different sketches of the stocky, cap-wearing assailant from the airport based on descriptions by three different eyewitnesses. None of them looked anything alike. She drew three blanks.

"Where's Lem Childs now?" Ray asked.

"Boston someplace."

"Did Childs and Sedgewick stay in touch?"

"Yes."

Ray asked the cops, "Do we have Sedgewick's address book?" The cops nodded.

"Check it for Childs," Ray said. He asked Laura, "Did Childs know that Sedgewick was going to Rome?"

"Possibly, probably. They talked a lot."

It was time to cut the widow loose. She'd come in with a packed suitcase. Ray didn't need to ask her why: Laura Zimquist was finally going back to California.

"Take her to Logan," Ray told the Homicide men.

"Not Logan," she said. "I couldn't stand to go there. Just take me to the bus depot. I'm flying out of La Guardia."

Ray stopped her at the door. "Did Sedgewick ever tell you why your husband came to see him just before, you know, the end?"

"Father said that Seth killed himself to protect me."

"From what?"

"Father said it didn't matter, because now I was safe. He said, 'Never ask why. Why won't help you. You're safe now—that's what matters.'"

9

Joe Mears skirted the landfill, coming down on the Gibraltar Street projects from the north. He crossed the street and crossed back, checking out the foot traffic. He saw a green Ford coupe sitting on F Street, pointed uphill. In the front seat, two white lunkheads washed down hot dogs with bottles of Pepsi. Driver: big and blond with a crew cut. Riding shotgun: some sobersides in a white sportshirt, black hair. Mears kept walking, around the back of 10 Gibraltar and up the fire escape to apartment 33, where he kept a stash pad. He found a pair of field glasses and took them to the roof.

The day was warm and the street was busy. The three project towers cast a jagged line of shadow on the neighborhood. Mears couldn't find the green Ford when he got to the roof and was almost done looking when he saw the big blond driver walk the block slowly, B Street to K, and disappear from view. Mears waited. Sportshirt was next, ducking into the laundromat. If these were city narcs, they were new blood—Mears had never seen them at Chico's with the others.

Patterns emerged. The big blond in the Ford cruised the block in tandem with a silver Dodge. Mears saw the Ford going north-south on Gibraltar, the Dodge south-north—Ford, Dodge, Ford, Dodge, stagger-shift, all day.

Mears looked for foot coverage. You got Sportshirt doing laundry. You got Big Blond buying a newspaper at the D Street tobacconist, then hanging out near the pawnshop like he's waiting for a bus, but there ain't no bus. The Ford comes by, Sportshirt driving now. He meets Big Blond on the corner. Blond knew he was coming; these motherfuckers have radios. All is quiet for twenty minutes. Mears wondered, *Show over?*

He thought, *Hello, narcs. You the B-team? You want to figure out who's pushing drugs out of Gibraltar? If you're good, you'll send an undercover in, and I'll be watching. If you're good, you'll go up the ladder to the source. I'm the source. Maybe you'll come for me.*

He had long since given up on meeting Caesar Raines; Caesar could get supplied tomorrow. Instead, he made moves. He caught a trolley down to Jamaica Plain. He took the plastic bags of Eucharist he had stolen from Sedgewick out of the priest's beat-up suitcase and ran them up to a furnished room on West Dedham Street. Mears pried up floorboards in the closet, wrapped the Eucharist under the priest suit, and hid them in the hole.

He went out. The spring dusk was going overcast. Boston looked shabby. Mears was checking himself for a tail, but he soon forgot about this, and got lost in his thoughts. He drifted north to the piers, then back to Park Square, which took about an hour. He was a fast walker.

He paid to see a movie and sat in the dark. The movie was something about the Navy winning World War II and the theater was almost empty. Mears watched as much as he could stand. When he had first come to Boston, he went to the movies every day. He saw *Bye Bye Birdie* dozens of times and devoured the *Beach Party* series. When he watched a movie, especially a musical, he could get inside it and not be himself. Maybe this was a backhanded gift from Portsmouth. He was always surprised when the lights came up and he had a body again. Church was that way too, and Cuban jazz in Chico's club. But as he watched the movie about the Navy, Mears felt every bit of his body. A headache came.

He got scared. The narcs were closing in, Chico's was long gone, and the movies were losing their power. Even church was changing—Latin to English, they said. The headache got bigger.

Mears hurried out and walked back to West Dedham Street through off-and-on drizzle. He let himself into his room and took the priest suit from the hiding place under the closet floorboards. Slowly, carefully, he put it on, white choke collar last of all. There was no mirror in the little room, so he went out to the street to see himself in a shop window.

He passed a man on the sidewalk, who touched his hat and said, "Evening, Faddah."

It was raining steadily now, and Mears was hatless. Other people said "Good evening" to him as they hurried home from work. It was what you did in Boston—not a big showy, kiss-ass thing, just a curt nod or a tip of the hat, and "Hello Faddah."

For a moment, Mears was giddy. He was a killer and a drug dealer, yet here was everyone giving him these respectful nods. He felt so light. He did a big sign of the cross in the air—he looked like an ump calling strike three—and made the rain into holy water which blessed every place it fell. People started looking at him funny, but he couldn't stop. He started to laugh. It was funny, wasn't it? People were crossing the street to get away from him now, so he started saying, "Hello. Good evening. Hi there. Nice to see ya—" He chased a few of them, shouting, "Good evening. Hello. Take care!"

The headache struck him savagely from behind, and he stopped in the middle of the street. He staggered to the iron fence in front of his building and stood there a long time, head down like he was looking at his shoes, getting drenched.

10

Manny Manning and his team worked the streets in Telegraph Heights, taking the pulse of Gibraltar. LeBlanc and Scanlon covered one end of the main drag, Butterman and Hicks the other. They switched positions hourly, shuffled cars, and mixed up the teaming: Hicks and Scanlon motoring down Gibraltar Street, Butterman flying solo on the side streets, LeBlanc on foot in between.

Shecky Bliss rented a room in a slummy walk-up, catty-corner from the projects, and started snapping pictures of the avenue in action. Manny blew up the photos and taped them to the walls of Narco's basement bomb-shelter office, grouped by time of day. Manny studied the pictures until he could give a guided tour of the ebb and flow of the indigenous dope trade. Gibraltar morning feeding, at noon, teatime, midnight.

Junkies kept dying—one or two a week, in the suburbs and the city. Manny called on the morgue to collect the contents of their pockets, looking for leftover bags—for samples, even small ones, of the fentanyl-laced dope flowing out of Gibraltar. The bags differed in size and color, and various cuts were used: mannitol, quinine, milk sugar, others. Purity and money were, as always, inverse: the lower the purity, the higher the profits. Somebody was making a mint off of fentanyl. Gibraltar was as busy as an anthill. Manny had at first assumed that many independent operators dealt there. But the careful, constant strength of the samples meant one standard was being enforced from above. Manny surveyed the nickel bags on his desk blotter. Somewhere on the block was one ant who ran the hill. That ant was Target.

Manny and Shecky went to see Bennie Anastasia, armed with photos of the crowds around the projects, hoping Bennie could pick out the two crucial men: the Negro spot manager and the Cuban Angel. But as they scoured Bennie's usual hangouts, Shecky got a feeling.

"Bennie's gone," he said flatly.

"He'll turn up," Manny said, from behind the wheel. "He always does."

"No," Shecky said, watching kids dart off the sidewalks. "Something's happening, something strange. Bennie's cleared out for real."

"Fuck him then," Manny said. "We'll ID the guys ourselves."

The narcs reunited after dark at the Triple Shamrock on Dorchester Ave. Biff got the first round, elbowing his way back from the bar with a tray of beer and shots and a lone ginger ale for Dave LeBlanc. The Triple Sham was cops six deep—mostly hoi polloi patrolmen, gabbing madly, drinking hard, awash in adrenaline, just off work. Biff knew a few of them from the Academy and collected congrats on the promotion to Narco as he made his way through the crush with his tray. He passed some geezers from Robbery, who lined the bar in the weird light of a Schlitz clock, empty glasses and packs of filterless Camels in front of them, talking to no one, not even each other, calling for drinks with their fingers. Biff put the tray down at a back booth, where the narcs were relaxing after a day of surveillance around the Gibraltar Street housing project.

"Gibraltar's active, that's for sure," Butterman said, taking a beer and a shot from Biff's tray. He roughed a napkin-map of the projects, making ink dots at the busiest selling locations and little stars for the teenagers standing lookout. Nat was talking trade-craft—tac plans and ob posts and good setups for rolling surveillance. The detectives in the booth took their drinks from Biff, nodding as Butterman talked. They were men in their prime, these narcs, more seasoned than the overloud patrolmen, but not yet burned-out like the Robbery stiffs.

Manny proposed a toast to new-boy Biff, and the table drank.

Manny wiped his mouth with his hand. "According to Bennie Anastasia, there's two faces to watch for at Gibraltar. The first is a Negro kid, name unknown. Bennie says he manages the spot. There's also a Cuban, name of Angel."

Manny smiled. "Let's have us a little shooting match. Hicks and Butterman, find the Cuban Angel. Bennie says he took a drug collar over the summer—you may be able to ID him through the arrest files."

Butterman cracked his knuckles. "Done."

Manny turned to Scanlon and LeBlanc. "You two do the Negro manager."

Scanlon's cast had come off that morning, and he scratched his wrist nonstop. "Not much to go on," he groused. "Gibraltar's a housing project, for chrissake. It's *full* of 'em. Let's ask Bennie for more details.

"Never mind Bennie," Manny said. "Shecky has a ton of good surveillance shots of the foot traffic outside the projects. The manager will be in the pictures somewhere."

"What about me?" Biff asked, pulling a chair to the fringe of the booth.

"It's too early to use an undercover at Gibraltar," Manny told him. "Meantime, fetch another round."

Which Biff did, many times. Butterman and Shecky told stories on each other, on themselves, and on everybody else, until the party started breaking up. LeBlanc was the first to go. Tight-lipped Jay Scanlon followed him. The Triple Sham was almost empty by then, the kids from patrol having gone home to their families or downtown to find girls. Only the Robbery geezers remained, sitting on bar stools and looking like woodcuts. When

Butterman and Hicks left for the suburbs, Manny and Shecky were alone with Biff.

"Have we bored you?" Shecky asked him.

Biff drunkenly banged his mug on the table. "More stories."

"More?" Shecky said. "You heard 'em all, I think."

"I haven't heard about Pressure Point."

"And you're not gonna, either," Manny said. "Shecky, tell a funny story."

"He's going undercover for us—for *you*," Shecky said. "Don't you think he should hear about our greatest victory?"

"*He should*," Biff brazened.

Shecky cleared his throat. "Pressure Point," he said.

"Shecky," Manny warned.

Shecky ignored him. "Once upon it time—actually, last summer—there was a busybody state legislator from Back Bay. He was an ambitious chap, and a reformer to boot. He kept giving speeches about 'alleged irregularities' in the senior ranks of the Narcotics Division. He was careful to note, this friend of truth, this budding Cato, that he wasn't accusing *any*one of *any*thing. Perish the thought. All he wanted was a simple look at Captain Gus Hanratty's operational ledgers, which didn't seem like a lot to ask.

"Well, Biff—are you awake?—what's Captain Hanratty to do? Let them look, then resign? Or just resign? A normal man, a man like you or me, would decide between these two equally bad choices. But not Gus Hanratty."

Shecky stole a look at Manny to see if he was listening, but Manny's eyes were on the wall across the bar, where six framed pictures remembered patrolmen killed in the line of duty, going back to 1901. Shecky wondered what Manny was thinking, and guessed that he was looking at the genuine heroes and hating the phony hero, Gus Hanratty.

Biff was waiting.

Shecky said, "Hanratty had already weathered one corruption

scandal—the mess that did in your da—and he had no intention of facing another one. So he fights back, our Gus. He puts a tail on the state legislator, looking for dirt. He sends out feelers through trusted intermediaries—discreet inquiries as to whether perhaps possibly the state representative might be interested in large campaign donations. Things of that nature."

Biff faced Manny. "Is this true?"

Manny said to Shecky, "Tell the story."

"Gus hits a brick wall," Shecky said. "Turns out the state rep loves his wife and acts like it. Turns out the man is rich as Croesus and doesn't need Gus's money. It's what's known in the trade as a big problem: how do you whore a man you can't blackmail or bribe? Any guesses, Biff?"

"Just tell the fucking story," Manny said.

Shecky said, "Hanratty assembles the largest operation anybody ever saw—eighteen separate observation posts, thirty catch units, seventy cops in forty-two cars and vans, gear and men begged and stripped from the rest of the department, talking to each other over a dozen frequencies, all cleared specially for the duration. A police juggernaut. Pressure Point, it was code-named."

Biff nodded, suddenly rapt, whispering the blood-and-thunder name to himself.

"Now, Hanratty deployed Pressure Point, where? Where would you put it, if you were he? Think, now, Biff. In the state rep's district, to win him as a friend?" Shecky touched Biff's arm. "You or I might have done that. But not Hanratty. Pressure Point gets orders: the South End, worst heroin country in Boston. Hanratty says, *Shut it down.*"

Shecky wet his lips with beer. "Fifth of December, we shut it down. We took twenty collars in five hours and kept it up, around the clock, for days and weeks. Nobody got to see their kids, their wives, their mistresses. Three hundred busts, we made. Or was it more, Manny?"

Manny grunted, eyeing the heroes.

"You invented Narco's street tactics, Manny. Pressure Point was your crowning glory. Or it should have been."

"Get on with it," Manny said.

Shecky got on with it. "Picture the scene, Biff: a blasted mile along the B&M right-of-way, south to Union Park Road, Narco everywhere, arresting everyone, a school bus running shuttle down to the back door of county arraignments, night court stretching into day court stretching into night court. Junkies collared early in the op were bailed a day later, arrested again, reparoled, then re-arrested. Spotlights, flares, bullhorns telling whole blocks to halt. Teams of cops with shotguns pulling late-night visits to every place where dopers were known to gather, sacking drug spots aplenty. We started calling it 'Prussia Point.' It was D-Day crossed with a circus. It was fucking *fabulous*."

Biff, in awe, dribbled beer.

Shecky lent him a napkin. "Heroin has been sold in the South End since before you were born, Biff. There are grandparents there who saw smack deals on the way to school thirty years ago. The locals figure it can never be stopped, will never be stopped, so they live with it. It's always been that way and will always be that way. Hope dies.

"You don't know what I'm talking about. I see it in your face. You're going undercover—maybe you'll learn. But for three weeks, Prussia Point *stopped the sale of heroin in the South End*. Little old ladies couldn't believe their eyes. Had Lincoln risen? White cops were saying no heroin here, and meaning it. The little old ladies baked us pies, gave us lemonade. We felt like Sherman's army liberating Georgia. *Us*, Biff: cops—the line of stinky fucking drunks you saw stretching to the men's room tonight. The question arose, what's gotten into Hanratty? Since when did he give a fuck about Negroes? What's his angle?"

Biff said, "His angle?"

"His angle," Shecky said. "You see, Biff, Prussia Point made it too hot to sell dope south of the B&M tracks, so the drug trade went *north*. Hanratty was herding the entire South End smack traffic into Back Bay, the state rep's lap. B&Es quintupled along the Charles. Christmas shoppers were getting mugged as they left Brooks Brothers. It was actually pretty funny seeing the pushers do deals outside the Cosmopolitan Club, jamming up the pay phones arguing with their girlfriends, slamming down the phone, turning to some blue-haired Yankee dowager and asking, 'Can you believe the balls on that bitch?'"

Shecky, chuckling bitterly, couldn't believe the balls. "We very nearly erased the richest, most historic neighborhood in Boston. And here's the brilliant part: if the state rep raised a peep, Hanratty could accuse him of not wanting the cops to protect Negroes equally, which would have put Gus in the deliciously ironic position of sounding like Adlai Stevenson. It's *genius*, really.

"Hanratty and the state rep sit down to talk. They realize they have much in common. They kiss and hug and fall in love. DA Johnny Cahill pronounces them man and wife. The state rep's probe of Gus Hanratty is shelved forever and, in return, the cops pull out of the South End, which had briefly been a place for decent people."

"That's fucked-up," Biff said.

"No," Shecky said, "but this is: Hanratty called us together just before the pullback. We packed seventy men into the high school gym we were using as a command post, all of us coffee-jagging and ready for more.

"Hanratty stood up front. He said, 'Pressure Point's over, boys. You have won a total victory over those scumbags out there. On behalf of this department, I thank everyone for their hard work.' He announces a week off for all hands and we whoop it up.

"Then he says, 'But before you go, there's one last thing. We got to clean up the mess we've made.'"

Biff asked, "The mess you made? What mess?"

"We all look at each other. *What the fuck is Hanratty talking about?*

"He says, 'We moved a lot of niggers into Back Bay. Can't have that. Move them back. Tonight.'"

Manny said to Biff, "I had nothing to do with it." He got it out fast, like an apology.

"Me and Manny left," Shecky agreed. "Came here and got potted, in fact. We didn't want any part of what was about to happen. 'Course, we didn't *stop it* either."

Manny said, "I couldn't stop it. How could I stop it? I'm just a sergeant."

"And I'm just a drunk," Shecky said brutally. "Yes, Biff, some men left and some men stayed. The men who stayed spent that night running every black face in their path back across the line. How many beatings did they administer? A few. The kids from the Howard University Glee Club pack-mugged by mysterious white men outside the Sheraton? Scanlon, Butterman, and Hicks did that. They aren't bad men—except maybe Scanlon. They just got bad orders at the wrong moment, and didn't stop to think."

Manny examined his beer.

Biff said, "Jesus."

Shecky raised his glass and tried to come up with a toast.

Manny's "shooting match" got started the next morning: Butterman and Hicks, working the Cuban known as Angel, versus Scanlon and LeBlanc on Gibraltar's night manager.

Nat Butterman found his Angel in the summer arrest files: Angel Alex Chacon, born in Havana in 1946, picked up in a Vice sweep of the South End in May 1964. Butterman and Hicks pulled the booking photo and started hanging out in Telegraph Heights. Angel Chacon didn't keep them waiting long. Bounding down F Street from the Broadway trolley, bowling bag in his hand, was a walking mug shot, the Cuban Angel.

Angel Chacon slipped into Middle Tower and stayed sixteen minutes by Hicks's watch, emerging with the bowling bag. He walked over the hill to Broadway and caught an inbound trolley.

Butterman caught it with him. Chacon sat in back, bowling bag on his lap. Butterman got on behind an old lady and found a seat next to her, toward the front of the car. Butterman launched into a random conversation with the old lady so the rest of the trolley would think they were together.

"Hi," Butterman whispered. "You probably think I'm some kind of perv, talking to you like this. But I need to seem like I know you. I'm a cop. You're part of my cover. I'm doing surveillance on that guy back there—the one dressed like Ricky Ricardo."

The trolley rattled over the saltwater channel to Dorchester. Chacon enjoyed the view of the skyline as the train went elevated, drumming on the bowling bag.

"Don't make a scene," Butterman whispered. "I'd show you my shield, but that would kind of defeat the purpose."

"You're a pervert," the old woman said. "You like to ravage old ladies."

Butterman started to sweat. "I swear I'm not a pervert—"

"*Pervert*," she hissed. "You'll talk your way into my apartment, which is right near the next stop, then you'll rip my clothes off. Your hungry hands will knead my ample, quivering flesh. You'll mount me forcefully, your rude rod driving deeper and—"

Butterman found another seat, to hell with cover, and stayed with Chacon through Park Street, where the Cuban changed lines. Butterman let him go. He called Manny from a subway pay phone.

"Everything okay?" Manny asked.

"Other than running into Shecky's mom on the train, sure," Butterman laughed. "I took Chacon as far as Park Street. He just scored at the location, Middle Tower, and he's on his way home.

This kid's definitely a customer. He's a live wire too. Betcha he'd sell to an undercover."

"Good," Manny said. "Find Hicks and come in."

Manny went back to Shecky's blowups of Gibraltar Street in action, big magnifying glass in hand. He was searching the crowd shots for the elusive spot manager, the nameless Negro kid, circling any male face which filled the bill, and numbering each with a yellow grease pencil. Manny lost himself in the pictures. He was looking hard at a tall, chubby kid who showed up outside Gibraltar early every morning and stayed late, loitering between the project towers and giving orders to the runners and the lookouts. Manny rechecked all the photos of Gibraltar. The chubby kid was always there in the same lime-green windbreaker, under which he jammed a large-caliber pistol, bulge shifting from his right to left side, depending on the day.

The gun bulge spoke volumes. Manny taught his men to pick a place where their sidearm sat best—armpit, ankle, waist, wherever—and leave it there, so they wouldn't be digging for their pistols like loose change when the time came. Uncomfortable with the gun, the chubby kid wore it all over his body. This told Manny that the kid in the lime windbreaker was new to the life.

"You're soft," Manny told the kid's picture.

LeBlanc and Scanlon set out to learn his name. They followed him from the projects to a social club near Boston City Hospital. They tailed him from the social club to a tenement apartment leased to a Mary Raines Clark. This took a whole day.

Mary Raines Clark's application for welfare said that she had been born in Virginia. She'd lived with a porter until he ran off, then worked as a seamstress until she went blind. She claimed six dependents: two daughters, a son named Wilbur, and three grandsons. LeBlanc did a workup on the grandsons, still looking for the soft kid's name.

"First, there's Alvin Clark," LeBlanc told Manny, cribbing from a file. "He's Wilbur's boy. He's twenty-five. Got a sheet for burglary from across the river. Mug shots are on order."

"He's about the right age," Manny said. "Who's the next candidate?"

"Garrett Hays. He's an interesting case. He was born in 1947 to one of Grandma Clark's daughters. The daughter was some kind of schizo, in and out of mental hospitals, and a junkie too. In 1960, when Garrett was thirteen, Department of Youth Services tried to put him in a state home, but Grandma Clark saved the day. DYS did a report, which I glommed."

LeBlanc read from the social worker's report: "'It is found that Mary Raines Clark maintains a stable, loving home, a vast improvement over that provided by Garrett's natural mother since her relapse. Wilbur Clark is Garrett's uncle, gainfully employed as a night watchman. Alvin Clark is Garrett's cousin. He presently resides in the Middlesex County Jail, Cambridge. Garrett's other cousin, Bo Norman, is twelve. He also lives in the apartment. Bo Norman is a fine student who dreams of becoming a police officer someday.'"

"Keep dreaming," Scanlon cracked.

The narcs had a laugh at the dreamer's expense, all except LeBlanc, who had found something else: a juvie arrest of Garrett Hays for heroin, May, 1963.

"How old's Garrett now?" Manny asked.

Scanlon shut his eyes to do the math.

"Eighteen," Shecky said, ruining the suspense.

"No," Dave LeBlanc said, handing Manny a photo from his folder. "He was seventeen." The photo was passed around, sobering all.

"Slit throat," LeBlanc said. "Found in an alley up in Brighton just about a year ago."

Manny studied the morgue shots of Garrett Hays. "Well," he said, "Rule Garrett out."

He picked up a surveillance glossy of the soft kid in the limegreen windbreaker. "Maybe this fucker's connected to the Clarks, maybe not. Either way, stay with him. He's the manager. He'll tell you his name eventually."

LeBlanc and Scanlon tailed the chubby kid from Gibraltar to an apartment in Roxbury leased to a Miss Smith. She was quiet and decent, the super said, and had a small son named Garrett Smith.

The chubby kid played hide-and-seek with Miss Smith's child in Washington Park, the gun still under his jacket. The child hid behind a tree, giggling and hushing himself. Scanlon and LeBlanc were across Paulding Street, windows rolled down, Scanlon devouring two hot dogs at once.

"Good practice," Scanlon said, chewing, gulping, chewing.

"Huh?" LeBlanc said.

"Good practice for the little jig—practice for hiding from us."

"Jay, shut up, okay?"

"Why're you so sore? All's I said was—"

"Just shut up. I'm trying to hear."

Soft was pretending not to know where Miss Smith's child was, searching everywhere except where the boy crouched behind a skinny sapling, knees knocking with glee, until excitement overwhelmed him.

"Here I am, Bo," the child shouted, jumping from behind the sapling. "Over here!"

LeBlanc started the car. "Guess Bo Norman didn't fulfill his dream."

The white hood said he was looking to push dope out of state. At first, Angel Chacon didn't trust him. "Who do you know?" Angel kept asking.

"I know lots of people," the white hood said.

That's not what Angel meant. "Who do you know that I know, so I'll know you ain't, you know—"

"A cop," the white hood said.

Angel said, "See?"

"I know Bennie Anastasia," the hood offered. "Me and Bennie A. got rich together. Ask him about me."

"Bennie A. dropped out," Angel said. "No one's seen him since the blizzard."

"Yeah?" Biff said.

"Yeah."

"Well, I know Gibraltar. I had my boy Garrett Hays over there."

"He's dead," Angel said, and made a slicing motion at his throat.

"I was with him like a fucking day before it happened," Biff said. "Garrett and me was *tight*, right?"

"You bought off Garrett?"

"All the time," Biff said. "Look, bro, you don't want to sell to me? Coo'. If Garrett was alive or Bennie was around, they'd tell you I'm solid, but whatever. The important thing is that we stay friends."

So Angel sold him dope. Biff was grinning, winking, chewing gum, dressing like Dean Martin's stunt double, and working Angel textbook: two, five, fifty, then a hundred glassines at four bucks apiece. Biff tipped Angel well, never quibbled over weight.

Manny signed the buy-money vouchers: four deals with Angel, $720 in fees and tips. Soon Biff was splitting takeout chicken with Angel, knowing he had the Cuban cold on four felony buys already in the evidence vault.

Scanlon and LeBlanc plodded on. They stayed with the spot boss, Bo Norman, putting him in the steady company of Caesar Raines, a retired pimp and bootlegger. Bo Norman was his nephew. Garrett Hays had been a nephew too.

Manny scrawled on his blackboard with squeaky chalk:

?

CAESAR

BO   ANGEL

RUNNERS   LOOKOUTS   INSIDE DEALERS

Manny pointed to the "?" and told his men, "That's the source, Mr. Fentanyl. That's the guy we're after. Caesar'll lead you to him."

Caesar Raines favored creased suits, walking sticks, and Chinese hand fans, and did absolutely nothing for a living so far as surveillance showed. He never went to Gibraltar Street, but always huddled with Bo before and after Bo's visits. Raines, unlike Bo, was a challenging mark—ponderous and cunning, passing lazy afternoons in and in front of the clubhouse, eating ample lunches in a soul-food place called Gilda's across the way, taking coffee in a pool hall down the street, buying papers and a shoeshine in the five-and-dime next door, but always watching the street.

On the second day of the extended Scanlon-LeBlanc tail, Raines met Bo Norman inside the clubhouse, then walked alone five blocks south to a liquor store on Norfolk, where he used a pay phone, speaking briefly. Raines waited fifteen minutes by the telephone. He picked up an incoming call on the first ring and spoke for five seconds. He dialed again, talked, consulted his watch, hung up. He waited. A taxi arrived. Scanlon and LeBlanc shadowed the cab to Walter's, a jazz bar on Mass Ave, where Raines remained until dark, four hours.

"Who else was in Walter's?" Manny asked LeBlanc and Scanlon afterward.

"We didn't go in," Scanlon said. "We'd have been made in two seconds."

Manny blew up. "Raines met somebody, right? Somebody big. So think it through. Who went in right after Raines? Who came out right before he left?"

The next day, Raines reverted to his country squire routine, and didn't break pattern again until the fourth day of the coverage, when he used the Norfolk Street liquor store pay phone to make a call and accept a brief callback. This time, however, Raines strolled to the clubhouse and sent Bo to a black Cadillac registered to the blind grandmother, Mary Raines Clark. Raines crossed the avenue to Gilda's and made a big pantomime of ordering half the menu.

LeBlanc and Scanlon shadowed Bo to a waterfront tavern in Italian East Boston. Scanlon followed him in and hunched over the jukebox. He punched up the Ventures' "Pipeline," Jan & Dean's "Dead Man's Curve," then—by mistake—"How Much Is That Doggie in the Window?" Bo sat alone at the bar, nursed a beer, and nibbled pretzels.

Caesar Raines arrived an hour later, and he and Bo walked down the block to Giampanelli's, a restaurant noted for its mussels and its mobsters. LeBlanc and Scanlon watched from a car across the street.

"Raines gonna eat *again?*" Scanlon marveled.

Learning from the Walter's lapse, LeBlanc scribbled the license plate of every wiseguy leaving or arriving during the Giampanelli's visit, coming up with half the made men in Boston, most of whom imported heroin. They were elated. Giampanelli's was dagos and docks. After two long months bogged down among the Negroes, they were finally onto Raines's Sicilian connection.

Or a wild goose chase, Manny thought. Bo drew the coverage to East Boston while Raines did what? Manny read the Giampanelli's surveillance this way: Raines lies low as long as he can before reaching out to his fentanyl supplier, probably hoping that the two sore thumbs in the unmarked sedan will go away, also knowing that he could use the duration of the tail to gauge how much Narco had on him. A short tail meant Narco knew nothing, and was fishing, or knew plenty, and wasn't curious. A long tail meant a case was being built. When Raines could wait no longer, he used Bo to draw LeBlanc and Scanlon to Eastie, then met the fentanyl source. Manny was getting a feel for Caesar Raines. Cop and Target thought alike. It felt like making a friend.

"We can't tail Raines anywhere good," Manny told Shecky after taking LeBlanc's report.

"Why?" Shecky asked.

"He'll ditch us. And he will never use the liquor store phone for real business again. It's a decoy phone from here on out."

"So what do we do?" Shecky asked.

"Simple. We watch that phone like hawks."

Which they did, in triple shifts—Manny and Shecky, Butterman and Hicks, Scanlon and LeBlanc—before finally hitting pay dirt. Raines and Bo showed up together at the liquor store. Raines, true to pattern, placed a call on the liquor store phone and waited for a callback, speaking ten words, less. Then, still true to pattern, Bo departed in the Cadillac, with Scanlon and LeBlanc three cars astern. Caesar Raines watched the cops follow his decoy. Manny and Shecky went too, but peeled off after a few blocks and circled back to Raines's home turf: the clubhouse, Gilda's restaurant, the pool hall, the five-and-dime. Manny spied Raines alone in the dime store, talking on a pay phone.

Shecky braked to set up for a tail, but Manny told him to keep driving.

"Where to?"

"DA's Office," Manny said. "We need a wiretap."

11

Ray got home from the courthouse as the first dinner guests were arriving. He dreaded the party of seven lined up for that night. He knew that Mary-Pat and her brother, Chipper, were recruiting a campaign manager from the old school, and he knew that Mary-Pat wanted Win Babcock for visions à la carte.

Vinnie Sullivan, the lawyer who had defended Da, and been a sort of rabbi to Ray ever since, was a family friend and as old-school as they came. Vinnie's clients included the patrolman's union and Morty Moore the Mortgage Magician. Vinnie had represented management during a recent threatened strike of strippers in the clubs along Route 1, and had broken the strippers' union by recruiting scab dancers.

Vinnie was chauffeured to the house by Biff, who brought a leggy date, Nancy Williams. The threesome settled in the living room as Ray got changed upstairs and Mary-Pat arranged the appetizers.

Vinnie turned to Nancy Williams. "You dance, hon?"

"No," she said. In fact, she coached Radcliffe's volleyball team and was working on a master's degree in physiology.

"You wanna dance?" Vinnie asked her.

"You mean right now?"

I mean in general. You'd be dynamite."

Chipper McCallion and Win Babcock pulled into the driveway. They kissed Mary-Pat in the kitchen as Ray came downstairs. Win gallantly carried a tray of herring, onions, and crackers into the living room. Chipper knew everyone except Miss Williams, and Win knew everyone except Miss Williams and Vinnie. Introductions were handled by Ray, and everyone sat down.

"So," Mary-Pat said, which was her way of bringing the conversation around to her husband, who watched from the corner.

Cued, Chipper said, "Vinnie, stop staring at Miss Williams and answer a question."

"Fire away," Vinnie said, staring at Miss Williams.

"Let's say Johnny Cahill retires and there's an election for DA in the fall. Would someone like Ray have a shot?"

Vinnie picked through the smorgasbord thoughtfully. "You'll have a contested primary on the Democratic line. There'll be two pie-in-the-sky liberals, maybe three, so they'll cancel each other out. The machine will back one guy, and that guy will win. So far, these are easy questions."

Chipper didn't blink. "What if Johnny picks his son?"

"Eddie's had a lot of problems," Vinnie said. "Everybody knows he'd probably be in jail now but for Ray over there. On the other hand, his da is a legend, and his ma was a saint. Eddie is, after all, a Cahill."

"So if Johnny picks his son, and Ray runs against them, who will the machine back?"

Vinnie decided on the least alien-looking hors d'oeuvre, a plain cracker. He popped it into his mouth. "Eddie," Vinnie chewed.

"Why not Ray?" Mary-Pat asked.

"First off, who's gonna pay for this campaign?" Vinnie asked the room.

"Assume money's not an issue," Chipper said. Ray's pulse quickened. They were serious.

Win Babcock, who was listening to Vinnie with medium interest, tensed when Chipper said money was no issue for Ray. Ray, as always, read Babcock effortlessly. *He doesn't want Chipper spending his money on anyone but Win Babcock,* Ray thought. *To him, I'm competition.* Babcock's tense look passed in a moment.

Chipper saved the prickliest problem for last and brought it up with brutal frankness. "What about the bag-man issue, Vinnie?"

"It'll come up," Vinnie said. "Not at first, and not directly, but they'll kill Ray with rumors. I mean, here's this guy talking about cleaning house, but his da was a bag man, and so's he."

Win Babcock protested. "You're talking the politics of the past, Mr. Sullivan. We'll tell the voters to look at Ray, not at Ray's father. Ray's got a track record. That's good red meat for the law-and-order mob. The city's in the mood for change."

Vinnie was skeptical. "That's certainly the message, Ray Dunn in a nutshell."

They talked about the campaign through dinner and coffee. By the end of the night, Vinnie was won over, and Win Babcock agreed to pitch in.

The next morning Ray went to the courthouse and was called on Johnny Cahill's carpet. Eddie Cahill sat in a red leather wing chair, tending to his cuticles.

"You're plotting my demise!" Johnny Cahill shouted at Ray. "You're a viper in my house!"

Ray said, "Calm down, boss. I'm not plotting anything."

Johnny called Ray a liar, and quoted some of the dinner-party conversation from the night before.

"I'm stripping you of your titles," Cahill told Ray. "From now on you're a line assistant, that's all. You'll keep the priest murder, and I expect results, d'you hear?"

Ray saw Johnny's angle on the priest killing. If Ray solved the case, he'd embarrass the Church, and earn a powerful enemy at the chancery. If Ray blew the case, Cahill could whisper that Ray was a deal-making phony.

Eddie Cahill got on the intercom to Ray's secretary. "Clean Mr. Dunn's office, please."

Ray stood up.

"You broke my heart," Johnny Cahill said to him.

Johnny Cahill led Ray across the carpet to the door. Ray went like a lamb, stunned. Johnny was whispering maliciously, "Win Babcock's quite a guy, huh? Talks a blue streak, wave of the future. Ambitious, though. Worse than me, even. Wouldn't trust him, personally. Tell the wife to watch herself."

Demoted and moved to an office in the basement of the courthouse, Ray did what he could to follow up on Laura Zimquist's story. He called the base commander in Portsmouth, who referred him to Washington. A Navy lawyer told Ray the entire matter was classified.

"I'm not looking for specifics," Ray explained. "I just need to confirm some facts. Did the Navy operate a special experimental mental hospital at Portsmouth between 1958 and 1963? Was it closed sometime that summer? Help me out on this."

"It's classified," the lawyer said, and that was that.

Through friends, Ray got a look at Dr. Lemuel Childs's file at the Massachusetts Board of Medical Overseers. Childs had been born in Keene, New Hampshire, had graduated from UNH and then from the Harvard School of Medicine in 1936, and had been licensed in psychiatric medicine by the State of New Hampshire in 1940. He'd staffed various hospitals in Concord, Manchester, and the north country until 1958, when he'd gone to work at Portsmouth Naval Hospital, where he'd served with Seth Zimquist as codirector of the Special Wing. Then Harlan Poole had died. Childs had quit the Navy, and had been appointed to City & County Psychopathic Hospital in Boston on June 1, 1964. City & County was a vast madhouse on a rocky island in the harbor, a Black Hole of Calcutta for the poor and the criminally insane. Child's title at the City & County was staff psychiatrist.

Ray called in Boston Homicide and gave them Childs's work number.

"Invite him downtown," Ray said. "Tell him I have some questions about George Sedgewick.

Manny and Shecky found Ray in his new basement office with two bulls from Homicide. The bulls headed out to brace Dr. Lemuel Childs, and Ray walked Manny and Shecky down to the courthouse canteen.

Ray was curt. "What do you want?"

"A wiretap," Shecky said.

"Four of them," Manny said. He gave Ray the short version of what Narco had learned. The Gibraltar Street projects were booming—pumping out a couple thousand bags of high-test dope a day to junkies from all around. Most of the takers were re- tail, except for a Cuban kid named Angel, who bought in bulk and peddled the bags out of his own little spot in the South End.

"Biff's got buys into Angel," Manny said. "If we play it right, Biff might be able to talk Angel into going partners. Then Biff'll start dealing directly with the crew at Gibraltar."

Ray kept walking. "Too dangerous," he said, his stock answer where Biff was concerned. "What do we know about Gibraltar?"

"The manager is a big softie, name of Bo Norman," Manny said. "The real boss is his uncle, an old bootlegger, Caesar Raines. Caesar buys the fentanyl from a source he sees a couple times a week. Caesar calls the source, the source calls back. Then he and Caesar meet. Caesar brings the product back to Bo, who oversees the mixing and the bagging, and sells it from Gibraltar to the world. Right, Sheck?"

Shecky was a pace behind. "Right," he said.

They came to the end of the corridor, turned around, and started back.

"You want the fentanyl source," Ray said. "That the point of the wiretaps?"

"We gotta get the source," Manny said. "We could bust up Gibraltar, sure, but for what? They'd just set up someplace else, OD a few junkies for advertising, and rake it in all over again. The only way to stop the ODs is to pinch the source."

Ray bought some coffee and a sandwich from a vending machine. "So follow Caesar," he said. "Bust him *and* the source when they meet."

"Caesar's too sly," Manny said, following Ray back to his office. "But he uses pay phones to set up the meets. That's why we need the taps."

They were back in the doorway of Ray's cubbyhole.

"How soon do you need them?" Ray asked.

12

Narco manned the wires from a listening post—called a "plant"—in a sweltering basement a mile inland from Gibraltar. Four phones rang endlessly—"slave" lines labeled in magic marker: "Gilda's," for the restaurant where Caesar Raines took lunch; "club," for the Suffolk Democratic lair; "dime," for the five-and-dime; "pool," for the pool hall. The slaves rang for incoming and outgoing calls both, and teletypes recorded every number dialed. The slaves jangled a total of 406 times on the first full day of eavesdropping, and the four teletypes never stopped. The narcs, were jumpy and hungry, and Manny reined them in.

"You will not take action in the field without my say-so," Manny told them the first morning. "You will not initiate a surveillance. You will not stop a subject, even to ID him. You will not do anything but listen to these four phones. Questions?"

Nat Butterman raised his hand. "Why?"

"Because cops pull bonehead stunts on wiretaps," Manny said.

Butterman, persisting: "Why?"

"Wiretaps let you hear through walls, hear for miles," Manny warned. "You'll figure out who Caesar likes, who he pretends to like, and who he hates. You'll think you know more about Caesar than anybody who really *knows* him, see?"

"No," Butterman said.

Shecky cut in. "Cops aren't used to intimacy. What do we usually do? We watch. We guess. We act. Listening's a luxury. It goes to our heads."

"Dang, you're deep," Butterman said.

"Take yourself, Nahum," Shecky said. "If I listened to your phones, what would I conclude? That Nat Butterman is slick shit with a bargain mortgage and a penchant for other men's wives."

"Lay off," Butterman said.

"I wouldn't hear the panic in the sales pitch," Shecky said. "I wouldn't hear how hard you work just to be the model American—"

"Lay off," Paddy Hicks said on his buddy's behalf.

"—I wouldn't know you lost two aunts at Bergen-Belsen, or that your whole life is a big defense against being singled out someday, as they were singled out."

"What's Bergen-Belsen?" Paddy asked Butterman.

"Nothing," Butterman said, eyes on Shecky.

"In fact, Nahum, I wouldn't even know your name," Shecky said.

"What's Bergen-Belsen?" Paddy asked Shecky.

"*Nothing, moron,*" Butterman screamed at Paddy. He was out of his chair and all over Shecky, and Hicks was all over Butterman. Butterman punched Shecky, a blur of little fists, elbowing Hicks's gut on the backstrokes. Scanlon got Butterman's knees, LeBlanc his waist, and finally Hicks peeled him off. Manny never moved from his desk.

Butterman stormed out. Shecky refitted his dentures, touched his face where it hurt, and tested his jaw left, right, up, down.

"See?" Shecky said to Paddy Hicks. "See how little you can really know about a person just by listening to them?"

For a week, they monitored chitchat, takeout orders, lovers' quarrels, and everything in between over four community phones in a neighborhood where few had phones at home. One male, drunk and never identified, told a woman he was coming over to beat her brains out. Another man called the same woman and asked her to a dance. A pimp used the five-and-dime phone to manage his affairs, and three others ran competing loan-shark books from Gilda's. The clubhouse tap was a font of bribes and petty ballot fraud.

"Nothing important," Manny said.

Raines came on only occasionally. He was out of the pross trade but kept in touch with former whores. He had a piece of several businesses in the area—a bowling alley, bootblacks, even a Chinese restaurant—and was a canny investor. He rescued his Chinese cook from a protection racket, and talked some guy named Kenny out of jumping bail. He got water turned on and child support paid.

Raines called Bo "Sonny." Once, in a slip, he called him "Garrett." Bo, too, used the clubhouse phone. He was marrying Miss Smith in September, and promised to move his new family down south. The boy he played with was Garrett's son, and Miss Smith had been Garrett's girl. Bo kept tabs on the dope business at Gibraltar Street, talking in elaborate code about "fried rice" and "chop suey" to a half-dozen unidentified males, saying as little as possible. Caesar Raines never called Gibraltar.

The wires looked like a wash until LeBlanc caught an outgoing call on the Gilda's phone to GA3-2832.

A male picked up, tinny music in the background. "Yeah," he said.

"Yeah," Caesar said. "He around?"

"Who?"

Caesar mumbled a name or a word, *near* or *here*.

The male said, "Nah."

Caesar said, "Tell him, call me. I'm up the store."

New England Bell said GAylord 3-2832 was a skid row hotel off Park Square. Manny, replaying the tape as they waited for the callback, heard a hitch in Raines's voice when he said "near" or "here." It was a name Raines hated, and hated saying, a name he was afraid of.

Hicks, on surveillance duty, radioed that Bo was keeping patrons away from the pay phone and Raines was chasing a hip flask with Pepto-Bismol. About forty minutes passed.

The Gilda's phone rang, incoming. Manny grabbed the headphones. Caesar answered on the second ring. "Yeah?"

A different male this time, same music in the background. "What's up?" he said.

"Not much," Caesar said, trying to sound unruffled and failing. "You?"

Silence followed, a beat too long Caesar blurted, "Gotta see you."

Another wrong-note silence followed.

The male said, "Come on up."

Hicks was on the radio, giving play-by-play. Raines and Bo huddled after the call. Then Bo went to his car and drove north, maybe back to Giampanelli's, another decoy hand job. Raines, now alone, squared the block twice looking for a tail, then started toward the clubhouse.

Manny sat back, headphones around his neck, cigarette lit. Shecky, Scanlon, and LeBlanc watched him thoroughly enjoy a Lark, clouds of blue-gray smoke making the basement even less breathable. Manny was savoring what he knew, and the fact that he knew it: Caesar's supplier is John Doe Near; Near sounds white and local; Near scares Caesar.

Manny had dragged his big office blackboard into the plant. Now he erased the question mark at the top of his chart with an air of triumph. He wrote:

THE WHITE MAN (NEAR/HERE?)
CAESAR
BO   ANGEL
RUNNERS   LOOKOUTS   INSIDE DEALERS

"We should follow Caesar when he meets the white man," LeBlanc insisted.

Manny said no. "Caesar will spot you, and when he does, he'll get to thinking: how did that detective know my movements? It'll take him five minutes to figure out this wire, and change his patterns. Stay invisible, and you're a secret. Show yourself, you lose your power."

Slaves rang and teletypes clacked as Raines's world got wider and deeper. Martin Luther King came to town that week and people on the restaurant pay phones could talk of nothing else.

"See him at the church?" a woman asked her sister in Brockton.

"Handsome man," the sister agreed.

The dime-store slave went off, and LeBlanc monitored the call.

"Outgoing," he told Manny and Scanlon. "Owner calling the cops. Says he's getting robbed at gunpoint."

LeBlanc threw down the headset and made for the door. Manny barred his path. "Bonehead stunt," he warned.

"I can be there in two minutes," LeBlanc said.

"And Caesar'll see you and start to wonder how and why a narc got there so fast."

LeBlanc twisted free of Manny. "Someone might get hurt."

Manny shoved him backward to a chair. The dime-store phone rang again. Outgoing. Five rings, then silence.

"He's calling for help," LeBlanc said.

The phone rang again. Three rings, silence.

By the end of the afternoon, the story was clear. Two brothers, Earl and Andy, had stuck up the dime store, taking four bucks and winging one of the checkout girls. Caesar Raines got wind of it, and tracked the brothers down. He called Bo from the clubhouse and gave him orders.

"You know them?" Caesar asked Bo, with LeBlanc monitoring through the slave.

"Earl, sure," Bo said.

"Andy's his little brother," Caesar said. "They're over at their momma's house right now."

"Yeah?" Bo said, uneasy.

"Go see them, Sonny, hear? You tell Earl he's been warned about this before, been warned too many times. You shoot him. Don't kill him. Shoot a finger."

Bo said nothing.

"Not a finger," Caesar said. "Man can't work without a finger. Shoot a toe. Little toe. Then give him a bus ticket someplace. Tell him, he comes back except to see his folks, I'll know it."

Bo said nothing.

"Make sure the little brother, Andy, watches. Make sure he knows it's a warning."

"Any particular toe?" Bo asked.

"Little one, I said."

"Yeah, but, like, right foot or left foot?"

"What damn difference could *that* make?"

Bo said nothing.

"Listen," Caesar said, "you're a gentle soul, I know, Gram raised you proper."

"Not like Garrett, you mean."

"Garrett was different, is all. And Garrett's gone."

"And I don't want to wind up like Garrett," Bo said.

"I know you don't like the gun part. I know that. But, listen, we're figures of respect around here. People expect us to stand up for 'em. You're doing Earl a service, running him out of town with just a toe blown off. And you may be saving his little brother from a life of stickups. Think of it that way."

Dave LeBlanc disengaged the slave just after Bo hung up. He told Manny about it.

"It's up to you," Manny said. "You can go save Earl's toe and flush the whole drug case. That's a lot of work for all of us, *flushed*, and over a little toe. But—and I mean this sincerely, Dave—it's your choice."

LeBlanc looked miserable.

"Fuck 'em," Scanlon said. "Earl, Andy, Bo, Caesar. Fuck 'em all."

"Clam up," Manny said. He turned to LeBlanc. "Dave, decide."

Scanlon gnawed a toothpick down to pulp. LeBlanc held his breath and stared at the four slave phones as if he wished they'd never come into his life.

Manny said, "Well?"

"Let it happen," LeBlanc said.

Manny stopped downtown to give Ray Dunn a progress report on the Caesar Raines wires. Ray was on the way out.

"Lot going on," Manny told him.

"Let's take a ride," Ray said. "You can tell me all about it on the way."

Manny got on the expressway, southbound, in a steady rain. Traffic crawled, halted, crawled some more.

"Where we going?" Manny asked.

"City & County," Ray said. The wipers beat as they inched past South Station.

"What's there?"

"A psychiatrist named Lem Childs. He's a witness in the priest killing. He's been dodging us, so I figured I'd surprise him at his hospital. Perhaps your glowering presence will jog his memory. How's the wire?"

"Good," Manny said, "but we won't nail the source with just a wire—the source and Caesar are too hinky. We got Caesar's MO pretty well mapped out, and we got a line on the source. He's male, and he's white, and he's scary. Caesar reaches out for him every other day, sometimes at an old hotel in Park Square, sometimes in bars or restaurants or on street corners. Caesar leaves a message and waits for a callback. The source gets back to him—usually in an hour or two. Him and Caesar talk, then they meet. There's no pattern to the phones the source uses, so you can't set up on 'em in advance."

"And you can't tail Caesar?"

"Not for any distance, no. Caesar's as good as they get."

Below Chinatown, the traffic cleared, and Manny made for Quincy in the breakdown lane.

"So what do you want to do with Caesar?" Ray asked.

"I want to take him down. If we nail him on a felony drug sale, he'll roll over on the white man."

"Are you sure he'll roll?"

"No."

"Do we have him on a felony sale?"

"No."

Ray thought this over for a minute until he got Manny's drift. "You want to use my brother," Ray said.

Manny had a little speech prepared. "Angel Chacon buys from Caesar, and Biff buys from Angel. So let's send Biff to Angel with a wad of cash, begging to do a big package. Angel could decline the deal, but he won't, 'cause he's greedy. So Angel will take Biff to Caesar."

"No," Ray said.

"Why not? It makes sense. Admit it makes sense."

"Biff's not ready to go in the deep end of the pool, and you know it."

"If Biff was just another undercover, you'd tell me to go ahead."

"Well, he isn't, so make a different plan."

"Ray, please. My whole life as a narc—which seems like my whole life period—I've been making shit-ass street-level cases. Thousands of them. Slam a junkie here, bang his dealer there.

The squarest, cleanest shit-ass cases, but still. Maybe, on a great day, I get Bennie Anastasia to rat out one of the brokers, and bust my rump for a month and take the broker out. Then some other broker fills his shoes and nothing changes. That whole time I've never seen pure, uncut product. I've never looked the source in the eye. Now I'm close, and I got to have it, whatever the cost."

"You sound like a junkie."

"Good narcs, always do. Besides, Biff wants to make the buy."

"Biff wants to make you happy."

"It's his life."

"Exactly," Ray said.

They were heading for the ocean on a winding road. A Corrections cop loomed from the fog in a yellow slicker, waving a flashlight across his knees. City & County was linked to the mainland by a rickety half-mile causeway with locked iron gates at the shore end. Manny pulled up at the gates and rolled down his window.

"BPD," Manny said, showing the guard his shield.

"We're here to see Dr. Childs," Ray added from the passenger side.

The cop jogged into his guardhouse and called out to the island.

"Childs'll know we're coming," Manny said, watching the cop talk on the phone. Ray watched him too.

The guard jogged back to the car. "Dr. Childs says he can't see you. He's very busy. Perhaps if you wrote him a letter—"

"Open the fucking gate," Manny yawned.

The guard hemmed. Manny got out of the car and the guard scampered back and opened the gate. Manny drove onto the causeway, waving to the guard as he passed.

City & County looked like the ruin of a war ministry behind the Iron Curtain. One wing was dark and boarded-up, gutted in a fire and never rebuilt. The rest was harshly lit, square against the fog.

They went inside the big front doors and stopped at a security desk, where Manny checked his .38 after emptying it, dropping the bullets into his pocket. The elevator smelled like muscatel piss. They got off on the top floor and buttonholed an orderly pushing a cartful of pills. A leather sap hung on the orderly's belt, next to jailer's keys and a rabbit's foot.

"Where's Dr. Childs?" Ray asked.

The orderly pointed down the ward at an old man smoking a cigarette and signing papers against the wall. Childs had the twitchy movements of a hare. He wore a shabby summer-weight suit and white sneakers.

Childs looked up from his papers, and saw Manny first. Manny folded his arms across his chest and did his best to glower. Childs looked down and saw that Ray was shaking his hand.

"You've been avoiding us," Ray said.

Down the ward, someone screamed.

Childs took them to a cramped office. Manny perched on the corner of the desk and grabbed the papers out of Childs's hands.

"Four lobotomies so far," Manny said, leafing through them, "and the night is young—"

Childs snatched his papers back and dropped them in his out box.

Ray said, "Father Sedgewick is dead."

"Did you come all the way out here to tell me that?" Childs asked.

"You've lost a lot of friends in the last few years," Ray said. "First there was Harlan Poole, then Seth Zimquist."

"Zimquist committed suicide," Childs said. "And Poole was hit by a car. George Sedgewick was my best friend. If I could help you find his killer, I would gladly do so."

"You and Zimquist ran the Special Wing in Portsmouth," Ray said. "Harlan Poole kept the patients in line, and Sedgewick took everyone's confession. You were all pretty cozy."

Childs's phone rang. He picked it up, listened, grunted, then hung up. "I'm needed in the ward," he said.

"Zimquist came east from California because the Navy promised him the chance to do something experimental with electroconvulsive therapy," Ray said. "You were Zimquist's partner, the pharmacology wizard, the man with the magic medicine chest. You and Zimquist were on the verge of a breakthrough—we're talking Nobel Prize stuff here. You called yourselves the Manhattan Project.

"It was a joke, our joke," Childs said to Manny.

"Don't sell yourself short," Ray said. "Remember the admiral's wife? She couldn't sleep. She felt as if she were choking and couldn't abide her husband's touch. She spent a month under your care and went home a new woman. How about the test pilot—remember him?"

Ray was drawing Childs out, playing up past glories.

"A decorated fighter ace," Childs said, "the fourth man ever to break the sound barrier, selected for the astronaut program, until they caught him stealing gravy boats from a department store."

Ray egged him on. "You cured the pilot."

"In two weeks," Childs said. "It was a very long time ago— seems like years and years. I felt about pharmacology the way Father Sedgewick felt about God. To me, there was no problem meds couldn't solve. I believed it was in our power to cure all mental illness."

"And the Navy thought so too," Ray said.

"The Navy hated counseling. Counseling was for homos and mama's boys, they thought. They loved drugs because pharmacology seemed like warfare to them. Soften up the sociopath with a round of Stelazine, and after that, send in the Marines. They could relate to it, you know?"

The phone rang. Childs answered. "In a moment," he said, then hung up. "I believed that electroconvulsive therapy, used together with certain drugs, could be a powerful therapy—a life-changing therapy."

"And you were right," Ray said. "You worked miracle cures."

"There are no miracles," Childs said, although the word clearly pleased him.

"Until Harlan Poole died," Ray said, coming forward in his chair. "They said it was hit-and-run, but everyone knew it was murder. You and Seth Zimquist had an argument over Poole's death, and never spoke again. Then the Navy shut down the experiments and kicked you all off the base."

"You've been talking to Zimquist's wife," Childs said.

"His widow," Ray corrected. "Seth Zimquist said that there had been a mistake. *One* mistake—that's all. Because of one mistake, your life's work was destroyed. Tell me, how did it feel?"

Childs assumed the tone of a particularly patient grade-school teacher. "You should know a few things before you make an even bigger ass of yourself, Mr. Dunn. Laura had a nervous breakdown after her husband's suicide. You interviewed her. Did she strike you as stable?"

Ray didn't answer, which Childs took as a no.

"More to the point, Laura's theories about Harlan Poole are drawn entirely from similar delusions expressed by Seth just before he killed himself. I wonder if Laura told you about her husband's other beliefs in his final months. Seth believed that John Kennedy was killed by a CIA sniper team, did Laura tell you that? He believed that UFOs routinely visit Earth and that the government was covering up hard evidence of this. He believed that cancer could be cured with avocado pits but, again, unseen forces were hushing up the truth."

Childs went to his file cabinet and pulled out a folder, which he gave to Ray. Inside were a dozen letters from September and October 1963, the months before Seth Zimquist took his last walk in the woods. Ray scanned the letters, handing them to

Manny one by one. They were typed on plain paper and signed
"Yours, Seth." In the letters Zimquist espoused many nutty theories—and never mentioned Harlan Poole.

Childs watched them scan the letters. "Seth Zimquist was a
brilliant man, but he lost his grip on reality toward the end. Laura
has never been the same since Seth took his own life. It's a pitiful
story—but that's all it is. If you've been conducting your probe
based on their views, you've got a lot to be embarrassed about."

Childs took the papers back from Manny. "I'll have my lawyer
send you photostats of these letters. In the meantime, may I sug-
gest you get back to the business of finding George Sedgewick's
killer?"

Manny and Ray pulled their car out of the parking lot. The rain had
turned to drizzle.

"You believe Childs?" Manny asked as they rattled down the
causeway.

Ray stared out the window, his chin in his fist. "Do you?"

"Those letters are pretty kooky," Manny said. "Could be the
Zimquists are soft upstairs."

They rode in silence the rest of the way to Ray's. Manny let
him off in the driveway.

Ray leaned into his window. "Are you going to use my brother
against Caesar Raines and his source?"

"Let's let Biff decide. He's a man. It's only fair."

Ray looked beat. "You can leave messages for me downtown,"
he said. "I'll be back in a few days."

"Where are you going?"

Ray said, "New Hampshire."

13

Joe Mears woke up and for a moment didn't know where he was. He'd scattered himself all over Boston: stored his books in a little house in Jamaica Plain, hid his money in a Gibraltar Street apartment, kept his stash in a hotel for hobos on West Dedham.

He opened his eyes. He saw a water-damaged ceiling and heard rummies arguing in the hall, which told Mears he was on West Dedham Street. Mears got up and examined the furnished room for signs of entry. The night manager had once let himself in while Mears was gone, checking a gas leak, he said. *Rifling my shit*, Mears believed. He jumped the night man in the basement and put a carving fork to his eye. After that, everybody left him alone.

Mears checked at the front desk for messages, and was told his friend had called. Mears knew this was Caesar Raines looking for product.

"He leave a number?" Mears asked the desk clerk. The clerk's hands shook as he gave Mears a scrawled-on matchbook. Mears crossed the lobby to a pay phone and called the number.

"Gilda's," a woman said.

"Caesar around?" Mears heard a busy restaurant in the background. He liked Caesar's methods: a few words on pay phones, all business, then a pickup. Never any bullshit about money. Not since Garrett Hays.

Caesar got on. "Yeah?"

Mears said, "You called."

Caesar got shaky-voiced, forever reliving his dead nephew, the way Mears liked him: "Can I see you?"

Mears let Caesar dangle, then said, "Okay."

Caesar: "Up the bar?"

Mears: "Yeah. Tonight, late."

The headaches had been fading since Mears came to Boston, but as Mears hung up on Caesar, a bad one hit. They struck in front, behind his eyes, then split like a cell and spread to both temples. Mears climbed the stairs of the old hotel like a blind man, finding his room by feeling the numbers on the doors. He lay in a ball on the floor. Mears thought that his headache was a message: get out. Cut off Caesar, cut off Bennie, go west. He dragged himself across the floor, sat against the wall.

The headache passed. Mears tried to think it through. If staying was a problem, so was leaving. Caesar was the weak link—the narcs' way into Mears. That was clear. But Caesar couldn't be killed, because his street network gave Mears access to the junkies, and but for the junkies, dope was just powder. Mears could find other outlets, but that was risky in a different way, and took time. If Mears was going to start fresh someplace else, he'd need to do a few more packages with Caesar to finance the move.

He could just flee, of course. He could be on a bus that night and be across the country in a week, but that wasn't right. Why should he scrape out of town like a beat dog? Years ago, Mears had promised himself that he would never again be the little man, the dipshit, the throwaway. This promise had gotten him through the electroshock and druggings in Portsmouth, and he couldn't go back on it now.

People should know what had happened to Joe Mears. People should know what the Navy had done, what the doctors had done, and people should know that priests went along too. Mears would do something big before he left. Something that would teach them all that he was not their victim.

He sometimes wondered why the New Hampshire cops had never come for him. In a sense, he'd been waiting for them all along. He had left enough clues to make it clear who killed Poole, and why. Mears had figured the murder would start a kind of chain scandal. Was it possible that no one cared?

People should know about Joe Mears, and if they knew and didn't care, they should suffer what he had suffered.

Mears caught a cab to Quincy Center, and a bus to the gates of City & County Psychopathic Hospital. He crossed the street and then crossed back, checking out the foot traffic, which looked innocent. He settled at a covered bus stop to wait. It got dark. He'd been there an hour when he saw the Chevy leave the island.

Lem Childs got off work, drove down the causeway and through the checkpoint. He came around a corner and put his headlights on. Joe Mears was in the road, standing with both hands up: *stop*.

Childs fought the urge to lock him out and run him down. Mears let himself in on the passenger's side.

"Get going," Mears said. He directed Childs off Squantum Street and south, through Quincy, to a golf course parking lot. Mears was looking for tails.

"Okay," he said. "Park here."

Childs killed the engine and the headlights. He had sweated through his shirt, and his shoulders ached from tension. The clinician in him said, *Face him, make eye contact*, but Childs couldn't. He looked across a dark golf course covered in old snow.

"There's plainclothes on Gibraltar Street," Joe Mears said. "And then I'm waiting for you and I see two more cops in a Chevy come through the gate. What the hell is going on?"

"They wanted to know about Sedgewick, Zimquist, and Poole. They came to me because I'm the last one left."

"What were their names?"

"Manning," Childs said. "The other one was a DA, Dunn."

"Manny Manning?" Mears asked.

Childs nodded. "Do you know him?"

"He's a narc sergeant. His men are tailing Caesar Raines. What do they got?"

"A hunch about Portsmouth." Childs was desperate to calm Mears down. Childs was the only living witness, and if Mears panicked, Childs would die.

"They got nothing more than the New Hampshire prosecutor had," Childs reassured him. "Without the records, they can't find you, and the Navy deep-sixed those long ago."

"They ask about Gibraltar?"

"No."

"Not at all?"

"Not at all."

Mears nodded. "Manny Manning," he said again and studied the parking lot.

Childs pushed a package wrapped in butcher's paper across the seat to Mears's thigh.

Mears kept his eyes on the parking lot. "That my dope?"

"Yes."

Mears took the package on his lap. "I need something special," he said. "Five hundred grams of the other stuff."

Childs was appalled. It was a massive order.

"Get it," Mears said. "Remember Poole, remember Sedgewick."

Childs had heard this veiled threat many times before. He had never called the bluff—if it was a bluff. "Nobody has that much product lying around," he said. "I'll need time. I'll have to go to the underground, call New York, maybe Switzerland—"

"Same price?"

"It's going up," Childs said. "The crackdown's coming. Everybody's stockpiling before the drought."

Both men were silent, letting a car pass.

"Give me some time," Childs said. "I'm not a miracle-worker."

"Sure you are," Mears said. "Look what you did for me in Portsmouth."

Mears made Childs drop him at the Ashmont trolley. Mears and his butcher's-paper package rode inbound to Park, doubling back on the subway to Copley. Mears hiked to the Back Bay train station, ducked in one door, out another, and was satisfied that he was alone. He walked into a drugstore on the corner of Dartmouth and Newbury, the dope still under his arm, and bought a box of chocolate-covered cherries, a roll of sappy flowered wrapping paper, a dollar in stamps, and a card that said *From a Secret Admirer.*

The girl who took his money smiled at the card. "Will that be all?" she asked.

"This too." Mears gave her a bottle of magnesium hydrochloride concentrate, the most powerful laxative in the store.

The girl rang it up. Mears wore the hangdog grin of a guy with a crush on a girl and big problems in the bowels.

He went to his place on West Dedham Street and unwrapped the package. He cut the fentanyl with milk sugar, closed the package, and slipped it in his coat pocket.

He took the box of chocolate-covered cherries from the shopping bag and got a fine-point hypodermic needle from the bathroom. He worked quickly, ignoring the dilution instructions on the magnesium hydrochloride, drawing a needleful of the creamy gunk. He shook the box of chocolates, then probed it lightly with his fingers, finding the candies through the sealed box. He gently sank the needle in the cardboard box bottom, where the pin-sized hole wouldn't be noticed. He felt the needle hit a soft chocolate and injected some gunk. He did this a dozen times until he was sure the candy cherries were good and dosed, then he taped the card to the box, wrapped it in the flowered paper, addressed it, first-class, to a girl in Squantum, and dropped it in a mailbox on his way to meet Caesar Raines.

Manny Manning came home from the plant the following evening and found the youngest of his seven daughters coloring on the kitchen floor. Her name was Louise. She was six.

"Where's dinner?" Manny asked her.

Louise shrugged. "Ask Mom."

"Where's Mom?" Manny asked her.

"Upstairs with Meg and Jo and Nancy in the bathroom."

Manny got a beer from the fridge and sat down at the kitchen table. He opened the can with one hand and drank. "All four of them are in the bathroom?" he asked.

Louise nodded, intent on coloring.

Manny rubbed his temples and sniffed his armpits, then took a swallow of beer. "Lu?" he said.

"Mmm."

"Why are all four of them in the bathroom?"

She colored carefully. "'Cause they ate the pretty candies that the mailman brought," she said.

14

Ray was knotting his tie and telling his wife why he had to go.

"I've got to follow a lead," he said. "Shouldn't be more than a few days."

She came out of the bathroom in a terry-cloth robe, her hair in a towel turban.

"I'll call," Ray said.

"Don't strain yourself. Just tell the baby-sitter what continent you're on."

"You going out?"

"I might," she said, affecting the airy hauteur of a bored Yankee heiress. She knew Ray hated that act.

He didn't ask where she was going. There were forbidden topics between them now. Ray's demotion and disgrace was one of them. Win Babcock was another. Was that two topics, or one?

"I think you're going because you want to go," she said. She rubbed her hair with the towel and sat down at her vanity.

"What's that supposed to mean?"

"Keep your voice down," she said.

Ray put his suitcoat on and paused at the bedroom door. "Be back in a few days," he said.

First he called on the Portsmouth police, which had sketchy reports on file about the death of the Navy employee, Harlan Poole, in July 1963. Rockingham County deputies questioned a handful of

people who knew Poole, then the state AG ruled the death acci-
dental, and Harlan Poole went to the archives.

Next, Ray found the landlord at the walk-up flat where the
Zimquists had lived three tortured months after Poole died and
the Navy shut down the Special Wing of the Portsmouth hospital.
The landlord remembered everything: Seth Zimquist's erratic be-
havior, his demand for extra locks on all the doors, visits from the
cops when Seth started shouting obscenities out his windows and,
finally, Seth's suicide, which ended the sad episode. The landlord
remembered Laura Zimquist most of all.

"Lovely thing," the landlord said. "Fell apart when her husband died. Heard she went to work for a priest down your way.
Hope her luck changed."

Ray finished up at the public library and pulled Seth
Zimquist's obit: Navy doctor, age thirty-two, suicide with a note,
October 11, 1963.

In his travels, Ray avoided the most obvious place to ask questions: the big base in the heart of the port. All the streets led to
the Navy's front gate. Ray found himself at the gate a dozen times
as he groped his way around Portsmouth, but he never stopped to
ask anything of the Marines on guard duty, not even directions.
Portsmouth was a major sub base and a brig. An oiler lay at anchor
where the Piscataqua River met the sea. Ray saw sailors in bars all
over town, drinking away the afternoon.

Ray took supper in a diner on the highway—scrod, squash,
fries, black coffee—reading a book about electroshock. What
little Ray knew about psychiatry he had learned beating insanity
defenses at trial, and that wasn't much. He knew that psychia-
trists put you on a couch and asked you how you felt. He knew
that some of them would take an expert's fee to say you couldn't
tell right from wrong. The world of electroshock was new to Ray.
He learned that standard electroconvulsive therapy was 110 volts

fed from a generator to the human brain through electrodes, once daily, never more, a fraction of a second, under local anesthesia and phenobarbital to cut down on convulsion injury. Electroshock relieved depression and schizophrenia, but nobody knew why. The prevailing view seemed to be that the voltage wiped the brain clean, erasing mental illness.

Ray turned a page to a black-and-white photograph of a man getting the treatment: electrodes on his temples, a black rubber mouthpiece in his jaws, eyes bugged.

Ray tried to picture kindly Father Sedgewick as chaplain to the house of horrors. Sedgewick had training in psychotherapy, so Zimquist and Childs let him in on everything. What does a priest say to somebody getting volts to the head courtesy of the government?

Ray looked up from his book as a waitress cleared his plates.

"Closing time," she said.

Ray paid and went back to his hotel, where he expected trouble sleeping.

After breakfast, Ray headed inland to the village of Stratham and met a gaunt man named T. K. Marcotte, who wore the khaki-and-green uniform of a Rockingham County deputy sheriff. Ray found Marcotte in the barbershop, which was also the post office, draft board, and town hall.

Ray shook the deputy's hand and explained his business. Marcotte walked him to a squad car parked out back.

"I was a new hire then," Marcotte recalled on the road out of Stratham. They passed rambling homesteads and dairy farms with stone walls. Ray rolled down his window and smelled wet hay and cows.

"Got a radio call from a construction crew digging foundations for new houses in the orchard," Marcotte was saying. "I'd never seen a corpse before."

Marcotte had a harrowed face from a Walker Evans picture and spoke with a Down East drawl—"orchard" came out *awe-chid*, "corpse" came out *cops*.

"Harlan Poole was a local boy, a roustabout, a drinker," Marcotte said. "Portsmouth PD knew him well. Poole spent a lot of time in the trailer parks with the Navy wives when the husbands were out to sea. Even his brothers hated him. We figured there was at least a dozen folks in the county with a motive to kill Harlan Poole, and this ain't a big county."

Marcotte pulled into a development of identical A-frames, cut-rate Swiss-style chalets for the Boston ski-season traffic, almost empty on the weekday. He parked near a cement-lined culvert full of fine sand and brown pine boughs. Ray followed him to the edge of the ditch, and both men looked in.

"Poole's body was just about here," Marcotte said.

"You guys investigate?" Ray asked, trying not to sound big-city.

Marcotte nodded, inscrutably matter-of-fact. "State police came down from Concord. Had me guarding the ditch for days. They found boot prints in the mud leading back to some tire tracks up there." Marcotte pointed back to the main road. "This was still dirtpack back then, hadn't paved it yet. This whole side of the county's new. Nothing but these little bungalows, all the way to Exeter."

Marcotte seemed to dwell on the little bungalows for a moment—the newness, the changes, all the way to Exeter.

"State police matched the tire tread to a car they found abandoned," he said. "The car had come from Portsmouth—stolen from the parking lot of the hospital the day before we found Poole out here. Seemed pretty promising for a while, but they never made an arrest."

Ray wanted to ask Marcotte if he didn't find the whole case odd: an Easter-egg hunt sending the investigation from Poole's roadside disposal straight back to a Navy mental hospital, then nothing. But Ray looked at the deputy's hollow face, and climbed down into the culvert instead.

"Federals showed up." Marcotte volunteered this from the bank. Ray turned and squinted up at him.

"You mean like the FBI?" Ray asked.

"Drove Navy sedans," Marcotte said. "Plymouths," he added, as if it mattered.

Ray scrambled out of the culvert, wing tips scraping cement, Marcotte pulling him up by the arm the last few feet.

"What kind of shape was the corpse in?" Ray asked, patting dust off his overcoat.

"Beat up bad—nearly busted in two. Had two black marks here," he said, touching his temples with each index finger. "Like bad burns."

Ray remembered the picture of the man getting shocked, electrodes on his temples.

They walked back to the sheriff's car.

"State police took the case from us," Marcotte said. "They closed it hit-and-run."

"Mind you," he said, walking faster, "it's nine miles to Portsmouth from here, and nobody saw a man along the road that night, though folks out here notice strangers. And, *mind you*, it's sixty-eight feet from the road to the ditch—I know 'cause I measured it myself. If a car ran him down and caused all them injuries, can't see him rolling that far, or crawling. Plus the burns on the temples . . ."

Marcotte was at the patrol-car door. He turned suddenly and looked past Ray to the ditch. "Still," he said, unconvincingly, "I suppose the state folks know better."

Ray understood that this was as close as T. K. Marcotte came to calling his own government a liar.

"Who closed the case?" Ray asked, hand on the car door. "Who do I see?"

"Feller named Woodrow Wilson Whitaker in Concord. He's a prosecutor up there."

"Something stinks," Ray said.

Marcotte climbed into the car. "That's manure," he said.

15

Manny waited in back of the church, reading the sports section by the light of the votive candles. The Bruins got shelled by the Maple Leafs, and the game ended in a brawl, which the Bruins lost by an even wider margin. Disgusted, Manny turned the pages noisily. A lady with five kids shushed from a few pews away. Other heads turned to Manny, who sank low. Biff had said this big suburban church was as far away from the dope trade as they could get. Last time Manny would let *him* pick the rendezvous.

"*In nomine Patris, et Filii, et Spiritus Sancti,*" the priest opened in a pinched tone, startling Manny, who was poring over the Bruins roster.

"*Dominus vobiscum,*" the priest sang.

"*Et cum spiritu tuo,*" the altar boys responded.

Mass was getting underway. Nothing like an hour of nasal Latin warbling. Manny thought, *I'll kill Biff for picking this stupid rendezvous.*

Biff finally showed, an hour late. He slid in next to Manny. The priest machine-gunned the Nicaean Creed: "*Patrem omnipotentem, factorem caeli et terrae, visibilium omnium et invisibilium....*"

Manny started whispering. "You done good so far, Biff, but now you got to take Angel to the next level. You got to get Angel to introduce you to Caesar Raines."

The priest sang, "*Et in unum Dominum Iesum Christum, Filium Dei unigenitum...*"

Biff glimpsed a genuflecting housewife's shapely ass. His knees began to jiggle.

"Pay attention," Manny said. "Any undercover can buy the street. It takes a great undercover to climb the ladder. Go to Angel. Tell him you got money to do a big package. Tell him you don't want nickel bags, even at a discount. Let Angel know he'll make out if he hooks you up. But insist: you want weight. Angel can't swing that on his own. He'll need to go to Caesar to fill your order. You follow?"

"Sure," Biff said, watching the sexy housewife purse her lips in silent prayer. "Angel."

"You done, what? Four deals with Angel?"

Biff added them up on his fingers, lost track, started again. "Yeah," he said, "four."

"...*Et incarnatus est de Spiritu Sancto ex Maria Virgine, et homo factus est*," the priest droned.

"Climb the ladder," Manny told him, standing up. "Get Caesar. Show him the buy money."

"*Crucifixus etiam pro nobis*," the priest said, "*sub Pontio Pilato; passus et sepultus est, et resurrexit...*"

Manny handed Biff a fat envelope, and Biff took it.

"Three grand," Manny said.

Biff and Angel Chacon sat on the hood of Biff's Ford in the South End. The BBQ stand was jumping. The elevated train rumbled by.

Angel licked his greasy fingers and chattered about pussy and relief pitching. He was telling Biff that back home he balled showgirls but that America was his number one country now. "*Number one*," he exclaimed, raising a wet finger. Biff was nodding fast, adding up the years Angel would do—twenty or so, if the judge ran him consecutive.

"This thing," Biff said, speaking clearly for his body mike.

"Yeah?"

"This thing."

"Um."

"I can't do bags."

"Um."

"Angel," Biff said, getting the kid's name on the tape.

"Hm?"

Biff's thinking: *Attaboy, asshole, answer to your name.* Biff's saying, "I can't make money on bags, see? I pay you four per. My people, they pay five. That don't cover my trouble."

"Um." Angel's chicken-chewing sounds.

"I'll need ounces, Ace. One a week maybe. I'll bag 'em myself."

Car horns up the block. Biff: "So can you handle me? Or do I gotta go elsewhere?"

"Sure," Angel says, a lie. Butterman and Hicks had tailed the kid making buys at Gibraltar Street and followed him to a shooting gallery on Harrison. A snitch had been inside the gal. There was no cut, no empty glassine envelopes, no gloves, bowls, strainers, or masks, none of the setup needed to package. Angel bought his dope from Caesar Raines bagged, always. Biff let the fib go.

"Cool," he said. "We'll get rich together, amigo."

Biff came back without warning a day later for his ounce, showing Angel the money in the envelope, Manny's money.

"Three grand," Biff said.

Angel kept Biff waiting by the BBQ stand while he scoured the South End trying to scare up weight. But Angel was a kid and lacked that kind of play. He returned an hour later with excuses.

"*Mañana,*" Angel promised.

"Fuck *mañana.* Who got?"

"They don't know you. And I got no credit."

"They know you, and we don't need no credit. We got cash."

We, that seductive Americanism. A proposition: partners, *oportunidad.* Angel tilted his head to the left, considering. Cars were double-parked outside the spots, waiting to score. Five G's a minute happened around them, and here was Angel's big shot to advance from four-dollar bag runner to powdered-ounce middle-man, bankrolled by this opportune dad. Dad wasn't no cop, Angel knew that just as sure as he knew where his ass was—Angel had four deals with him and never took a bust. Angel had a feel for people.

"Okay," he decided. "But I go with the money alone."

"Ixnay," Biff spat. "You can rap. But I hold the green."

Angel walked him to a barbershop on Norfolk Street. Biff watched him fall all over Caesar Raines. Nobody mentioned dope.

"Help me out," Angel begged.

A barber stood by with a cup of cream and a straight razor. Bo Norman ate a candy bar in the open doorway. Angel took the en-velope from Biff, and showed Caesar what three thousand dollars looked like. Caesar ignored the money and gave Biff the once-over.

Angel blurted, "He's okay. I know him months and months. We go partners all the time. He knew Garrett. He knows Bennie A."

Caesar addressed Biff. "You knew Garrett?"

Biff took his money back from Angel and nodded.

"From where?"

"Juvie lockup," Biff said. "Garrett went in for dope, couple years back, and I was there with him."

Caesar thought it over. "What did you two talk about?"

"Different things," Biff said. "I got a sister in a nuthouse, and Garrett's mom was in one too. Garrett told me about his cousins. He said one was a jailbird and the other was a big pussy." Biff said this as if he didn't know Bo and Garrett were cousins. Biff was thinking about the electric fan and the blaring radio, and knew his body mike would get none of this.

Caesar nodded at Bo and returned to his shave. Bo led them outside and told them to wait.

"You sure of this?" Biff asked Angel.

"Yeah, yeah, yeah. These guys supply everywhere. I know them way back. They my partners just like you. Don't worry. They businessmen. They big."

"Their shit is good?"

Angel quickly blessed himself, four touches, respectful of very pure product.

Biff should have aborted. Bo kept them waiting a long time. He came and went and started asking all the wrong questions, going in and out of the barbershop, using pay phones, stalling. Biff figured they were trying to check him out through the grapevine. Bo told Angel to take a hike, and Angel left. Biff was alone.

Bo finally walked Biff into a shabby brownstone at 5 Norfolk. Swaggering Biff eyeballed the thick walls down the first-floor corridor hoping Butterman, Hicks, LeBlanc, and Scanlon waiting in panel trucks two blocks off saw him leave the street.

"Follow me." Bo grinned, leading Biff downstairs to a dark basement, and out into an empty lot behind the building.

"Where's my fucking package?" Biff was demanding as he came up from the basement into the daylight. Caesar was there. He stuck a sawed-off shotgun in Biff's face. Bo lifted Biff's snub .32 out of the back of his pants. Bo gave the .32 to Caesar, who handed him the sawed-off. Everybody gulped.

Caesar reached into Biff's shirt and pulled out a wire and a tiny microphone. He yanked them free and threw them away. Caesar said, "You are a policeman."

Bo Norman watched the street while Caesar loaded Biff in a little Chrysler coupe. They snuck out of the South End. Biff had never seen the coupe before and figured his field team wouldn't recognize it either. As Bo Norman drove north on the expressway, Biff knew the panel trucks would wait another fifteen minutes before getting creeped and only then start uselessly combing empty streets. Biff would be dead by then.

Caesar sat next to Biff in the backseat, snub .32 digging into Biff's ribs.

"Gimme the money," Caesar said.

Biff thought fast. "You want this?" he asked Caesar, taking the wad from his jacket pocket. He thrust it out the window and let the three thousand dollars blow off into roadwind.

Greedy Caesar grabbed at the bills with his free hand, reaching past Biff. Biff went for the .32 and got it. Bo, behind the wheel, swerved in and out of oncoming traffic, plowing through a roadside construction site. Biff would lose the pistol to Caesar in a moment, and Bo was fumbling with the shotgun up front. Caesar was twisted across Biff, and Biff's arm was around him, gun now jammed in Caesar's left side, Biff on his right. Biff squeezed Caesar's trigger finger, gambling that the slug would enter Caesar on the far side and slow down before exiting into Biff's lung. Caesar jumped, organs stopping the bullet, free hand letting the money snow the highway. Biff jammed the .32, angled up, into the soft part of Bo's neck as Bo tried to steer and bring the sawed-off over the top of the seat. The sawed-off went off in his hands. Biff let a round go, splattering Bo's screaming face across the windshield.

Biff reached over a slumping Bo and grabbed the wheel. The car slowed. From the backseat, Biff worked Bo's legs to brake.

Bo was dead. Caesar wound up in Boston City with a wound in his side. Manny and Shecky went to him there, shooed his nurses, and pulled a couple of chairs up to his bed.

"You know me?" Manny asked him.

Caesar closed his eyes. "You're the undercover's boss, I 'magine."

"I am," Manny said. "I want to nail your source—the guy who sold you that killer dope."

"You offering a deal?"

"Give me your source, and you plead to the drug sales. No kidnapping, no attempt to kill a police officer, which is mandatory life."

"And you'll take care of Bo? Bury him and all. Someplace nice, where his gram can visit."

"I can do that," Manny said.

"And Garrett," Caesar said. "Take care of him too."

"Garrett's already buried," Manny said.

"Garrett Smith, I mean. The child. Bo was moving to Virginia with the child and the boy's mother."

"I'll get them some money," Manny said. "Enough to get to Virginia. Anybody else, Caesar?"

Caesar had nobody else. "This can't be traced back to me," Caesar said.

"Tick-a-lock," Manny said, making a key-in-keyhole gesture at his lips.

"I ain't bullshitting."

"You got my word. Now, out with it."

"Joe Mears," Caesar said. "That's your man. Showed up like maybe a year ago, year and a half. He's talking about how he's got connections, how he can pull anything he wants. Morphine, pills, pharmaceutical cocaine, all of that. At first, I didn't want to know this guy. I thought he was a fucking cop—he was the coppiest-sounding motherfucker I ever dealt with. He tells me he can get synthetic heroin. I'm like, 'Why not just use real heroin?' He explains that synthetic heroin's much purer—you make more money off it."

"He killed Garrett," Manny said.

Caesar looked away. "Yeah," he said.

"That's when Bo started managing your spot?"

"Yeah."

Shecky said, "How did you know that Biff was a cop?"

"Mears told me. He'd been saying for weeks that there was

surveillance all over Gibraltar. He also said you were following me to meetings with him, or trying to. I thought he was paranoid."

"When did Mears tell you Biff was a cop?" Shecky asked.

"Just before Biff did the buy, when he was waiting with Bo. Mears was down to see me, and he spotted Biff in the street. He said, 'He's a cop.'"

Shecky didn't understand. "How did he know?"

Caesar said, "Mears has somebody inside Narco. Somebody who tells him what the cops are looking at, what they're doing."

Manny had heard enough. "Where do I find this Joe Mears?"

Caesar gave them an address: 10 Gibraltar Street, apartment 33, in the Heights.

16

Ray parked in front of the gold-domed statehouse on the corner of Center and Main in Concord, and found the AG's office on the second floor.

Assistant State Attorney General Woodrow W. Whitaker had resigned a few years before, so Ray made nice with the attorney who handled extrajurisdictional contacts. The attorney gave Ray two minutes of his time, then left for a hearing a hundred miles away, telling the receptionist to find the closed file on Harlan Poole. She returned from the basement with two binders that smelled of pine disinfectant.

Ray settled in the corner of an empty law library and started reading. He built a time line as he read. Poole was last seen on July 9, 1963. T. K. Marcotte found him dead in the ditch on July 10, notified the state AG that afternoon. Troopers hit Stratham before the autopsy was over and went to work establishing Poole's movements on the day he died.

Poole got off work in the Special Wing at two in the afternoon, haunted waterfront taverns until five, when witnesses saw him pick up a Navy wife as she punched out at a local fish cannery. The wife called the witnesses gossips and liars, until Woody Whitaker's men threatened a polygraph. She admitted taking Poole back to her trailer court, where she claimed they played gin and drank rye, until he left just before seven P.M. She was the last witness to see Poole alive.

Next came the alibis, and again the troopers covered ground. Townies known to hate Poole were in bars, or jails, or out of town, or with their families, or working nights at paper mills and canneries. The husband of the cardplaying wife was under the Mediterranean in a nuclear submarine. Poole's own brother looked like a suspect for a while, although little pieces of the case—the twin burns, the stolen car abandoned Boston-bound—didn't jibe. The brother cleared a polygraph with ease.

The Navy circle checked out too. Seth and Laura Zimquist saw a movie in town at seven-ten, *The Great Escape*, with Steve McQueen. The trooper running the interview had seen the movie and quizzed them about the ending. The Zimquists were home by ten, in time to share tuna casserole and table wine with Father Sedgewick.

Lem Childs had worked late on July 9. He was home by half past ten, and went to sleep reading Sarwer-Foner's *Dynamics of Psychiatric Drug Therapy*. Sign-out logs and a night watchman backed him up.

Father Sedgewick was the last man interviewed by the troopers. He had said mass with another priest in town from five to six, kept an appointment with a sailor going through a divorce from six to eight, talked on the telephone with friends in five different cities from eight to ten, then saw the Zimquists for dinner. Woody Whitaker felt the hospital staff had sound alibis and no motive, and Ray, reading Whitaker's notes two years later, agreed.

The second binder got interesting fast. Whitaker had made up his mind that the killer had come from the Navy hospital, and now the investigation doubled back. Father Sedgewick was re-questioned, not by troopers, and not on Navy turf, but rather by Whitaker himself, in Concord. The priest was almost totally useless. *No*, Sedgewick didn't know of any mental patients released from Special Wing. *No*, Sedgewick hadn't heard that Poole had enemies.

Next came Lem Childs. Ray had somebody's notes of Whitaker's cross-exam of Lem Childs, and Ray imagined the scene.

Whitaker asked if Poole had enemies among the hospital staff.

Childs said that he had no enemies.

How about the inmates at Special Wing? Did they like Poole?

Childs pointed out that Poole handled security, and Special Wing was full of men suffering from severe mental disorders. Delusional men, violent men. Poole made few friends among them.

Did Poole ever get physical?

Childs sat pat. He made few friends.

Was Poole ever threatened by inmates?

These were men who saw the devil in the mirror, Childs said. These were men who thought you emitted signals and would gouge out your eyes to get at the transmitter.

Had any inmate ever threatened Poole and then been released?

Childs launched into a lecture: Nobody violent was ever released. Some came in violent, but these were treated and they improved. A few who were incurable were removed to other secure facilities. Only the cured were released.

Whitaker showed Childs pictures of Harlan Poole's curious temple burns. Recognize these?

No, Childs said.

Ray knew that Seth Zimquist was interviewed too—the index in the front of Volume One listed a Zimquist deposition—but there was nothing in the file. Ray found the tab where the depo should have been, and saw that it had been razored from the binder.

Whitaker petitioned the Navy for a roster of Special Wing patients. He opened politely, and the Navy, citing the confidentiality of medical records, politely declined. Whitaker responded that he only needed names of ex-patients, no details of the treatment sought or given, nothing medical at all. The Navy replied, by hand delivery, that the Special Wing had been terminated the previous week, and the records were "unavailable." Whitaker and the Navy were on a collision course.

Ray reached the end of the second binder and asked the secretary for the rest of the Poole file.

"The rest?"

"I've got Volumes One and Two in here, but the file's incomplete."

She went down to the basement and came back apologizing. "You're right," she said, smiling, and gave Ray Volume Three, a single binder, very thin. Ray opened it and found a typed form closing the case over the signature of Woodrow W. Whitaker, Assistant State Attorney General, September 18, 1963.

Ray stared at the signature, trying to figure it out. Woody Whitaker had run a nice case. He took the probe to the patient population, likely an ex-patient, and knew he had struck oil when the Navy shut the Special Wing down. Then, *closed*. Had the Navy gotten to Woodrow Whitaker? Was there any other explanation?

Ray returned the binders in a stack to the secretary.

"Hope it helped," she said.

"Helped a lot," Ray told her. "Woody Whitaker knew his job."

"Woody was the best we had," she said. "For twenty years young prosecutors came in and tried to be just like him."

"Where can I find him now? He's not dead or anything, is he?"

She smiled. "Oh no."

Ray smiled back. "He got an office in town?"

"No," she said. "Woody inherited some money and moved back home—a little place called Warsaw, up north."

"Inherited money, huh?"

"Yes." She laughed. "We should all be so lucky."

They agreed they everyone should be that lucky. "When was that?" Ray asked.

She thought back. "It was in September, I remember—couple years ago now."

Warsaw, New Hampshire, was a clapboard church, a general store, and a monument to the Civil War dead. In the store, an old man wearing bib overalls was stacking tins of Quaker Oats.

Ray said, "I'm looking for a lawyer."

The old man stopped and rubbed his bald head. "Ain't got none," he said. "Thank God."

"His name is Woody Whitaker," Ray said.

The old man shook his head. "He's gone. Just last year." The man said this as if a year were an hour in Warsaw, New Hampshire. "He was living at his folks' place when he moved back from Concord. Didn't take, though."

"Didn't take?"

The old man hooked his thumbs in his overalls. "Woody in trouble ?"

"No," Ray said.

The old man gave Ray directions to the Whitaker place, and Ray headed up the valley on a narrow turnpike. In a block, Warsaw was gone.

The Whitaker farm was a spent-looking spread on stony land off the road. Ray parked his car in a patch of mud between a ramshackle house and a barn that sagged in on itself. The pastures were empty. A light rain fell.

Ray knocked on a screen door, and a woman opened up. She wore a housedress and work boots and took Ray at first for a tax collector.

"I'm looking for Woody Whitaker," Ray said. "I'm a prosecutor."

She kept the screen door open with her leg. Cats curled around her ankles and chased each other across the floor. She ignored the cats and looked at Ray's mud-spattered car, or maybe at the empty pasture and the sagging barn.

"Do you know him?" Ray asked.

"He in trouble?" she asked. This seemed to be the first question everybody asked about Woodrow Wilson Whitaker.

"He might be," Ray said. "I need to talk to him. If I can't find him, he might be."

The woman disappeared inside the old farmhouse, letting the screen door hang open. Three cats escaped between Ray's feet. They ran halfway to the barn and stopped there, confused, then walked in circles. The woman came back with a mauve envelope, torn open, ink smudged.

"Woody came home after he left the attorney general's," she said. "Stayed a few months, then he moved on. He sent that letter last year."

Ray turned the envelope over in his hand. A sheet of cheap notebook paper, folded once, poked out. Drops of rain fell on the paper as Ray held it, and the ink ran. Ray hunched to protect the writing from the rain and saw the words *sorry, mistake, goodbye*. Ray looked at the torn flap and saw the return address: c/o Postmaster, Great Nor'n Timber Co, Chute's Gap, NH.

The woman took the letter back and pulled the screen door closed. "Mind the cats when you leave," she said.

"If I find Woody . . ." Ray said through the screen.

"Yes?"

"Well," Ray said, "you got a message for him?"

"Tell him you saw his little sister," she said. "Tell him we got foreclosed. Tell him I'm living on apples. Tell him I'm the last one left."

Ray backed off her place and got on the road. Woody Whitaker hadn't retired on an inheritance; his family was broke. Ray wanted to ask Whitaker why he had taken a bribe from the Navy to close the Poole killing as an accident. Ray pulled over to find Chute's Gap on his map. His finger traced a route a hundred miles into an empty corner of New Hampshire, the wedge between Quebec and Maine. Chute's Gap was on the fringe of the Northern Tier, huge concessions ceded to the timber syndicates a lifetime ago. On Ray's map the empire was labeled simply PRIVATE.

Ray had dealt with the locals up here once before. A Boston gunsel named Curly McCarthy skipped bail and ran for Canada. A month later, Ray got a call from a man who identified himself as a game warden for the Great Northern Timber Company. The warden said they had Curly McCarthy.

"Found him at an Indian camp," the warden said. "He was stirring up trouble."

Ray asked the usual questions, basic facts he would need to extradite McCarthy, but the warden was vague. The Indian camp was either in New Hampshire or in Maine, or possibly Canada, the warden wasn't sure. He said he didn't think the company would be pressing charges, as if the company held the powers of prosecutor, grand jury, and judge.

"Just come get him," the game warden said.

Ray told him it might take a week to get a DA's investigator up to the Northern Tier. The warden was unfazed. "He ain't going nowhere."

When Ray's men finally got to where McCarthy was, they found that he had been shot—it was never clear by whom. Two bullets in the back.

"Tryin' to escape," the game warden said, as if it happened all the time.

Ray later told a law school classmate who was originally from Bangor about the Curly McCarthy episode.

The Maine lawyer laughed. "Doesn't surprise me," he said. "The statute books refer to the top half of Maine as 'unorganized land.' It is, to my knowledge, the only place east of the Rockies with no form of local government whatsoever. Takes up an area bigger than Massachusetts and Rhode Island combined."

The valley turnpike became New Hampshire 3, and Ray went north and east seventy miles through mill towns and mountain hamlets too small to name. At Lancaster, the state road met the big river in these parts, the Connecticut. Barges from the Great Northern floated downstream to the pulp mills, riding low.

Ray left New Hampshire 3 in Clarksville, heading east on a narrow asphalt ribbon, a straight shot, thirty miles through a dense forest of firs. He was nearly forced off the road by trailer-trucks hauling logs and doing forty. He expected to find Woody Whitaker somewhere around Chute's Gap by nightfall. There was a lot at stake, but Ray was in no hurry. He pulled over and let the logging trucks pass, knowing he was on Great Northern's land now.

The asphalt turned to well-maintained gravel and forked in four directions just beyond a cabin. Ray could see a dozen shacks in a cleared acre of woods where the road forked.

Ray parked his car in front of the cabin. A weathered sign hung over the porch:

TRIBAL AGENT FRONTENAC-HURON PEOPLES
US POST OFFICE, CHUTE'S GAP, NH
JUSTICE OF THE PEACE

COMPANY STORE—CHITS ONLY

ROYAL STUBBS, JR.
Prop

A dog barked miles away. Someone in the settlement was burning pine.

The cabin was unlocked. Ray stepped inside a cramped, shed-like room full of canned food and mothballed woolens, mapling pails, mousetraps and bear traps, a case of shotgun shells, a barrel of nails, spades and shovels, coiled hoses, snowshoes, old calendars, skis—it was the contents of a large farmhouse had been stacked inside one room.

The back of the cabin was one big room with no door. Ray put his head in and saw a man lying on a canvas cot in a flannel shirt and long-john bottoms. On the floor next to the cot was a bottle of no-name bourbon. A lantern hung on a nail over the cot, filling the room with jumpy light. The place smelled of compost, rotgut, and kerosene. A small transistor radio played softly, the crop report in French. The man on the cot was pie-faced drunk.

"Hello?" Ray said.

The man sat up. He was fifty or sixty, with a face of silver stubble. He swung his feet around, felt for the bottle on the floor, nudged it aside, and brought a well-oiled German Luger from someplace under the cot. The pistol and the radio were the only modern things in sight.

"Who in blazes are you?" the man said.

"My name is Ray Dunn. I'm with the DA's Office in Boston. Are you Stubbs?" *Or are you Whitaker?*

"Got ID?" the man asked.

Ray held his creds open for the man across the room, who squinted at them.

"Toss 'em here," he said.

Ray underhanded the leather shield case onto the cot. The man looked it over, inside and out, and threw it at Ray's feet. Ray stooped and picked it up.

"I'm Roy Stubbs," the man said, laying the gun on the blanket by his thigh. "Drink?"

Ray said no and pulled up a crate.

"Nobody told you to sit down," Stubbs said.

Ray sat down. "I'm looking for a man who lives up here."

"Frontenac?" Stubbs asked.

"No."

"White man, huh? He a logger?"

"No. His name is Whitaker. He came from Concord by way of a little town called Warsaw. He was here as of a year ago."

Stubbs knew the name and knew the man; his face said so. "There a *reward* on Whitaker?" he asked.

"No," Ray said.

"Then I don't know him."

Ray said, "I'll give you twenty bucks to show me where he lives."

Stubbs's face was red and sweaty, but his features were composed. His eyes followed the lantern light playing on the eaves. "*Hunnid*," he belched.

"Twenty-five," Ray said.

Stubbs pulled on Army trousers and laced up his work boots. He took a blue wool greatcoat from a peg and tucked the Luger in his waistband.

Ray followed Stubbs up the gravel road toward the shacks. Three teenaged boys sat in battered lawn chairs, drinking cans of Pabst and giving Ray and Stubbs the evil eye. The teens looked shifty and tough. Ray couldn't tell if they were Indian or not, but he knew they hated Stubbs.

"Whitaker showed up last March," Stubbs said, as they passed the teens. "I seen his type before. Looking to wind up someplace nobody knows him, the end of the earth. He found it here, and settled in."

Stubbs stopped in front of the shacks. "This here's the Indian camp. Sorry place for a white man, huh?"

Stubbs walked between the shacks to the last one, which stood against the woods. He knocked on the door and hiked his pants to expose the pistol butt.

The woman who opened the door wore a plain skirt, a shirt big enough for a burly man, and cracked black wing-tip shoes, also outsized. Over her shoulders, like a shawl, was a man's worsted wool suitcoat, charcoal gray, nicely tailored, and scrubbed threadbare.

Stubbs called her Sissie. "Meet Mrs. Whitaker," Stubbs said to Ray. "Sissie, this is Mr. Dunn from Boston. He's paying me a hundred U.S. dollars—"

"Twenty-five," Ray said.

"—to see your husband," Stubbs said to Sissie. "Is Woody available?"

Stubbs slapped her rump as she passed. Sissie walked a little ahead of them down a path, under laundry on a line, through a stunted garden, past a rusted-out De Soto, to a fouled creek where an old woman drew water in a plastic pail.

On the far side of the creek, all alone in a small clearing, was a single new grave, marked with a board stuck in the soil:

WOODY WHITICKER
1917–1964

"Woody stepped out—you *just* missed him," Stubbs cackled. The joke was on Ray, and Stubbs made the most of it. He laughed until he coughed. Sissie bent over and pushed the plank deeper into the ground.

"How did he die?" Ray asked her.

Stubbs answered for her. "Smallpox," he said. "Runs riot among the Frawnts, don't it, Sissie? See, the Frawnts don't have an immune system like us, and sometimes a white man goes with the Indians and he loses his immunity too."

Ray realized that Sissie was wearing the remnants of Whitaker's civil servant clothes—the shirt, the wing tips, the suitcoat, all from good haberdashers in the state capital. Ray wondered what Sissie had first made of Whitaker when he showed up in Chute's Gap with his lawyer talk and his suit and tie and his fancy shoes. Ray wondered what she made of Mr. Dunn from

Boston, with his suit and tie and fancy shoes, and expensive questions about the dead.

Back at Sissie's shanty, Stubbs cleared his throat. "How 'bout it?" he asked Ray. "You can't talk to Sissie's husband, but you can do whatever you want with her."

Ray avoided everybody's eyes. He noticed that the teens were still in the lawn chairs by the road, watching everything Stubbs did.

"It's a long, cold trip back to Beantown," Stubbs said. Sissie stood in the bad light by her shanty, and pulled the suitcoat close.

"Thank you, ma'am," Ray said and walked off.

Stubbs followed him. "Now," he said, "About the *reward*."

Ray said, "Deduct it from Whitaker's money."

Stubbs's eyes narrowed. "What money?"

"The money you stole off him after he died, or maybe *before* he died—it doesn't matter. I'll bet it's all in a box under your cot. Am I right, Roy?"

They were standing in front of Stubbs's cabin. Ray looked over and saw the pistol leveled.

"Hit the road," Stubbs said.

Ray smiled. "Scared of robbers, Roy? Damnedest thing about money: when you have a little, you're scared of losing it, and when you have a lot, you're *more* scared of losing it."

Ray got into his car, and Stubbs went inside. Ray looked up the gravel road toward the shanties. He was thinking about a prosecutor who sold out, and couldn't live it down, not inside, not where it counted. He was thinking about Whitaker fleeing from his self-disgust from Concord to Warsaw to here. That was Whitaker's route and, later, Ray's. That was what happens to tainted lawmen: they corroded inside out and wound up easy pickings for Royal Stubbs or Johnny Cahill. Ray sat in his car a long time as the light faded in the deep woods. He started his car and let it idle.

Before he left, he would do something in memory of Woodrow Wilson Whitaker—not the man who took a bribe and called it "inheritance," but rather the other man, the younger man, the one who knew his job and did it. For him, Ray drove up the gravel road and pulled over in front of the three teens still killing time in the secondhand lawn chairs.

"He has a lot of cash in the back room," Ray said to them, leaning out his window. "I just saw it with my own eyes. If you wait a few hours, he'll be too drunk to aim the pistol."

It was a seven-hour drive to Boston. Ray got back to the state highway by eight and took a room in Lancaster. That night, for the first time in his life, he saw the aurora borealis.

He was up again an hour before dawn and drove fifty miles before he found a place with the lights on and coffee brewed. At Franconia, he hit the interstate. He began picking up Boston radio stations as he came out of the mountains near Plymouth, New Hampshire. Ray played the dial, getting odd patches of reception, a few seconds of Top 40, radio mass for shut-ins, a snippet of Morty Moore the Mortgage Magician screaming *"Sixty-Five in '65,"* then static. As Ray drove south, the radio reception improved. He was twenty miles above Massachusetts when he tuned in, steady and clear, to WEEI-Boston, all news, all the time, and the big story of the day:

"In police tragedy in Boston," the announcer said. "A raid by Narcotics detectives erupted in gunfire this morning. One man is dead, and another is wounded. We'll give you details as soon as they are available...."

17

As Ray followed in the footsteps of Woodrow Wilson Whitaker, Manny Manning was going to battle stations for a raid on Joe Mears's pad.

Paddy Hicks scared up vests and shotguns, enough for a full entry team. Butterman called Housing PD, telling them Narco would be on their turf, as was protocol. LeBlanc and Scanlon sat on Gibraltar Street in case Mears came or went.

Manny worked at his desk, drafting an entry plan for apartment 33 at 10 Gibraltar. Biff stayed with him, getting a crash course in warrant tactics. Caesar Raines swore that there was one way into the apartment—the front door—and one way from the front door to the back bedroom, where Mears slept: a narrow hallway ten steps long. Mears would have something like seven seconds to ready himself for the lead cop, who had to come at him through the bedroom door at the end of the hall. Manny tested this estimate in his head: two seconds to sledgehammer those sturdy steel Housing Authority doors, another second to enter, three more to cover the length of the hallway, one second in the doorway of the back bedroom to get the picture and react. If Mears comes up blasting, the first cop through the door risks at least a point-blank torso hit. Mears has a .25 or a sawed-off, the vest would save that first cop, good bet. Mears has a Magnum or a special load, no. Mears lucks out with any kind of face shot, that's that. Mears nails the lead cop low, below the vest—which is likeliest, since Mears will be lying down or crouching—maybe the cop bleeds to death depending on the carry distance to the near-est ER, and if it's snowing, and traffic.

"We call it 'raid roulette,'" Manny told Biff.

Manny knew that poor people usually had only one door, and that drug dealers almost always slept in the bedroom farthest from that door. He preferred the one-door entry plans because Target would kill, die, or submit. In freak, streaky luck, despite a hundred raids and a dozen shootings in ten years as a narc, Manny had never lost a cop.

"You *that* lucky?" Biff asked him.

"It ain't luck," Manny said. "Ever had your place kicked in at dawn? Fucks you up. Be Target a minute. Your front door ex-plodes. You got to wake up, figure out you're being raided, by who, take cover, then you got to choose. If you fight, you got to find your gun, hope it's loaded, find the safety, aim and pull, and you got to hit that first shot, because now I'm on you. I've seen targets come up with lamps in their hands, or clocks, or mops. I've seen them blow holes in the ceiling or the bed or themselves or their wives. I've seen them go through all of that, hit perfect chest-center shots, and get vest. Then it's my turn."

Manny himself had killed or wounded fourteen men in raid-related gunplay, and along the way taken five slugs in his vest, one through his forearm, another through his shin, one in each elbow, and buckshot in his hip.

By dawn, Manny's team was assembled in the street over the hill from Gibraltar. Housing was on the radio saying they were in place on the roof outside Mears's bedroom windows, in case he jumped for it. Paddy Hicks handed out vests, walkie-talkies, and shotguns. There was nothing left to do but gather around Manny and take a playing card, facedown, from a deck on the roof of Manny's car, queens and jokers carefully removed in advance. Shecky kept the deck. He had it shuffled before every Narco warrant by Donna, the bosomy Triple Shamrock barmaid who thought Butterman a dreamboat. This was mandatory prewarrant ritual: whoever got the three of clubs would be the first man down the hallway, Target's target. They chose the three of clubs as the fateful card because nobody ever wanted it, just as nobody wanted to be lead guy.

Other teams took volunteers or took turns, or sent the guys with no families in. Some bosses even punished men for minor infractions by sending them in first, a practice Manny deemed lower than low. Manny always said that the first guy in could only be picked by Lady Luck via Donna the barmaid. Manny was a thorough, careful field man who drilled his team incessantly on shooting rules, blocking out angles like a director rehearsing a play, eliminating the chance of a friendly-fire wounding. If Manny caught a cop deviating from the entry plan, he made the offender wear a handlettered sign. I CAN'T FOLLOW AN E-PLAN, for three days. If it happened again, that cop was gone. Men felt safe with Manny Manning. This draw-a-card voodoo was Manny's sole concession to quirk, and most of the team secretly hated it. They would rather be *ordered* into a shooting than pick it for themselves from a deck of cards shuffled by a barmaid, especially a barmaid Nat Butterman had balled.

"Skip the cards this time," Manny said. "I'm going in first. I got a score to settle with this bum."

The narcs shifted uncomfortably in the street. Shecky, as always, spoke for them. "You can't do that," he said.

"Why the hell not? I say *I'm* going down the hall first."

"And if you draw the three of clubs, you will go first," Shecky said. "But we *always* pick a card."

Manny glared at him. "I thought you hated picking cards."

"Believe me, I do," Shecky replied evenly. "I suppose every man here hates it. But we *always* pick cards even though we *always* hate to, and you can't change it now."

"Sure I can. I'm the fucking sergeant."

"We don't pick cards, we don't go in," Shecky said.

"Yeah," Nat Butterman seconded.

LeBlanc, Scanlon, and Hicks nodded grimly at the pavement. Biff, about to do his first raid, nodded too, thinking nodding was part of the ritual.

So they picked cards. Biff, reaching across the car roof to the deck, drew from the middle: eight of hearts. Shecky picked next: ten of clubs. Paddy Hicks took the ten of hearts.

"That's two tens in a row," Butterman grumbled. "That bitch needs to shuffle better." He drew the three of spades.

They went around the circle, then around the circle twice. Nobody spoke, nobody smoked. Housing was on the radio wondering where Narco was.

Biff drew. "What do I win?" he asked, showing everyone the three of clubs.

"Biff can't go," Manny said. "He's never been on a raid before."

The cops ignored him, giving their cards to Shecky and drifting off to their cars for the short drive to the designated setups around Mears's building.

Manny was saying again, a little frantically, *"Biff can't go."*

Shecky took Manny's cards and Biff's cards, leaving him the three of clubs. "We reunite your card with the deck after the raid," Shecky told Biff, then whispered in his ear, "That means we're all gonna make it." He patted the back of Biff's head, a good-luck tap, then jumped in Scanlon's car and rode off, leaving Manny and Biff alone on the empty street. Dawn streaked pink over the top of the housing projects.

"Now what?" Biff smirked. This was fun.

"Stay close to me," Manny said.

Scanlon felled the door to Joe Mears's apartment, two blows from a sledgehammer. He dove right, and felt Biff's leg brush past him. Biff set sail for the back bedroom in the dim dawn light. Manny followed Biff down the hall screaming *"Ahhhh,"* scare tactics, kicking the first door he came to off its rotting hinges, an empty bathroom. The rest of the team rushed in behind. Butterman, Hicks, and a housing cop, loaned for the raid, took the other doors along the hall, throwing each open: a closet, empty; a bedroom, empty. Hollering Manny, waving his shotgun, stormed the empty kitchenette.

Biff, three of clubs safety-pinned to his chest like a bull's-eye, sprinted through a living room, also empty. Biff heard rustling in the back bedroom, Mears's bedroom, now three paces ahead of him, door closed. Biff rushed the noise inside the bedroom, shouting *"Cops!"* He tried to kick the door, but misjudged his momentum. His knee banged the knob.

Then Biff did an insane thing: he stood at the closed door for one full second. Manny was screaming. Butterman was screaming. Hicks was screaming. Biff was thinking, *So this is what this feels like.*

He opened the door by turning the knob. A white man was in the sheets.

"Freeze," Biff shouted from the doorway, leveling his twelve-gauge. The white man dove across a night table. Biff let a shell fly, spraying the man with buckshot and mortally wounding a lamp. A lightbulb blew up. Biff, seeing blue stars from the flash, stepped into the bedroom. He heard movement behind him. He turned and was shoved by unseen hands, tumbling over the bed.

"Gun!" Cops were shouting someplace else in apartment 33. Biff found his feet. His face was dripping. With sweat? He blinked his eyes clear. There was blood on the floor and on the windowsill. The other man was gone, but he was wounded.

"Biff!" Manny cried from the hall.

"Out the window!" somebody yelled from the living room.

Manny arrived at Biff's shoulder in the back bedroom, seeing him unhurt. Butterman and the Housing cop gawked helplessly out an open window, back bedroom now filling with narcs.

The Housing cop was on a walkie-talkie: "It's Mears. He went out the bedroom window. He's escaping across the annex roof."

Housing was supposed to cover the roof.

"*Goddam incompetent asswipes,*" Butterman roared at the Housing cop.

Biff handed the cop an armful of raid gear and two-hand-vaulted out the window.

Manny screamed, "*Biff get the fuck back here!*"

Biff landed hard on the roof below Mears's bedroom window. Manny was shouting at him to wait for backup, but Biff found his feet and lit out after Mears.

Butterman and the Housing cop were at Manny's elbow fighting for a walkie-talkie. Manny grabbed the radio from both of them and dispatched LeBlanc to the far end of the projects to cut off Mears and Biff. LeBlanc roger-copied the order as Biff hit the far end of the roof and disappeared down what Manny assumed was a fire escape. LeBlanc's ETA was two minutes. Biff and Mears would be alone until then.

"Biff, get your ass back here, copy," Manny sent over the radio. "Biff, copy."

Biff and Mears were gone from the roof. Beyond the roof was a vacant lot, and beyond the vacant lot was a line of deserted factories. Manny thought it through: once Mears and Biff got into the factories, Mears could lie and hide, forcing a building-to-building hunt, or run for the docks, or cut inland through the neighborhood, swim a broad saltwater canal, and vanish into downtown Boston. Biff could let Mears go; that would be smart. Or he could follow him into what Manny considered nasty ambush country. Unless LeBlanc cut them off.

"Biff, copy," Manny tried again. Waiting for Biff to reply, Manny looked at the walkie-talkie he had wrestled from the Housing cop and Butterman, who were still next to him. The three of them had four radios. Manny was hailing Biff on Biff's radio.

LeBlanc called in. He had covered the lot which lay beyond the roof. Mears and Biff were gone.

"Secure this place," Manny told Paddy Hicks. "Rest of you, let's find them."

Manny lost control of the show the moment he called Special Operations Division to request boats and dogs and more searchers. He was patched through to the duty boss, a lieutenant, and Manny took orders the rest of the morning. He briefed the lieutenant as best he could: botched warrant, the target at large, a single cop in pursuit on foot without a radio, whereabouts and status unknown. The lieutenant asked Manny what the fuck he thought he was doing, the first of many reprimands to come.

The morning dawned sunny but chilly, ten-knot wind from the harbor. Hapless Housing PD brought in their K-9 unit with German sheps. Radio cars helped out, and Harbor Unit steamed the length of the docks and the Ship Channel, looking for Mears. BPD's K-9s arrived, and took the deserted mills, starting at the waterfront, inching north. Housing's dogs were still in the empty lot, baying whenever they saw their rivals from the BPD. Even Housing's *dogs* were stupider than other dogs, Manny noticed. The BPD handlers started their pack with trace scents from the ransacked, shot-up bedroom in apartment 33, but Manny, who hunted ducks with mutts better than these, considered K-9s useless for finding anything except the strongest-smelling trails— fresh-fired guns, coke, wet blood—and the handlers were on the Special Ops Division frequency bitching that something in apartment 33 had messed up the dogs, blaming Narco for running a butcher shop. For all anybody knew, the German sheps were running around the deserted mills looking for the Housing dogs, who were in the apartment twenty minutes earlier, or for Manny, whom they'd sniffed on the way in, or for buried bones. Manny found his car, switched to Narcotics' frequency, and told his units to call in.

The narcs were in separate cars, trawling from the north end of the neighborhood to the south, crossing and recrossing each others paths, like lacing up a boot. Manny found a pair of binoculars under his car seat and grimly scanned the uneven line of brick mill buildings.

Biff had now been out of radio contact for over an hour. Manny forced himself to think that there was some operational reason why Biff hadn't called Central from a telephone. That was what the book said you should do. Chasing Mears, Biff couldn't get to a phone booth, *anywhere*, to call in. Or perhaps Mears had turned on Biff somewhere in the abandoned mills, and, yes, perhaps Mears had taken Biff out, but hadn't hurt him, not really. Manny pictured Mears punching Biff, knocking him out smartly, like in the westerns. Sure. Cruising up Navy Avenue, Manny couldn't let himself imagine the alternative. From far away he heard: *pop* and *pop*.

Shecky's voice, over the radio: "Leader, Leader. *Shots fired. Copy.*"

Manny: "This is Leader." Manny scanned channels as the radio exploded: Housing, Special Ops, K-9, everybody sending *gunshots*.

Manny, back on Narco radio, sent again: "Shecky, Manny. Copy?"

Many heard a distant burst: *pop-pop-pop*. He cut a wild U-turn on Navy and floored it, missing, just, a garbage truck that suddenly filled his windshield. The units lacing the boot with Shecky were closest to him, and they were hailing Shecky willy-nilly, radio discipline gone, sending over each other, sending over Shecky. Manny told everyone to clear the fucking air, took a deep breath, sent again: "Shecky, this is Manny. Where are you?"

The streets flashed by as his speedometer climbed, Manny driving with one hand, mike in the other. Manny chanced the intersection blindly, swerving around a streetcar and into a woman in a station wagon, her mouth making a memorable O. He bounced off her and down C Street, and floored it again. A siren started somewhere ahead, angry car horns everywhere behind.

"K-9 Leader, this is K-9 One," Manny heard. The dog handlers were calling in, but why were they on Shecky's frequency?

"This is Narco Leader," Manny sent. "Copy me, K-9 One." Manny was a block away from Shecky's last location.

"We found them, Narco Leader," K-9 responded, a dog snarling in the background.

The first thing Manny saw as he skidded up to the crowd of cops was Shecky saying something to a K-9 guy, who had let go of his dog to hold Shecky with both hands. Shecky bled in pulsing gushes from where his nose had been. He stopped talking and slumped in the kid's hands.

The dogs and their handlers were in the alley. One of the handlers was telling the dogs to heel, another was shouting "*Attack*," and a third was shouting, "Joe Mears, you're under arrest—"

The dogs wheeled and bared teeth at Manny as he strode up. Manny saw Biff standing alone in the alley, cornered. Biff had his Pistol in his hand and poked it like a stick at the crowd of cops. He was trying to speak but couldn't.

Manny stepped in front of the cops. "Biff," he said.

But Biff didn't know him.

Manny took a step. He was ten feet from Biff. Behind him, the cops were redeploying. Dogs to the back. Men to the front, guns drawn.

"Get out of the way, Sergeant," the SOD lieutenant said.

"He's a cop," Manny said without taking his eyes off Biff, who stood alone, his gun in two hands, the shooter's stance. If Biff shot, they'd shoot, and Manny would get blasted from both sides. If Manny stepped out of the way, the lieutenant would tell his men to open up.

"Biff," Manny said. "Put the gun down."

"Biff," Manny said. "They'll shoot us both in about five seconds.

"Biff," Manny begged.

Something changed in Biff's face. He seemed to hear Manny's voice.

"The gun," Manny said, holding out a hand.

Biff handed the pistol over, and Manny threw it against the wall, then grabbed Biff by both shoulders and held him. Biff was shaking. The three of clubs was still pinned to his coat.

18

Joe Mears slumped against an alley wall and heard police dogs converging a block away. Mears was gut-shot from when the cop nailed him in the bedroom and his hand was mangled. He wiped blood from his palm and saw the bones of his hand, a sickening glimpse as the gash refilled with red. The tenements seemed to curve and meet in the sky above his head. He closed his eyes and went into shock.

He was in a hospital bed. A tall man in a lab coat sat by the window. The man seemed handsome or perhaps just calm. Mears got out of bed and fell, buttocks spreading on the cold tile floor through the hospital gown. The man helped him up. Mears shuffled to a mirror on the wall. His head was shaved. He had twin half-dollar-size scars, silver-pink, just above the temples. He ran his stubby fingers over the scars. He looked out the window, which was bolted shut and covered with iron mesh. Snow fell on a patch of brown grass. Sailors in peacoats walked in twos and threes. It was cold enough to see their breath. A car passed and made no noise.

He listened for the dogs and heard none.

The man in the lab coat said, "You're in the secure wing of the United States Naval Hospital, Portsmouth. You've been with us almost a year."

Mears sat on the bed.

"I'm Dr. Seth Zimquist," the man said. "Do you remember coming here?"

Mears shook his head.

"You were a very sick man, Joe. Mentally, I mean. You've undergone treatments. We have, in effect, erased the old Joe Mears and built a new one in its place. Don't be afraid."

A second doctor joined them, closing the door. Mears noticed that it locked, a muffled click. The new doctor said his name was Lemuel Childs. He asked Zimquist if Mears remembered anything. Zimquist made a zero or an okay with his hand.

Childs opened a fat folder on his knee. "You are ten years old," he said. "A family farm. Ohio. Winter. Dawn. Crows skim over a bare cornfield. Your father is named Nimrod Mears. He's a lay preacher, reformed Mennonite. He's cold and distant, like the fields."

Mears knew what a farm was, but he knew he had never lived on one. He heard the dogs somewhere outside. He tried to get up, but couldn't.

"You enlisted in the Navy to get away," Childs said. "Your father objected, Mennonites being pacifists. You did it to spite him, probably. You served on cruisers and destroyers. Your principal home ports were Subic, Guam, and San Diego."

Mears knew what Guam and San Diego were, but only as words on a map. He had never been to sea.

"You had a girlfriend in San Diego," Childs said. "She was tall, a swimmer. She'd worked as an extra in Esther Williams movies. Very pretty, this girl. Do you remember her long brown hair?"

Esther Williams he remembered. She dived into water for Hollywood. He knew what water was, what movies were. But he'd never been to San Diego.

"In 1956, she told you she was pregnant. You raped her to induce a miscarriage. Other things came out at the trial. There was a suggestion that you had raped a girl in Los Angeles, one in Manila, two in Hawaii. There was also an unsolved rape-strangulation in Ashtabula during one of your Ohio leaves, but the evidence was weak. Do you remember?"

He'd never raped a girl to kill his own kid, never raped the others. *Had he?*

"You were found guilty of the San Diego rape," Childs said. "You served six years in a Navy jail before escaping. The shore patrol found you working on the docks in Boston. They brought you here. For your own good. Do you remember?"

Mears sobbed. The dogs were walling, on his scent, closing in.

"You are violent," Childs said, closing the folder. "Accept that you are violent."

Zimquist spoke up, softening the tone. "Don't believe your head, Joe. Accept that you are Mears. Accept that you are violent. If your head says otherwise, it's lying to you."

The rest of what Zimquist said was drowned out by barking. The dogs were in the next street, dragging him back from Portsmouth. He found his feet and forced himself to move. The alley opened on a courtyard where laundry hung on a line. He grabbed a workshirt, buttoned it up with one hand, and took a pillowcase to wrap the other. He went through the basement of the next building and fell over something in the dark. He lay on his side, and pain overwhelmed him again. In his head, Zimquist said: *Accept that you are Mears. Accept that you are violent.* He struggled to one knee, then both knees, then stood up, feeling his way along a mortar wall.

He came out of the basement on a street by the Ship Channel, which was fifty yards across. He could swim it, but he had to shake the dogs. He saw a car at a stoplight up ahead. He snuck behind it, duck-walking, staying low, and unwound the pillowcase from his hand. The light turned green. Mears looped the pillowcase around the bumper, and stayed low as the car pulled away. He could hear barking in the basement of the building just behind him. He dove over the bank into the channel as the dogs rounded the corner. The baying of the pack grew fainter as the dogs followed the pillowcase on the bumper of the car and Mears started swimming away.

The Secure Wing of the Portsmouth Naval Hospital had a lounge. The doctors called it a solarium. It was the only place in the nuthouse that Mears remembered fondly. He liked the big glass ashtrays and cheap paintings of famous naval engagements on the wall. On Mears's first day out of his locked room, maybe a week after he woke up, he found a woman sitting alone in a corner of the lounge. She wore a housecoat and galoshes and lipstick, deep red and crookedly done.

She smiled at him as he sat down. "I'm going to church today."

Her name was Mrs. Shepard. Her hubby was some kind of admiral. "He loves me very much," she said. "They tell me I'm nearly cured."

Mears watched a patient get wheeled into a room at the end of the corridor. Mrs. Shepard told him this was where the electroshock happened.

Mears said, "Electroshock?"

She leaned over and touched one of Mears's fading silver-pink scars. An odd gesture. They were just a couple of mental patients in an empty lounge, strangers to each other, yet she was touching the scars on his head. For some reason, he never forgot that.

"They'll heal," she said.

The head guard, Harlan Poole, shackled them together and marched them to the base chapel, where they sat through early mass. The chapel was empty except for Mears, Mrs. Shepard, Harlan Poole, and the priest, who sang, "*In nomine Patris, et Filii, et Spiritus Sancti...*"

Mears knew the correct response: "*Amen.*"

"*—Introibo ad altare Dei...*"

Mears said, "*Ad Deum qui laetificat juventutem meam...*"

Juventutem meant "youth," and *youth* was a gang of boys, orphan boys, and a nun standing with them, catechism in one hand, ruler in the other. The orphans fell into line in the street and marched up a hill to church. Mears saw himself. He was the smallest boy. The nuns kept moving him from family to family, telling him as they dropped him off: "This one will work, this will be home now forever. . . ." But he always wound up back in line sooner or later, marching up the hill to early mass. He saw a priest and heard Latin echoing everywhere. He could see this and hear this and know it all meant *church* to him; he was no fucking Mennonite.

He must've been talking to himself, because Mrs. Shepard gave him a look and Harlan Poole rapped him in the shin with a song book. Afterward, when the priest was leaving, Mears shouted at the priest until Poole slugged him in the gut.

The priest came over, scolding Poole. "How dare you strike him here?"

Mears was on the ground. "I need to see you," he told the priest. Poole stepped on Mears's fingers. The priest shrieked; Mears didn't.

"He's going back to lockup," Poole told the priest, dragging Mears away.

Later that day, Mears was in the lounge. The priest came to him.

"I'm George Sedgewick," he said. "Your name is Mears. I've spoken to Dr. Zimquist and Dr. Childs about you. They are hopeful." Father Sedgewick wore a black raincoat and carried books under his arm. He was older than the doctors. His face was open and gentle. He sat down without taking off the raincoat, books on his lap.

"Help me," Mears said.

Sedgewick folded his hands on top of the books. "The doctors are here to help you," he said.

"The doctors?" Mears came forward to whisper, "They say I'm from Ohio, a farm with crows and somebody named Nimrod, but I never been there. They say I raped a girl in San Diego, but I never been there either. You saw me in church."

Sedgewick shifted in his chair. "Yes."

"I know the Latin."

"Yes, you do."

"Well, *where* do I know it from?" Mears told Father Sedgewick what he had seen when he heard the Latin: orphan boys and a nun marching up the hill to early mass.

Sedgewick said it was all very fascinating.

Mears touched the priest's knee. "I'm not the guy they say I am."

Sedgewick moved his knee and acted as if he'd heard all of this before. "Who are you then?"

There was the stumper. Thanks to a year of Zimquist and Childs, he knew who he *wasn't*, nothing more.

"Were you here when I came in?" Mears asked Father Sedgewick.

"Yes."

"The very first day I got here?"

"Night," Sedgewick said. "It was late at night."

"Did I do anything? Did I say anything?"

"You beat up half the shore patrol," Sedgewick said. "They called you Mears, and you kept saying, *'That's not my name.'* We had quite a brawl that night."

"They found me in Boston," Mears whispered. "Childs said so."

"You were a fugitive there."

"Well," Mears said, "what if the shore patrol got the wrong guy?"

Sedgewick stood up, swinging the books under his arm. "Listen to your doctors," he said. "It's for your own good."

So he said whatever they said to say. *Accept that you are Mears. Accept that you are violent.* He did whatever it took to convince Zimquist and Childs that they were geniuses and that he was cured. After a few months, they gave him some money and a bus ticket to Cleveland and a paper saying Joe Mears was free to leave the base.

He shook everyone's hand the day he left the ward, even Harlan Poole's. He walked alone to the depot; he insisted on going alone. He cashed in his ticket, scaled the wall of the Navy base, and stole a car from the parking lot. He jumped Poole that night outside a trailer park, and began a new life as whatever he was.

Now he leaned on Dr. Childs's buzzer and hugged the wall. Childs opened the door.

"Shotgun," Mears said, indicating his side. "Clean me up."

Childs helped him in, and Mears fell on the couch. Two logs were burning in the fireplace. A pot of tea sat under a cozy.

Mears refused anesthesia; he couldn't let Childs put him under, not after Portsmouth. Instead, he bit a dishrag and watched Childs carve shot from his torso and clean his palm. He squirmed as Childs stitched the flaps of skin together, jerked his hand away, ripping the wound open again.

Childs reached into an old house-call bag and produced a syringe. "It's ethyl chloride," he promised. "Strictly local. You won't go under. Can I?"

Mears nodded. "Hurry up."

Childs daubed a vein with rubbing alcohol and shot him up. Mears knew that he'd been lied to as soon as the dose hit. He thought that maybe Childs was the sort of guy who could only kill a sleeper, but he lost this thought, falling back into the couch and into something deeper than the couch. He was awake but he couldn't move. He watched Childs sew his hand and pick Narco lead from under his skin. Childs dropped the pellets into a glass candy dish. The only thing Mears could move was his eyes.

When he woke up, the fire was out and the couch was covered with splashy stains, dried blood. Childs was packing up his instruments. Mears sat up.

Childs said, "What happened today?"

"The cops raided my place," Mears said, inspecting his stitched-up hand. "Boston's too hot now. I'm getting out. That means a last score, a big one."

"I'm working on it," Childs said.

"One of the cops saw my face," Mears said. "I don't need to tell you what happens if I get collared. I'd have to tell them *everything*. We'd both go down in flames."

"Yes," Childs said.

"The cop who saw my face got messed up. They'll have to stash him someplace. Probably in a nuthouse, maybe City & County. His name is Biff Dunn. You got that? If he's at City & County, I want you to find him and fix him so he can't testify against me."

"Are you asking me to kill this Biff Dunn?"

Mears pulled on a clean shirt Childs had fetched him. "If you could kill somebody, you'd kill me. Just fix Biff Dunn so he can't recognize me."

"Fix him?"

"Fix his brain like you fixed mine," Mears said, wobbling to his feet. "And don't forget my package: five hundred grams of the wonder drug. One more deal, and then I'm gone forever."

At the door, Mears paused. He said, "Accept that I am violent."

19

Ray made his way down the hall of Mears's building, past by-standers and reporters and uniformed cops doing crowd control. Ray stepped inside apartment 33, ran a finger over the dented doorframe where the raid team had sledged their way in. Down the hall, he saw a bathroom, its door kicked off, a closet, a bedroom, and a kitchenette in shambles. The place had been hit hard.

Dave LeBlanc was the only narc left at Gibraltar. He wore his bulletproof vest from the raid and cradled a shotgun in his arms. He still looked newly surprised, though the raid had been over for six hours.

"Shecky's dead," he said to Ray.

Ray took his arm.

"Shecky's dead," LeBlanc repeated, as if it couldn't be.

Ray steered him down the hall. "Dave, what happened?"

LeBlanc filled Ray in. He told Ray how the Caesar buy went down wrong. Somehow Bo and Caesar knew Biff was a cop. Biff had to shoot it out with them. Bo died and Caesar was hit. Manny had cut a deal, and Caesar had rolled over on his fentanyl source.

LeBlanc took Ray to the back bedroom. "The source is named Joe Mears," LeBlanc said. "Caesar knew Mears lived here off and on, so we hit the door. We found ID in Mears's name here. There were traces of fentanyl and cut. Mears did his mixing here."

Ray picked through the empty plastic beakers, tap water in Visine bottles, the wreckage of a high-volume drug operation. "Mears was sleeping when we arrived," LeBlanc said. "Biff got a round off, and hit Mears, judging from the blood on the floor. Mears went out that window and Biff went after him."

Ray took a look at the drop to the roof below. Ray turned to LeBlanc. "Where's my brother?"

Biff had been stomped by cops and mauled by their dogs after the shooting. He had been rushed under sirens to Carney Emergency, where he had cut himself on the Coke machines, raving as they dragged him in. Six cops had barely been able to hold him down. That was the word: Biff was a crazed animal after the shooting, berserk.

"The press was going nuts," LeBlanc said. "You know, the cop-shoots-cop angle. The brass wanted Biff on ice until they figured out what to say."

"Where is he?"

LeBlanc said, "City & County."

At City and County, Ray found Manny with Hicks, Butterman, and Scanlon, and most of the senior commanders in the Boston Police Department.

Biff was alone in a guarded room. He lay in a large white bed, legs, arms, and head swollen and stitched. He stirred when Ray came in.

Ray said, "Tell me what went down. Start from the beginning."

"Manny got a tip Mears was in the apartment. So we go with a raid team. I'm leading the charge. I get to the bedroom. I see Mears in the sheets. I shoot at him and I think I hit him. Did I, Ray?"

"There's blood in the bedroom. Maybe you did."

Biff looked pleased. "So I'm in Mears's bedroom, right? I hear a scuff noise behind me. I get shoved back and land on my ass. Mears tosses water in my eyes."

"Water?"

"Yeah, like to blind me. Felt like water, anyway. The rest of the raid team piles in. I hear the Housing cop saying that Mears went out the bedroom window and there's nobody covering the roof. So I go."

"Go where?"

"Out the window after Mears," Biff said. "Hey, Ray, what the hell's going on? Why won't anybody talk to me?"

Ray realized he was still standing. He sat down by Biff's bed.

Biff said, "What?"

Ray said, "Look, Biff, I need to know what happened when you went out the window."

"I fell," Biff said. "That's what happened."

"It's serious," Ray said.

"You act like someone died."

"Someone did."

"Mears?"

"Shecky."

"They get the shooter?"

"Your gun," Ray said quietly.

Biff's blank face wrung up. Tears squeezed out of his squint.

"There'll be an investigation," Ray said. "You could get charged with manslaughter or even murder. Tell me what happened when you went out the window."

"The drop was farther than it looked," Biff said. "I guess it fucked me up. I saw Mears at the far end of the roof, starting down the fire escape. By the time I got there I saw him crossing the empty lot, running. He cut down an alley, away from the harbor. I didn't see any cars covering the street. I knew if I let him go, he's gone. So I stayed with him.

"I figured he slipped into one of the old mills, so I picked the nearest one, and did a vertical sweep, floor to floor, trying to be real quiet. I hear him—or somebody—above me, on the stairs, moving around.

"Every floor I sweep, one, then two, then three, I'm getting closer to him. He's above me. Finally, I kick open the door to the roof, big hollow tin door, makes a much louder noise than I expected, like a cannon. And I'm out in the sunlight again and I'm crouching, doing three-sixties with my gun.

"*'Mears!'* I shout. *'Give it up!'*

"It's so quiet up there, seven floors above the street. That's when I remembered that it was Sunday morning and everybody's still asleep. It was peaceful, you know? I can remember hearing an airplane up in the sky. For a moment, it seemed real silly, us chasing powder. We boom a door, I try to off a man in bed, then hound him across rooftops. How did I get here? For a minute, it seemed silly." Biff started crying.

"Calm down," Ray said. "What happened next?"

"I started hearing things. The light looked all shaky. I couldn't see. Took me about an hour to go down the stairs to the street.

"When I get there, I see Shecky in a car. I flag him down. He says, 'C'mon,' so I get in. I get this crazy feeling that Mears is right there, like right behind the car, watching us. I'm telling Sheck I must've whacked my head when I went out the window, because I feel wrong."

"Feel wrong' how?"

"In my head. I felt *off.* The light was shaky and I could hear everything—heartbeats of people sleeping in the buildings, and sirens on the other side of town."

"Go on."

"We're driving, me and Sheck, looking for Mears, right? Sheck says, *'There he is.'* He's pointing and handing me the radio, shouting at me to give Manny our position, tearing up the street headed straight for the Channel. I shut my eyes because I think Sheck's gonna drive us right over the bank into the water.

"Sheck's yelling at me, *'Call it out, call it out.'* Let the field know where we're at, that's what he meant.

" '*We're gonna crash,*' I'm yelling back.

"Then Shecky swerves up on the curb and we're running Joe Mears down on the sidewalk. He's running next to the wall, looking behind, running between us and the wall, looking and running, and we're next to him. Shecky floors it, pulls ahead of him, fishtails in front of Mears, smashing into the wall. Sheck's out of the car and draws on him, '*Cops! Freeze!*'

"Mears stops short, breathing heavy. He's naked, muscled up like a jailbird, fucking crewcut redhead. He smiles real slowly, like he's finally catching on to a joke. Shecky says, '*Hands in the air!*'

"Mears is standing there, ten feet from where we smashed into the wall, panting, grinning. But he won't put his hands up.

" '*Get 'em up!*' Shecky yells. 'Cuff him, Biff,' he says to me. I can remember hearing the cracked radiator dribbling onto the sidewalk. That's how quiet it was, like everything's exaggerated."

Biff stopped.

"It was quieter *than quiet*," he finally said. "It was the weirdest fuckin' thing. I couldn't *move* it was so quiet. Mears just looks at us and won't put his hands up.

" 'I'll count to three,' Shecky says. 'Biff, for chrissakes cuff him,' he says to me, then Shecky starts counting, 'One. Two. Three.' Mears doesn't try to break, but he won't put his hands up. 'Cuff him, for chrissakes!' Shecky's screaming. I don't know how long the three of us stood there like that. I could hear Manny on the radio in the car saying, 'Got who? Shecky, got who?'

"Mears won't put his hands up, and Shecky, who never shot nobody, won't pull the trigger on a naked guy who's just standing there.

" 'Move and I'll kill you,' Shecky says. But Mears just smiles at him. The light's all jumpy-like, and the radio's loud inside my head. I covered my eyes. I hid. I'm fighting somebody, but my eyes are closed, and I can't open them."

Ray asked, "Do you remember hearing gunshots?"

Biff shook his head. "I was hearing a lot of things," he said.

"Listen," Ray said. "There'll be an investigation. Guys will come to see you soon—maybe cops, maybe DAs, maybe people you trust. They'll be asking questions, like this. Okay?"

Biff nodded.

"Don't tell them anything. I'm getting you a lawyer. Just clam up, okay?"

As Ray left, the men in black raincoats from Internal Affairs were rolling their tape recorder up to Biff's door.

The boys were asleep and Mary-Pat was on the carpet in the living room, stuffing a thousand preaddressed envelopes with letters from the Committee to Elect Ray Dunn District Attorney. Ray sat on the couch.

"How is he?" she asked.

"Not good," Ray said. "How are you?"

Mary-Pat stuffed four envelopes, making Ray wait for an answer. Ray watched Mary-Pat take another mimeoed letter from the stack, fold it in thirds, slide it into an envelope, lick across the seal, close the envelope neatly, then stack the envelope in a box with three hundred others. She had signed his name all night long. Her fingertips and thumbs were paper-cut. She knew he was watching her, but she wouldn't stop folding, licking, closing, stacking. She wouldn't turn around and face him.

"How are you?" he asked again.

"Been better," she said, licking along an envelope flap.

"Anybody call?"

"Yes," she said.

"Anything important?"

"I don't know. I didn't answer."

"Probably more reporters." Ray picked up a letter from the stack next to Mary-Pat and read it:

Dear Fellow Bostonian:

Allow me to introduce myself. I'm Ray Dunn, and I'm running for DA. The 1960s are a time of hope and change...

He put the letter down. "Hon, it's over, you know."

Mary-Pat stacked an envelope in the box, and paused. He saw her neck and shoulders shudder, bottling a sob. She folded a letter in thirds and slid it in an envelope.

"It's over," he repeated.

"It can't be," she said, still facing away. "We'll tell the people Biff's shooting Shecky was an accident. He's mentally ill. He couldn't help it, and besides, it's got nothing to do with you. People will understand. People will forgive."

She stuffed an envelope viciously, tearing it in half. She turned to Ray. Her eyes were red-rimmed and puffy. "You never wanted it," she said.

"Does it matter?"

"It matters to me," she said. "I had this idea that we would tell everybody that...that...that..."—the sobs spilled out—"that progress was possible, you know, and everybody would get excited and forget about Johnny Cahill and everything he stands for. I had this idea that you'd run for Congress next, and we'd go to Washington, and have an exciting life."

She threw the two torn halves of the letter and envelope. They caught air, fluttered, and fell.

"What's so wrong with what we have right here?" Ray asked.

Mary-Pat hid her face.

"We're not enough for you anymore, are we, me and the boys?"

She sobbed and shook her head.

"No?" Ray asked. "No what? No we're not enough anymore or no we're *not* not enough?"

She didn't mean it, Ray thought. She'd say so in a moment.

Mary-Pat said, "What the hell did I know?" She tried to stuff envelopes, but she was crying too hard, blinding herself, and fumbling with the piles.

For a moment, Ray saw his marriage from outside, saw himself and Mary-Pat as two people. The moment startled him. He had never done that before. He wondered if this was how divorces began.

20

Manny had served with Shecky almost ten years and considered him a close friend. Yet Manny realized in the days after Shecky bled to death on a sidewalk in Telegraph Heights that nobody really knew Shecky after all. Shecky sometimes mentioned sisters in Brookline whom he rarely saw, and didn't like. They were his only family. The one other thing Manny knew was that Shecky had left a will with a nice young lawyer on Beacon Hill, and when Manny called the lawyer with the fucked-up news, the lawyer asked him to come over.

"You're the executor," the lawyer said when Manny arrived.

Manny and the lawyer unsealed the will in the presence of one of the lawyer's secretaries. Manny gathered that this was some kind of ancient legal requirement.

The lawyer read it out loud. It was brief; Shecky didn't have much beyond a checking account, which he wanted split between two women Manny had never heard of, old flames. "There's one other thing," the lawyer said. "It's an old book which had belonged to Shecky's father, an Orthodox rabbi, who's long dead. The book is in a safe deposit box at Shecky's bank. I think it might be quite valuable, this book. It's a very old collection of Torah commentaries."

"What did Shecky want me to do with it?" Manny asked.

"He wanted you to give it to someone," the lawyer said, running a finger over the will. "Yes, here: you're to give the book to a Nahum Butterman."

The lawyer looked up. "Do you know anyone by that name?"

The will included some instructions, "Things to do if I am killed LOD," line-of-duty. Shecky didn't want a hero's send-off. No flags, no uniforms, no muffled drums, and no one from the police department above the rank of sergeant. Shecky wanted a memorial service, quick and simple.

What he got was a maudlin, showy sob fest, nothing like the service he had asked for in his will. The sisters took over and carted a hundred of their friends in from the suburbs, none of whom knew who Shecky was.

The men from Narco were the pallbearers: Scanlon. Butterman, and Hicks on one side, Manny and LeBlanc on the other, and some pimply kid from the undertaker's filling in to make six. The narcs wore dark suits with narrow lapels, thin black ties, spit-shined shoes. Strangely, it was Shecky's nemesis, Nat Butterman, who took it the hardest. He cried straight through the service.

Manny bribed the undertaker to tuck Shecky's shield inside his suit pocket, loaded service .38 on Shecky's left ankle, a pair of cuffs through a back belt loop, because you can't send a narc to the next world naked.

By the time Shecky was buried, Vinnie Sullivan had been retained on Biff's behalf. It was Vinnie who brought word to Ray that the DA's Office, at the very highest levels, was bent on indicting Biff for murder.

"That's ridiculous," Ray said. "Let's assume Biff shot Shecky, although I think it's far from clear that he did. It's obvious that Biff had some kind of mental breakdown during the raid. He was delusional when they brought him to Carney—seeing things, hearing things. A dozen cops can testify to that."

"I don't think this is about Biff," Vinnie said.

"What do you mean?"

"I think they're out to dirty you up, Ray. I think they still see you as a threat."

"Are you saying they'd indict Biff to punish me?"

Vinnie said, "Johnny Cahill feels betrayed, and you know Johnny—he believes in an eye for a tooth."

"Maybe I should go to Johnny. Pledge my fealty—whatever it takes."

Vinnie shook his head. "Don't go near Johnny. They got Biff committed to City & County on a thirty-day observation order. After that, Biff'll be cut loose and we'll have our own shrinks take a look at him."

"*Thirty days* in City & County?" Ray said. "That place is a hell-hole. Get him out of there, Vinnie."

"I'm working on it," Vinnie said.

In the hospital, Biff lost ground. Ray was permitted to see him once a day. Some days Biff was half sedated, chain-smoking Lucky Strikes, and remembering less and less about the morning he had chased Joe Mears out the window of the back bedroom in the Gibraltar Street projects.

He would ask Ray, "Why am I here?"

Ray would explain that there had been a shooting and Biff would ask, "Who got shot?"

"Shecky Bliss," Ray would tell him.

Biff would strain to remember who Shecky Bliss was.

Ray explained to his two oldest sons what had happened, because they might see it on the news or hear it on the playground.

"Your Uncle Biff was in a shooting," he told Ray Jr. and Timmy. "He's okay. But he has to be in a kind of hospital for a while. Another man was killed—a good man named Shecky Bliss."

Ray waited for their questions, but none came. Perhaps they saw this sort of thing on television all the time, or maybe it was just too big a tragedy for them to comprehend. They were either too young or too old, Ray didn't know which.

"Shecky?" Ray Jr. finally asked. That a foreign name?"

"Not really, no," Ray said.

"Sounds foreign," Timmy said. He pronounced it to himself. "Glad *I'm* not named Shecky."

Whenever he was alone with his wife, Ray felt *he* had shot Schecky. Mary-Pat's papers and files and mailings prepared in anticipation of their joint plunge into politics had been burned or sent to the dump. All of it was suddenly *gone* one night when Ray straggled in from the courthouse, and neither of them ever mentioned it.

Ray started staying away, sleeping in Biff's flat by the bay in Dorchester. Biff's place was close to City & County. Ray could get out to see his invalid brother pretty easily—at least that's what Ray told himself. Mary-Pat didn't ask.

Mostly Ray kept busy. He and Manny went to the Charles Street lockup and reinterviewed Caesar Raines, who had taken a plea to drug charges and gotten, as promised, a walk on the kidnapping and the shooting. He was looking at five to ten years. Caesar wouldn't even see them until Manny supplied proof that the rest of the deal had been honored—that Bo had been suitably buried, and that Miss Smith and the child, Garrett, had been suitably moved to Richmond.

Caesar didn't have much to add. Mears had showed up in early '64 from nowhere. He had claimed to have connections into fentanyl and any other lab drug Caesar might covet, but he had demanded payment in full, on time.

"Mears had a source inside Narco?" Ray asked.

"Mears was talking to someone who was in touch with y'all," Caesar said. "He knew what you were working on, knew who was who, that sort of thing." He had names: Manny Manning was the boss, Mears knew that. 'Shecky,' 'Butterball,' 'Hines'—were names Mears knew."

"Do you think he had a cop on the payroll?" Ray asked.

"Nah," Caesar said. "He had some inside knowledge, but not that kind. After the blizzard, Mears warned me that Narco was asking questions about fentanyl and Gibraltar and I'd better keep my head low. He said Narco knew about Angel and to be careful of anybody Angel brought to me. When the undercover came 'round, Mears saw him in the street waiting for Bo, and asked, you know, 'Who's he?'

"I say he's some little gangster name of Biff. Has cash, wants product. Mears gets keyed up on the name, Biff.

"He says, 'Did Angel introduce him?'

"I say, 'Yeah.'

"He says, 'That white boy's a cop.'

"I says, 'Yeah, sure, fine,' but Mears won't let it sit.

"He says, 'That cop knows too much. Kill him, Caesar.' Now, after Garrett, I do what Mears wants. I do what I got to do to protect the family I have left. You still lookin' for Mears?"

"Yes," Manny said.

"Don't bother," Caesar said. "He's long gone."

Ray and Manny started to ask the same question. Ray let Manny ask it. "How do you know he's gone?"

"He said he was leaving even before you sent the undercover in. He'd been saying that since the blizzard. Plus he hit me up for money maybe two-three weeks ago."

Manny asked, "How much did he want?"

"Ten big ones," Caesar said.

Ray said, "What did Mears need it for?"

"He was planning some big thing. Needed ten grand."

"'Some big thing,'" Ray repeated. "Like what?"

"Revenge, pro'bly," Caesar said. "That's what got Mears up in the morning. Whatever it was, he had to do it before leaving Boston."

Ray and Manny went from the Charles Street lockup to Mears's apartment, which had been sealed by Crime Scene on the day of the raid. The heat was off and the place was cold. Manny walked from room to room, smoking nervously.

"Crime Scene already searched this place," Manny said from the kitchenette, pushing a drawer in and out. Cans of baked beans rolled across the floor.

Ray took his head out of Mears's squalid bathroom. "They don't know what to look for," he called down the hall.

Manny mumbled, "Do we?"

Ray put his head in the hall again. "You say something?"

Manny stood in the kitchenette. "The 'big thing' Caesar was talking about—the 'big thing' Mears had to do before he could leave Boston. What was that, do you think?"

Ray talked through the walls. "Don't know," he said.

Manny stepped over splintered pieces of the bathroom door and into the back bedroom, where Mears had been sleeping when the raid team hit. The room filled Manny with dread, but he forced himself to look at every inch of floor, wall, and ceiling, under the mattress, behind the curtains, and in the drawer of Mears's table. He tapped every space for false walls or false bottoms, winding up on his hands and knees in Mears's bedroom closet, a flashlight in his armpit. He saw a glint of metal as he played the light around. He brought it back and saw the glint again.

"*Ray!*" he shouted.

Ray came to the open closet and looked in. By the baseboard in the back of the closet was a stiletto knife, open, blade broken off at an inch. On the handle of the stiletto was a design: an all-seeing, wide-awake eye.

"I've seen about a thousand stilettos in my life," Manny said, "but I've only seen one like that. It was Bennie Anastasia's pride and fucking joy."

Manny got home late that night. His wife was waiting in the foyer. She told him that a small gift box had come in the mail during the day, addressed by name to Manny's oldest daughter, care of "Sgt. Manny Manning." Dot Manning gave the box to her husband in the driveway, unopened. Dot crossed her arms and said, "What's happening?"

"Lighten up," Manny said. "It's a prank. That damn Butterman."

"And the chocolates? This was also Butterman?" Dot shook her head. "Tell me what is happening."

Manny told Dot he was going out for smokes and left her in the driveway.

He put the suspicious box in the back seat of the car, in case it blew, and tried to figure out how much trouble he was in. *I'm Mears,* Manny began, *and I feel the cops closing in on me. So what's my next move? I stay off the phone, that's for sure. I move around a lot. I only deal with one customer, maybe two, guys I control, guys like Caesar. That way I'm safe—unless Caesar gets sloppy and sells to an undercover, unless Caesar rolls on me.*

Mears had to protect Caesar because Caesar was his firewall against the cops. If Narco had an undercover cop somewhere around Caesar, Mears *had* to ferret the uncle out, by name and by face. Mears probably thought he could *smell* the undercover if he ever met him, but to do that, he'd have to meet him, and Mears met no one—that was the whole point of Caesar. So, how?

Manny was stumped again, until he remembered what Caesar had said: "Manny Manning was the boss, Mears knew that." Mears did what Manny would've done: he worked from what he knew to what he didn't know. Mears used Manny to find Manny's undercover. *Mears knew my name and he worked from that,* Manny thought. *Mears found the street address for Narco—it's in the goddam phone book—and sat on the place. Mears's looking for me. He doesn't know much, but he knows I'm plainclothes, so he forgets about the uniformed cops. He knows I'm a narc, so he focuses on the plainclothesmen in the precinct who work like narcs, the ones who prowl around slums all day in unmarked sedans—these'll be narcs. Mears picked the oldest guy, and followed him home. Maybe Mears guessed Shecky was the sergeant, and maybe he shadowed Shecky home to an apartment with* BLISS *on the buzzer. After that, Mears picked the next-oldest guy, and that's how he found me: by finding the house I went home to, the one with "The Mannings" written in scroll on a piece of fucking driftwood over the mailbox.*

He tailed me into a meeting with Biff. He was with us in church the day I briefed Bill on the big buy. That's how Mears made Biff for a UC, by playing me as a mark. Mears investigated the investigators.

How had Mears gotten Biff's name? Manny was stumped again, until he thought of an answer. *Mears went down to the Academy, looked at the pictures of the graduating cadet classes hanging outside Combat Cross Auditorium, the Hall of Heroes, till he found Biff's face from 1958.* Biff at eighteen, crew-cut and crooked teeth, barely shaving, proud in blue. Underneath the, screwball smile: "Dunn, Biff." On the day of the fateful buy, Mears saw the same face, older now, buying dope from Caesar Raines.

Manny finally understood why he couldn't stop driving: *Mears tails me. Maybe he's with me right now.* Manny faced three awful truths, one after another:

Mears knew where Manny lived.

Mears knew his wife and his daughters.

Mears was hunting Manny.

Manny was appalled and, strangely, thrilled.

He wound up at Wollaston Beach Park. He walked through the pines to the surf, and threw the box that had been mailed to his daughter up the sand, figuring if it was booby-trapped, this would set it off.

Manny should have called bomb disposal, but then he'd have to explain that he was being quietly terrorized by a drug dealer, which would have snuffed the Manny Manning warhorse legend. Never ask for help. Instead, Manny stood in the drizzle on an empty beach, throwing a small box up the shore.

The package didn't blow. So he soaked it in the chilly sea and sat on a park bench under an orange streetlight. He opened the box at arm's length with his pen knife. Inside was a pair of testicles, shrunken and badly discolored, dark dice. Manny shrieked, stood up, ripped his pistol from his shoulder holster, scanned the stunted pines, draped in shifting drizzly mist.

Nothing, nobody.

He reholstered his gun and sat down with the box. The panic passed and Manny was just plain curious.

Whose are these? he wondered. He tried to be Mears. He reviewed the possibilities. Angel was in jail; Butterman and Hicks had scooped him up the day after the raid on apartment 33. Garrett Hays was dead. Bo, dead. Caesar, good as dead.

Were these Biffs balls? New panic, until Manny got a grip. The box had been mailed days ago. Manny had stopped in to see Biff at the hospital that morning. Biff had balls when Manny saw him.

It didn't matter whose balls these were. Manny got Mears's message anyway: stay away from me, I'll stay away from you. Manny shook the little box, heard a soft rattle of its contents, or was it drizzle falling through the pines?

"These are mine, Manny realized as he drove back to his house. *He's giving them back to prove that he took them."*

When he got home, he woke everyone up—Dot and his seven daughters, who ranged in age from nineteen to six—told them to pack light. Manny told the girls some story about a gas leak.

"I called the firemen," Manny said when his family was in the driveway. "They'll fix it right up. Take a little while for the place to air out, though."

"I didn't smell any gas," Louise, the baby, said.

"That's because you're short," Manny told her. "Gas rises and only tall people smell it."

The oldest girls were scared. "I have school," one of them said.

"Forget school," Manny said.

"Is there a gas leak there too?" Louise asked.

"There's some kind of leak," Manny said. "Let's go."

He piled everyone in the station wagon, drove them to a motel in the southwest suburbs, and checked his brood into three rooms under the name Kelly. Dot followed them in Manny's Chevy. When the girls were asleep, Manny and his wife went out to the station wagon to talk.

"There's a guy," Manny said. "Red hair, crew cut, well-built. He'll kill you and the girls if he can. Don't go back to the house. Don't let the girls go to school. Don't let them out of your sight."

Dot didn't ask who the man was, or why he wanted to hurt Manny's family, or how it had come to this. She just watched her husband light a cigarette.

"You'll find this man?" she said.

"I'll find him."

"You'll make it so he can't hurt us?" It was like her question of a thousand years ago, when the feds arrested Tim Dunn and the rest: *You'll protect my girls?*

Manny gave her a kiss. "I'll kill him," he said.

21

Manny launched a full-scale roust of every known Bennie Anastasia haunt going back to Mattapan and the war. Butterman and Hicks took the South End, Bennie's old stomping ground. They found that Bennie's former pad had been vacant since about the first of the year. LeBlanc and Scanlon strong-armed Bennie's friends in the beatnik scene, the regulars at Walter's and the Onion and the Hi-Lite. Nobody had seen Bennie since the blizzard.

Manny worked alone, his steady partner, Shecky, missing from his side. He covered the flophouses, quizzing closemouthed skags, none of whom admitted even knowing Bennie's name.

"How 'bout a white boy, Joe Mears?"

"Nope," they said.

"Hung with Caesar Raines."

"Caesar who?"

"You know big Bo, right? Caesar's spot manager. Everybody knows Bo."

"Don't know him."

"Angel Chacon?"

"Nope."

"Spanish Angel. Cuban Angel."

"Nope."

Manny got annoyed. He showed them a Bennie mug shot, circa 1952. "Know him?"

"Nope."

Manny flashed a Bennie surveillance photo from last year. "How 'bout him?"

"Nope."

Manny showed them a ten-dollar bill. "Him?"

"Hey, yeah, that's the Ten-Dollar-Bill Guy."

Manny snatched it back. "Talk," he said.

The skags said Bennie had cleared out after the blizzard and ditched the dope biz altogether. Rumor put him in Cambridge, near the Square. Rumor said he'd grown a beard and got religion. Rumor got paid ten dollars.

Butterman and Hicks ran Bennie to ground on Kirkland Street, Cambridge, where he was taking classes in African history at Harvard.

"What the fuck is Bennie Anastasia doing at *Harvard?*" Manny Manning asked the wall when he read Hicks's field report.

Manny met Ray for coffee in Harvard Square. "We need to talk," Ray said when Manny arrived.

"So talk," Manny said.

"Outside," Ray said. He walked Manny around Harvard Yard. "When did you sleep last?" Ray asked.

"Sleep?" Manny said. "This what we need to talk about?"

"I'm hearing rumors."

"Rumors," Manny said. They followed the wrought-iron fence. An early-April cold snap was in the air. Their breath puffed as they talked.

"Yeah, like I'm hearing that after the raid at 10 Gibraltar, you picked up your family, cleaned out your house, and *moved.*"

"Moved," Manny said.

"Will you stop that, please? Yes, *moved.* I went by your house, Manny—went down to Squantum where you've lived for the last twenty years, remember? Know what I found?"

Manny, walking, pulled a pack of cigs from his overcoat and paused to light up. His hands shook badly.

"Nothing," Ray said. "No furniture, no cars, no Manny's daughters, no Manny's wife, no Manny. I'm hearing rumors that you leave work at the end of the day *in disguise* and that you wear a flak jacket everywhere you go, like right now, for example, Manny." Ray tapped Manny's bulletproof sternum. "I'm hearing that you and your family—" Ray paused for emphasis—"are living in secret *under assumed names.*"

"So?" Manny said. "Lotsa people move."

"And change their names?"

"Sure. Rock Hudson, for example." Manny walked away.

"You're in deep shit," Ray told his back, "and me and Biff are in it with you. Now tell me what the fuck is going on."

Manny faced Ray, exhaling smoke and steam. "The shit is deeper than you know," Manny said. He told Ray about the laxative that had made his daughters sick. He told Ray how it felt to have a pair of nuts mailed to your house. He said, "Mears knows my family. He can strike back at me through them. I'll kill the motherfucker, Ray."

"You got to find him first," Ray said quietly.

"Tell me how."

Ray put an arm over Manny's shoulder. "Let's ask Bennie," he said.

Manny drove Ray to 505 Kirkland, Bennie's new home, a clapboard rooming house painted like a rainbow. An unfamiliar design graced the front door:

Manny and Ray examined the design for several seconds. Manny spoke first. "Bennie," he said, sorry for him.

A blond waif opened up. She was sixteen, barefoot, and high.

"There a Benjamin Anastasia here?" Manny sweetly inquired. She smiled vaguely.

"Mind if we take a weensy peek?" Manny asked, shouldering past her. 505 Kirkland was a flop, and looked it. Scruffy college kids, appeared in every door along the hall. A young man asked Manny and Ray to identify themselves.

"I'm Manny," Manny said. "He's Ray."

"Well, I'm a law student. Where's your warrant?"

"Sergeant Manning," Bennie Anastasia called from the top of the stairs. "What took you?"

Bennie walked them into a side room, stirred a girl and boy from a sleeping bag, and closed the door.

"We're all old friends here," Ray said, seeking a neutral tone, feeling Bennie out.

"Nice, huh?" Bennie asked, gesturing to his whole world at Harvard. "Why you here?"

"Why *you* here?" Manny said. "You used to be okay, Bennie. A junkie stoolie, but a stand-up junkie stoolie. A man of the streets. What the hell happened?"

Bennie said, "I have turned a page in the Book of Life."

This saddened Manny. "You were the best rat in the history of the Narcotics Division. I mean that sincerely."

"Gee, thanks. What does that mean, to be the *best* rat? Means I get to pal around with you and your cops. Means I get to shake the hand that knocks the shit out of some fucking choirboys just 'cause they're black. I know it was Butterman and Hicks and Scanlon who did that." Bennie laughed. "Operation Pressure Point. Please."

"I wasn't part of that," Manny said, "and when I found out what they did, I kicked some ass."

"No, you shouted. That's not kicking ass."

"You did okay with me," Manny said. It seemed important to him that the ex-informant accept this.

"Wanna see okay?" Bennie said. He rolled up his sleeves, palms to the ceiling. He was indisputably clean. "There's a good thing going on here: books to read, people treat you decent. A prof over at the Div School wants to write a screenplay about my struggle against oppression. Who do you want to play you in the movie, Manny, assuming King Kong's unavailable?"

The fearless backtalk stunned Manny.

"We did what we did," Bennie said. "No hard feelings. But the party's over. I ain't working for either one of you ever again."

"You don't have to talk to us," Ray said. "That's true. What happened back in Narco—well, that's the old days, and the old days are obviously gone, for better or worse. But we need to find Joe Mears."

"So?"

"So whaddaya know, prick?" Manny cut in, despising Ray's soft sell.

Ray cut him off. "Narco raided Mears's place on Gibraltar Street. There was some gunplay and Shecky Bliss died."

"It was in the papers," Bennie said.

"We found *your* trophy knife in Mears's closet," Ray said. Manny took the stiletto from his jacket pocket.

Bennie looked at them, deciding. "I knew Mears a little here and there," he said. "He was in the beatnik scene. I saw him at the clubs. I sold him that stiletto over the winter 'cause I was tight. I never did business with him, so if he was dealing, that's news to me."

"Where's Mears now?" Ray said.

"Fuck if I know."

"Find him," Manny barked.

"Find your mom—I bet they're together."

Manny caught Bennie backhand across the mouth.

In the car, Manny uncorked. "He's dirty. He's got a house full of stoned runaways, he's spending money, and he has no job."

"You saw his arms."

"So he sells but don't use. Or he shoots it in his balls. He's dirty, Ray, and you were in there kissing ass."

"And we're out-of-county and you hit him. That was bright."

Manny was sheepish about the slap. "He knows a lot more than he's saying."

They inched down Brattle through dinner traffic.

"We need Bennie, don't we?" Manny said as he drove.

Ray was tired. "Maybe Bennie's telling the truth. Maybe he just knew Mears here and there."

"Maybe not," Manny snapped.

"The only way we'll ever know for sure is to get Bennie talking."

"How do we do that?"

"Same way we always did: make a case on him and threaten prosecution. If Bennie's dealing smack out of 505 Kirkland, we got to nail him for it. A real case, no malarkey. That means you tail Bennie until he scores, *if* he scores. *If* he's in Boston when he does, take him in nice and easy."

Manny's arms were rigid, two hands on the steering wheel. They crossed the Charles into narrow downtown one-ways. Manny pulled over by the courthouse to let Ray off.

"What are you gonna do?" Ray asked.

Manny looked at his knees. "Bust Bennie. Make him my rat again, use him on Mears. Nice four-corner drug case, just like the Narco glory days. Remember them days, Ray?"

Vinnie finally sprang Biff from the county nuthouse after Biff had served half of his thirty-day commitment. Ray went to pick his brother up on that last day, and had to help him to the elevator.

"Where we going?" Biff asked him.

"Home," Ray said, meaning Biff's flat off Dorchester Bay.

Biff was quiet, thinking about this, until they were past the security gates and off jail island. Then Biff turned to Ray and asked, "Where's home?"

22

Manny set up in a laundromat diagonally across from Bennie's rainbow crash pad until he conned a vacant apartment from the landlord, a John Birch type, who believed Manny was investigating Harvard's Russian Department. Manny camped by a window upstairs the rest of Monday and all Tuesday. He walked around the block. He sat in his car. He read the funnies, smoked devoutly, and couldn't remember when he'd been happier. This was your basic stakeout, something Manny was the best at.

At least fifteen people were staying at 505 Kirkland. Three times that number came and went each day: short visits, strange faces, few repeaters. Nerves going in, some even counting money; smiles coming out. Classic drug-related foot traffic, another Gibraltar.

Wednesday, early: Bennie left the house for the first time since Monday lunch. He was wearing white jeans, paratrooper boots, and some kind of African shirt thing Manny had once seen on the Nigerian ambassador at Logan.

Bennie went northwest on Kirkland toward Harvard Square. Manny followed in his Chevy, staying a block back, making like he was hunting for parking, and feeling very obvious. Bennie was heading for a meet in the Square, Manny guessed, so Manny left Kirkland and came around on Sumner. He set up behind a wall, back to Kirkland, rearview mirror catching the corner. He waited a tense minute thinking he'd lost Bennie, until the white jeans appeared in the rearview mirror, right where they should be, cutting across the fire station lot, heading for the Yard.

Manny was thinking pickup. Bennie sold smack. He was a pro. He wouldn't keep more than a few hundred decks on hand at a time. Assume half the foot traffic is legit. Bennie sold to twenty, twenty-five kids a day, for three days, averaging two nicks a kid. Every three days he'd meet a guy, pay him off, re-up.

Manny watched Bennie slip behind the firehouse, neon African shirt flapping like a sign: BUST ME. Manny had run Bennie as an informant for six busy years. He'd spent more time with Bennie than he had with his wife. Bennie's defiance shook Manny's confidence. *Find your mom*—the balls of the guy. Now Bennie would get his. The afternoon presented known ground: buyers and suppliers, weasels walking green into meets, easy tails on suckers in loud shirts. Sitting in his Chevy, untuned engine arbitrarily gunning, Manny felt a surge of what another man might call joy.

Bennie beelined for the China Bowl, a pink-painted chow-mein monstrosity that Manny remembered from Intelligence Division reports as a pusher hangout. Bad food too, Intel said.

Manny chose his play. No way to see the handoff from inside the China Bowl without being made and queering everything. Manny would have to stay in the street and jump Bennie after he scored. This meant the supplier would walk. Okay. The bag Bennie'd get in the Bowl would have a few hundred decks of heroin in it, too big for Bennie to put in his pants pockets. So Bennie would go in, sit down, talk future deals with his man, pay, score, maybe eyeballing the decks quickly in the dim light, probably not, then step into the street carrying the bag in his hand. Manny would wait here, roust Bennie with the junk, then reminisce about Mears.

Manny parked his car and lounged near a Rexall's across Dunster, his back to the China Bowl, watching its flamingo reflection in the storefront glass. Ray wanted the case against Bennie to be clean. "Nail him with the dope in Boston," Ray kept saying. "If

Bennie's in Cambridge, call Cambridge PD. No stunts this time."
Manny agreed, although even as he did, he knew Ray was in
dreamland. Bennie would stay out of Boston, and Cambridge PD
would observe all the legal niceties if they arrested Bennie. Manny
hadn't sorted everything out yet, but he was clear on this much:
Shecky Bliss was RIP, and Bennie knew something about it. For
that, Bennie would get hammered, and Manny didn't give a fuck
where it happened.

The door of the China Bowl swung open and Bennie stepped
into the light. Manny ducked behind a newspaper stand and
craned to see the telltale package in Bennie's hands. Bennie was
walking and pedestrians were everywhere; Manny couldn't see.
Bennie turned, now thirty yards away. Manny couldn't take the
package in front of half the Harvard student body. Manny stepped
into Rexall's and pretended to admire the corrective girdles.

Salesgirl: "May I help you?"

Manny, furtive, startled, sweating: "Just looking."

He peeked out the store window, hearing the salesgirl dial the
Cambridge cops. Bennie was gone. Manny's brain was firing on all
pistons: *He'll go straight back to 505 Kirkland, no detours.* Manny
stepped out of Rexall's, ringing the shop-door bell, and, gambling
that Bennie wasn't now tailing *him*, ran-walked a quarter mile by
an indirect route back to his Chevy parked on Trowbridge. Manny
drove like a maniac, hacking and winded, to the corner of Trowbridge and Kirkland. He needed to grab Bennie before Bennie
made 505 with all those law scholars around. Manny waited,
checking both mirrors, hoping no Cambridge PD prowl cars
would make him for the Rexall's girdle perv, then he turned and
saw Bennie sauntering up the block carrying a brown paper bag.
Now Manny knew everything any narc ever needed to know: the
bag held heroin and Bennie was running it over to 505 Kirkland.

Manny waited the time it took to inhale his cigarette deeply
and let smoke out, glanced right and left for Cambridge cops. All

clear. He stomped the gas. Bennie saw the Chevy hit Kirkland, saw the face behind the wheel, and streaked across the lawns. Manny caught up to him, flattening Bennie with an open driver's door. Manny backed up quickly but carefully, missing the precious informant's head on the pavement by about nine inches. He piled a knocked-out Bennie in the backseat, tucking the brown paper bag in his own jacket pocket, and drove, sweating like a speed freak, over the Charles Street Bridge, back to where he was a cop.

Manny made for the Callahan Tunnel and East Boston. He took Anastasia to the Skyway Motel, a dive hard by the airport, popular with the plainclothesmen. Vice questioned suspects at the Skyway and Homicide used the rooms for naps and adultery. The BPD got a group rate, smashed furniture thrown in free.

Manny double-cuffed Bennie to a chair and upended a pail of toilet broth on his head. As Bennie came to, Manny hit him on the ridge above the nose, bone-on-bone jar running up Manny's arm. Rage and frustration at everything that had gone wrong since Jay Scanlon broke the door at 10 Gibraltar swamped Manny from nowhere. For a moment, he was close to killing Bennie. He stepped back. Bennie drooled Harvard colors.

Manny pitched the brown paper bag onto Bennie's lap. His trembling fists lit a Lark. "*There*," he said, ugly-triumphant. "I got you with your junk pickup. You're a fucking career persistent fucking felony fucking offender, and that bag makes me your landlord. Welcome back."

Anastasia moved his face as if to talk.

"Shut the fuck up. Where is Joe Mears?"

Anastasia spat out teeth, blood, and shredded tongue. His jaw was shattered. "Luk im da bug," he said.

The bag was full of confetti.

Bennie grinned lopsidedly. Manny turned the TV on loud and gave Bennie the single worst beating he'd ever given any man. This took fifteen minutes. *Romper Room* was on.

Bennie was a mess. Manny had once heard from some visiting New York narcs that heroin could be soaked into clothes, then later, somehow, distilled out again. It sounded like Buck Rogers to Manny, but he was sure that Bennie was dirty. 505 Kirkland was a drug spot, he'd seen that on Monday and Tuesday. Why walk into an obvious pickup to score a bag of confetti? Bright boys like Bennie sometimes did fake pickups to smoke out a sting, but why had he run from the Chevy if he wasn't in possession?

Manny left Bennie cuffed to the chair at the Skyway Motel and drove over to the police lab. He bribed a bored young chemist to test the confetti while Manny waited.

"What am I looking for?" the chemist asked.

"Opiate family, including fentanyl," Manny said. "If not that, try everything else. All I know is, that bag breaks the law."

"Bullfighting?" the chemist mocked, eyeing Manny's bloody shirt, then disappeared into the lab.

Manny sprawled in a chair like he was back in the maternity ward, his poor war bride of a wife yet again in labor and yowling for the knockout drops. Manny's head spun. If it wasn't drugs in the bag, he had nothing on Bennie, nothing he could prove, and that meant a career-ending brutality suit. The ex-rat was probably just coming to in the Skyway Motel, Mr. Bennie Double Concussion.

23

The chemist had an answer. "Nothing," he said, two pudgy hands making zeros. "There's no dope or morph or smack or any opiate, or anything else that breaks the law. Thank you, come again."

Manny wanted to grind the snotty little shit out like a cigarette. What the fuck was he supposed to do now? *Apologize* to Bennie? He could picture that: kneeling to unlock the double cuffs, "Hey, ha-ha, sorry about running you down and tuning you up. How's the noggin?"

A doctor Manny knew met him at the motel and worked on Bennie.

"Can he talk?" Manny asked the doctor.

"Not for a while," the doctor said, closing his bag. "Feed him through this straw. Give him codeine and don't be stingy. Call me day after tomorrow, and we'll see."

The doctor's brother had been a cop with Manny, so the house call only cost a hundred dollars in cash.

Manny swallowed hard and called Ray at Biff's flat. "I'm at the Skyway," Manny said. "You better get up here."

"Who's covering Bennie?" Ray asked.

"Bennie's with me," Manny said.

"Is he talking?"

"Not in so many words," Manny said.

Ray arrived at the Skyway Motel with Biff, who immediately turned on the TV and started watching a cartoon. Manny had smoked his way through a pack of butts by then, and Bennie was out cold on the bed, one hand cuffed to the bedstead, his face misshapen from the beating and from the hasty jaw-wiring job afterward. Ray walked around Bennie several times, almost on tiptoes, as if Bennie were a Jackson Pollock hanging in a museum. Then Ray turned to Manny and very quietly said, "What have you done?"

"I worked him over," Manny said. "Go cry in the corner if you're so upset."

Ray hunched awkwardly as men who are not accustomed to fighting often do just before they throw a punch. Manny saw the punch coming before Ray even made a fist, and Manny decided that he would take a shot from Ray. Manny watched as Ray worked himself up to it, then worked himself back down again.

"If we let him go now, he'll rat me for police brutality," Manny said.

"And if we don't, he'll rat us all for kidnapping," Ray said.

It felt like the end of the line. Both men sat down and watched Biff watch TV. Manny glumly studied the brown paper bag as if it would tell him how to get out of what it had gotten him into.

"How much property gets used in lab tests?" Manny asked.

"Couple percent of gross weight," Ray said.

Manny stood up. "This bag's half empty."

They left Biff with Bennie and blasted crosstown to the lab. The chemist had gone off tour an hour earlier. Ray stood lookout while Manny burgled personnel files and found the chemist's home address: 12 Perry, Cambridge. They crossed the Charles and took Memorial Drive.

A light was on in an upstairs apartment. Manny shoulder-popped the door. The chemist wore a flowing saffron robe. Manny's confetti spread in front of him on a low Japanese table, surrounded by rings of lit candles.

"You told my friend the confetti wasn't contraband," Ray said, closing the door.

"It isn't."

"What *exactly* is it?" Manny inquired, a frightening lilt to his voice.

"*D*-lysergic acid diethylamide," the chemist said. Manny and Ray were silent. The chemist looked rewarded, as if stumping them were the point.

Manny grabbed a fistful of saffron robe and hoisted the chemist to whisper at him, "Explain."

"Relax," the chemist gulped. "Jesus. It's a drug, okay? Actually, it's an ergot-based synthetic compound invented by Sandoz in Switzerland during the war. Takes about forty-five minutes to set in. I swallowed a rather ambitious dose, oh, forty minutes ago. So no more violence. I'll tell you what you want to know. Just don't send me on a bad trip."

Ray and Manny thought he meant a prison term.

"It's called different things," the chemist said. "LSD, acid, whatever. But it's all the same splendid shit. Half of Harvard has tried it. You guys narcs from Antarctica or something?"

Ray was flashing back to monthly newsletters he got from the USBN, the federal narcs. The bulletins were constantly hyping new drug epidemics with headlines like *Hashish Horror* and *Morphine Menace.* They were filled with "case studies" about Iowa coeds who puffed on a joint and wound up lesbian. Ray had always thought the newsletters were useful—for starting fires and training puppies. But maybe the feds were finally on to something. Ray remembered reading an item in one of them about a strong hallucinogen invented in Switzerland catching on in bootleg form on college campuses. He remembered the funny name, "acid."

"So it's like marijuana then?" Manny asked.

"Yeah, sure," the chemist said, "except five to ten million times more potent. That's if pure. Pure LSD is supposed to be crystal. I've never seen it pure—only accredited researchers can get their hands on pure crystal."

"Why?" Ray asked.

"You are not dealing with grass here. Acid is way the fuck too powerful. Take that pack of butts there," the chemist said, pointing to the Larks in Manny's shirt pocket. "What's that? Five grams? Five grams of pure crystal LSD is five million micrograms."

Manny said, "So?"

"So a street-standard LSD dose is something like seventy-five micrograms. Think about it. Five lousy grams would be enough to supply Boston for a year. Sandoz'll only ship pure LSD to doctor types with FDA import licenses."

Manny said, "Is it dangerous?"

"If not controlled, very. There are hospitals in the Haight in San Francisco that see ten cases of LSD-induced psychosis a day, climbing all the time. Bad trips are easy to have. The guy who turned me on to acid used to steal it from the Psychology Department at Harvard. There was a prof over there. Tim Leary, big LSD guru, kept a few grams around at all times. Later my friend flunked out and couldn't steal the stuff anymore. So he mixed up a batch in his kitchen sink and tried a dose. He miscalculated purity by just a little bit and wound up in a locked mental ward."

Ray was remembering the USBN bulletins—something from over the winter about acid getting outlawed. "Is it still legal?" he asked the chemist.

"For another week. New laws go into effect on April 12. After that, possession's a big felony. In six days acid goes criminal and the whole psychedelic scene changes forever. That's why every hustler up and down the East Coast is scrambling to get an LSD stockpile together."

"And that's why you stole our bag," Manny said.

"Yeah, I stole your bag. I can only imagine how *you* got it. After April 12, Sandoz stops shipping and the only acid on the streets will be unstable homemade shit which has put a lot of hippies in the hospital."

"Who are the hippies?" Ray asked.

"This a put-on? Alan Funt, come out."

Manny grabbed an armful of saffron and annunciatingly asked, "Who are the mo-ther fuck-ing hip-pies? Give me names. Nicknames. Descriptions. Hangouts. KAs. Start with the leaders. Speak slowly. Go."

"They're everyone," the chemist sputtered, shutting his eyes. "Jesus Christ, you two. Go to the Common any Sunday. Ever wonder who those kids are, the ones flying kites, playing guitar, wearing floppy hats?"

Ray, come to think of it, *had* noticed college-age youths in public places dressing strangely.

"Well, that's my generation, dig it? We are tuning in and dropping out, attacking the evils of capitalism."

"You mean like the Commies?" Manny asked.

The chemist ignored him. "Hippies are just a bunch of kids who don't like what's been happening to this country. I mean, is this why we fried Nagasaki? So you two could kick in my door, no idea what you're chasing, and strangle me? You probably aren't bad men, just caffeine junkies with B-movie minds. *You* are what the hippies don't like."

Ray was beginning to understand.

"You ever hear of a light-skinned Negro guy named Bennie Anastasia selling LSD out of a house over on Kirkland?"

"Heard of him," the chemist said. "His product is strong, man. They say he has a connect inside."

Manny: "Inside?"

"Yeah, like a university lab."

"Or a mental hospital," Ray said. He described Mears. "Do you know anybody like that?"

"No," the chemist said.

Ray and Manny ransacked the chemist's place.

"What am I looking for?" Manny called from a bedroom closet.

"Who knows?" Ray said, maniacally rifling a desk.

They found the chemist balled up like a scolded tot in the corner of his kitchen, eyes squeezed shut. They left him a handful of tabs. Ray stopped at a sign on the wall, the circle with the interior lines like collapsed crosshairs from the front door of 505 Kirkland.

"What's this mean?" Ray asked.

"Peace," the chemist smiled, tripping.

"Now what?" Manny asked. They were on Memorial Drive, Boston-bound.

"Follow the drugs," Ray said.

"Which drugs? Mears's fentanyl or Bennie's acid?"

"Mears is the source for both of them. Think about it. Mears flees Gibraltar after tossing *liquid* in Biff's eyes, giving Biff symptoms that sound a lot like an LSD dosing. Bennie Anastasia was in with Mears from before the beginning of your case against Gibraltar. Remember, Caesar Raines said Mears had a source inside Narco—a source that told Mears what you were up to. That source has to be Bennie. He's been fucking you all along."

"No way," Manny said. "Bennie wouldn't do that. I know him."

"You don't know him. He was your informant, not your friend. Owning a man and knowing him are two different things."

Memorial Drive was deserted, now past midnight, and Manny was behind the wheel. They had been in this part of a case before, straight from a meet with a new source, heads abuzz with fresh answers and fresh questions.

Back at the motel, Bennie was groggy but awake and rattling his shackles against the bedframe. Biff sat in front of the television, volume off, room bathed in blue-gray flicker.

Manny unlocked Bennie's cuffs. Bennie stood up, massaged his wrist, and glared. He sputtered a curse, or tried to, and drooled.

"Listen carefully," Ray said. "We know you trafficked LSD with Joe Mears."

Bennie stopped sputtering.

Ray said, "We know you tipped off Mears to Narco's moves, and we know you told Mears that Biff was a cop. Mears told Caesar, and Caesar nearly killed Biff."

It was Bennie's turn to panic.

"That's a ton of shit on your head," Ray said. "Conspiracy to murder a police officer is mandatory life. So here's my offer: you answer a few questions, forget that Manny smashed your jaw, and in return you get to go home tonight."

Bennie nodded.

"How long has Mears been selling you LSD?"

Bennie held up a finger.

"One month?" Ray asked.

Bennie shook his head.

"One year," Ray said.

Bennie nodded.

"Who is Mears?" Ray asked.

Bennie shrugged.

"I mean, is he a Boston boy, an ex-con, a member of the Elks? What the fuck was he before he showed up offering fentanyl and LSD to the highest bidder?"

Bennie screwed up his face up, as in *Got me.*

"Did you ever meet Mears's source?"

Shrug.

"Did Mears ever mention the source's name?"

Shrug.

"Any guesses about the source?"

Bennie had no guesses.

"Where is Mears now?"

Bennie spread his hands, palms up.

"Don't lie to us," Manny snarled.

Bennie spread his hands even wider, palms still up.

"Was Gibraltar Street his only pad?" Ray said.

Bennie shook his head.

"Where else?" Manny asked. "Where else do I find him?"

Bennie tried to pronounce an address, but his jaws wouldn't move. Shiny drool hung from his chin.

Ray took a pen from his inside jacket pocket and they hunted for some paper, finding none. Bennie was hopping up and down, trying to spit out Mears's other address. He took the pen from Ray and wrote in big letters on the wall of the motel room:

JP OFFCENTER
RED HOUSE, ROCKY HILL
VIEW OF FIELD

Bennie topped it off with a childish drawing of a house on top of the Alps.

Manny stood behind him, deciphering what Bennie had written. JP meant Jamaica Plain. OFFCENTER meant near Centre Street, JP's main drag. The rest meant nothing to Manny.

"What *kind* of field, you idiot?" Manny said.

Bennie wrote. YOUR MOT

Manny thumped Bennie's face against the wall before he could finish the *H*.

"Knock it off," Ray said, helping Bennie off the floor. "Bennie, what kind of field?"

Ray and Manny watched as Bennie wrote in big letters, FOOT-BALL.

They pumped Bennie for more, but this was all Bennie had. He capped the pen and gave it back to Ray.

"Okay," Ray said. "Get lost. But remember, we got a deal."

Bennie didn't nod or shake his head or make any kind of gesture. He just took the brown paper bag of LSD tabs from the bed and went to the door.

Ray stopped him there. "Deal?"

Bennie nodded. He gave Manny a last look, part hate, part guilt—their strange six-year marriage ending, unexpectedly, in stalemate. Bennie limped out to the parking lot and started walking to Cambridge.

"I'll run Biff home," Ray said. "We could all use sleep."

Manny finished his cigarette in the open doorway, watching Bennie disappear. "Sure," he said.

After Ray and Biff left, Manny took a long hot shower in the motel room, then crossed the expressway to a truck stop, where he ordered up a huge meal, pancakes, fried eggs, double bacon, grapefruit, and a bottomless cup of coffee, black. As he ate, he stared across the expressway at the half-dark neon of the Skyway, VAC NCY. He finished the feed, had a cigarette, then walked back to the Skyway. There were two hours of dark left. He got into his car and headed for Jamaica Plain.

24

Boston English High School was not off Centre Street, as Bennie had said, or even near Centre, but it had the only football field in Jamaica Plain. Manny prowled Washington Street, Call Street, and McBride, all of which were lined with houses with a view of English's field. Manny parked and started checking out the area on foot. Everything was quiet. He found the rocky ground Bennie had remembered along the ridge above the football field, and picked the most run-down-looking house on the street. It was gray, not red—a little clapboard saltbox on a brick foundation that had settled unevenly.

Manny stole across a patch of crabgrass to the corner of the house, flattened himself against the siding in a shadow, and listened. The place was dark. Nothing stirred. Manny took Bennie's stiletto from his pocket and scraped the wood. Underneath the gray coat of paint was an older coat, almost maroon. Manny reached into his pocket and took out a safety pin. He reached into another pocket and took out a playing card, the three of clubs, and pinned it to himself.

There were many reasons why a one-man, best-guess showdown with Joe Mears was crazy. Mears had every advantage here: he knew the layout inside and he'd be used to the dark. Manny needed numbers and firepower to overcome Mears's edge, and Manny could get both by calling Nat Butterman at home and telling him to bring the rest of the team and an assault kit—ram, radios, and pump-action shotguns. Fully armed, Narco could take this place properly, from the front and the back, and clean it out with buckshot. If Mears fought, they would kill him. If he ran, they would kill him. If he surrendered, Manny would take him to the basement and kill him.

But Manny wasn't phoning Butterman or anybody else, because Manny couldn't face his men, not after leading them into the last raid, and getting Shecky shot and getting Biff worse than shot. Manny couldn't lead them anywhere until he had put the death of Shecky right. He reached inside his overcoat and drew his .38 from its holster. His hands were cold, but the gun was armpit-warm. He opened the cylinder with a sharp outward snap of his wrist and rolled the chambers with his palm. Six ugly bullets. He closed the cylinder, thumbed the safety off, and kicked in the front door.

The only thing he knew about Mears's front room was that it must have four corners, and he found one of the corners with his shoulder blades. The door hung open, slightly off its hinges, and let a shaft of streetlight down the middle of the room toward a dark hall leading to the back of the house. Manny had only a few seconds of surprise to work with, and let these seconds pass backed into the corner, gun barrel against his nose, waiting for Mears to charge down the hallway toward the open door.

Mears didn't charge. Manny came out of the corner slowly, took a step into the hallway, and listened. Nothing. The hallway sloped with the lot toward the back. Manny stole past a string of cramped, odd-sized rooms. His eyes adjusted to the dark. He relaxed.

He came at Manny low and caught him in the midriff. The man was running for the front door, which stood open just ten feet away, but Manny got a foot in his feet and tripped him up. The man fell hard and let out breath, but crouched to sprint. He pushed off as Manny landed on his back. The man twisted around and found himself staring at the mouth of a .38, Manny's big-knuckled hand, and Manny, in that order.

The man said, "Are you Joe Mears?"

He was a drifter who had squatted in the house for a few nights because it looked abandoned. He knew the name Joe Mears because he had seen it on ID stashed inside. He thought Manny was Mears, back to reclaim the place. Manny never bothered to straighten the drifter out.

"Find another place to squat," Manny said.

When it was light, Manny called Ray and told him the story. Ray drove over and together they questioned the neighbors about the occupant of the house on the rocky ridge.

The neighbors didn't know his name. He came and went, was often gone for weeks, and didn't seem to drive a car. He kept to himself. The only thing they knew for sure was that he was a Catholic priest—they had seen him several times in the last six weeks wearing a priest's black suit and Roman collar. It was a funny place for a priest to live, and a funny way for a priest to act, but who could tell what was normal these days.

Manny and Ray searched the house. Mears had definitely been here—the discarded ID proved that much, as did five cases of laxative and a mixing setup in the pantry. Manny found a receipt for the laxative in a wastepaper basket. Mears had bought the lax from a wholesale pharmacy two weeks before, paying cash. The brand of laxative matched the cut most commonly found in Caesar Raines's fentanyl.

Manny picked through piles of clothes, mostly war-surplus, turning every pocket inside out, dumping lint and pennies on the floor. Cigarette butts were everywhere, and so were cockroaches.

Ray found a single dirty mattress in the back of the house. Next to it were an old hi-fi, some record albums, and a dozen books. Everything else in the crash pad was messy and random, except the books, which were lined up along the floor against the wall.

Ray opened each book, looking for anything. He fondled a secondhand copy of *Gray's Anatomy* with a busted spine, and hefted some textbooks stolen from the Boston Public Library: Page and Russell. *Electroconvulsive Therapy*; Cronholm and Molander, *Memory Disturbance In Electroconvulsive Therapy*; Holmberg, *Biology of Electroconvulsive Therapy*; Bellak, *Manic-Depression*; and *Chemistry Today!*, fifth edition, which was heavily underlined. Ray tossed *Chemistry Today!* on top of *Manic-Depression* and crossed the room.

Next to the mattress was the stub of a candle and a dog-eared Latin Bible, Roman Catholic Vulgate, *nihil obstat* 1928. The Bible was open to Luke 8:26, a story Ray remembered from elementary school: a man, possessed by a legion of demons who drive him to bestial acts, is bound in chains until freed by Jesus when Jesus casts the demons out and drives them into a herd of pigs. Why had Mears kept his Bible open to this passage? Did he see himself as the man possessed, freed by Jesus? Or was he Jesus, freeing others?

Under the open Bible was another book—a hardcover novel called *The Island* by Aldous Huxley. Ray flipped through *The Island* to a random page and read about a man who took a drug and had a vision while listening to Bach.

The Allegro was revealing itself as an element in the great present Event, a manifestation at one remove of the luminous bliss. Or perhaps that was putting it too mildly. In another modality this Allegro *was* the luminous bliss: it was the knowledgeless understanding of everything apprehended through a particular piece of knowledge.

Tonight for the first time, his awareness of a piece of music was completely unobstructed. Between mind and sound, mind and pattern, mind and significance, there was no longer any babel of biographical irrelevance to drown the music or make a senseless discord. . . .

Manny came into the room and saw Ray sitting on the floor, surrounded by books. Ray said, "There's a Latin Bible here, Manny, and three books on electroshock therapy. Plus there's the priest suit—"

Manny cut him off. "Take a look at something."

In a pantry cabinet Manny had found a large gray suitcase of pebbled vinyl with both locks pried open. The suitcase was empty. Manny held it up and shook it, and a single white object, round and flat and an inch across, fell to Ray's feet like a snowflake. Before it hit the ground, Ray knew what it was. The wafer sat on the tip of Ray's left shoe, and Manny held the suitcase up as if he expected Mears himself to fall out next.

Manny heaved the mangled suitcase aside and dusted his hands. "Okay," he said, almost affably, "I'll ask: what the fuck does *that* mean?"

Ray looked the Eucharist over. "The suitcase belonged to a priest named George Sedgewick."

"A real priest or a drug dealer who dresses like one?"

"A real priest," Ray said. "You know about him, Manny. Sedgewick's the guy who died at the airport over New Year's. He was bringing Eucharist from Rome to Boston. It was a publicity stunt to ease the way for the first English-language mass. He was jumped at Logan—"

Ray looked around the pantry, making sure every detail fit what he was about to say. Ray said, "He was jumped at Logan by Joe Mears."

Ray walked through the house. Eucharist still in his hand, putting the facts together as he spoke. "Before Mears came to Boston he was a patient in a Navy mental hospital in Portsmouth. There were some hotshot doctors there running experiments on people, horrible experiments, and Mears was one of their failures. They went too far with him or made a mistake, I don't know which. But when Mears got loose, he started killing the hospital staff to pay them back. Remember Childs—the guy we interviewed at City & County?"

"He was one of the Portsmouth people," Manny recalled.

Ray nodded. "There were three others: a goon named Poole, a doctor, Zimquist, and Father George Sedgewick."

"And they're all dead?"

"As doornails," Ray said. They were in the bedroom, surrounded by books. "Mears winds up in Boston, and so does Childs," Ray said. "Mears could kill him at any time, and what can Childs do about it? Call the cops? Tell the truth and implicate himself in God knows what? It's an option, a crappy option."

Manny lit a cigarette and said, "He cuts a deal instead."

"A deal with Mears," Ray nodded.

Manny was nodding too. "Childs supplies Mears with product and Mears starts selling fentanyl to Caesar."

"And LSD to Bennie," Ray added. There was a logic to it. *Of course* Mears winds up in the drug business—it's all he knows. *Of course* he specializes in the exotic, to make the best use of Lem Childs. Ray looked at the Eucharist in his hand, and showed it to Manny as if something were written on it.

"Childs knew Sedgewick was coming in from Rome on New Year's Eve," Ray said. "Childs told Mears. It was part of the deal: the priest dies."

Manny tried to take it one step further. "So let's go to Childs and make him tell us where Mears is."

"Won't work," Ray said. "Childs doesn't know where Mears is except when they meet to hand off a package. Besides, if you lean on Childs and he plays dumb, what's your next move?"

"I arrest him for the murder of Sedgewick, and for the drug sales too."

"Based on what?" Ray said. He brandished the Eucharist. *"This?"*

"You got a better idea?"

Ray said, "Mears will have to meet Lem Childs at least once more. They'll do another pickup before this drug goes criminal, so Mears can dominate the LSD shortage. Be a narc, Manny. Stay with Childs, and he'll lead you to Mears."

Ray went back to Biff's apartment and found his brother lying on the kitchen floor and listening to three different radios, tuned to opera, news, and surf music. A kettle whistled on the stove, and an alarm clock had been ringing for some time. Ray went around the apartment, shutting off the radios and the stove and the alarm clock, and sat Biff at the kitchen table.

"You need to hear this," Ray said. "Manny and I have been working on Mears, and I think we're getting the picture."

Ray talked slowly and paused often, hoping Biff was hearing him.

"Mears is into a new drug called LSD. This drug is a million times more powerful than anything Narco has ever seen. It makes you act nuts, see things, do things. You said Mears threw 'water' in your face in the back bedroom. Remember? Do you remember?"

Biff looked at Ray as if he could still hear the opera in his head.

"That wasn't water he threw at you, Biff. That was this new drug. It didn't show in the tests they performed on you in the hospital because nobody knew to test for it. It won't even be illegal for five more days."

Ray put his hand on Biff's hand. "You didn't fuck up in the raid. You were drugged. Shecky Bliss isn't your fault."

Ray searched Biff's face in vain for a flicker of recognition. "Mears is still in Boston," Ray continued. "We had him at the China Bowl selling LSD to Bennie Anastasia, but he slipped away. He's supplied out of City & County by a man named Lemuel Childs. He's a doctor there."

Biff stared at the table.

"We're gonna tail Childs," Ray said, "and we're gonna grab him and Mears with a package when they meet. That package of drugs will prove that Shecky Bliss wasn't your fault."

Ray had no idea if any of this sank in. He went into the bedroom and called his office. He asked a secretary to type a subpoena for the bank records of one Lemuel Childs back to the first of the year. As Ray hung up, he heard Biff hit the shower.

Ray sat alone in the bedroom, listening to the shower go, glad that Biff was cleaning himself up. Ray made some soup for lunch and knocked on the bathroom door.

"Biff," he said, "you hungry?"

He knocked again. "Biff?"

The shower was running ice-cold and it was empty. Ray found Biff's wallet and shield on the toilet seat.

Biff was gone.

25

It wasn't as if he had a plan. He simply understood, after weeks of getting no place in his skull, what had to happen next. He didn't know, or care, much more than that. So he waited until Ray got on the phone, pulled the shower trick, then hit the street. He thumbed a lift on a grocery truck and rode with a thousand dozen eggs through the tunnel and south on the expressway to the Quincy side of the Neponset Bridge. He banged on the cab of the truck to be let off, and said goodbye to the driver. He waited until the truck was out of sight, waving inanely because he had forgotten where he was and why he had come here. Then he tried very hard to recognize street signs, buildings, anything, and he remembered that if he walked toward the smell of the salt marshes, he would come to the guardhouse that led to the causeway that led to the nuthouse jail island. He had a couple miles' walk to the guardhouse. It was becoming a hot morning—the first hot morning of the spring. He took his coat off and laid it carefully over a mailbox, then started his hump to the sea.

His feet hurt. A streetcar ran west, crackling along overhead wires. Biff kept walking. The morning got hotter. He was past the Naval Air Station and coming up on the guardhouse. A little jimmy in a Corrections getup stepped out of the shed into his path.

"I'm hearing voices," Biff said. "I'll see Dr. Childs now, please."

The guard started jawing, so Biff hit him in the ear with a pretend karate chop that hurt his hand but dropped the jimmy nicely. Biff started past him onto the causeway, squeezing through the iron gate, and was halfway to the island when the Corrections boys came screaming down the causeway from the island in a trashy carpool Rambler. They piled out, four gorillas making for him, slamming four doors, nightsticks banging against car and leather belts and thighs and wooden gun butts, a comforting sound at that moment, just an old cop sound. He gave the fat sergeant, who led, a lazy grin and got cracked in the teeth with the tip of a sap. He slumped, thinking, *Here we go, BoSox, here we go. . . .*

They stomped him until the fat sarge gave himself a charley horse. Biff yelped to make them think they were getting somewhere, but he mostly felt dreamy and sleepy. They loaded him into the back of the Rambler and drove him out to the island, leaving him manacled to the wall in Receiving.

He sat on the floor for an hour before a nurse came over. "Name?" she asked.

"Mears," Biff said. "Joe. I'd like to see Dr. Childs."

The nurse disappeared. Another hour passed. Two orderlies came in asking for the job who beat up the cop. Biff tried to stand. They uncuffed him, and joshed, one taking each arm, calling him Sugar Ray, until he was down a long corridor and behind two locked iron doors. Then one orderly pinned his arms behind his back. The other orderly stepped in front, fished for brass knuckles in his pockets, slid them on his right fist lovingly, and sent five bolo shots into Biff's breadbasket. Biff crumpled to the filthy floor.

"You in the Open Wards," the hitter said. "I'm boss here. You and your voices fuck up again, Mr. Joe Mears, and you'll never walk off this island on working knees. Dig?"

Biff dry-retched on his new boss's scuffed steel-toed shoes and got kicked in the back of the head.

"Dig?"

He was nodding feebly at the shoes. They dragged and carried him through another security door, and shackled him to a bench bolted to the floor. He passed out.

When he woke up, all his joints hurt. He'd pissed in his pants some hours before. He was in a room big enough for half-court basketball, and one of the fifty-odd loons gawking at him had stolen his shoes and socks and tried to take his soiled shirt but hadn't been able to get it off over Biff's wrist shackles. He moved his arm. He could tell that he'd been given needles in his shoulder.

After a while, the orderly who had pinned his arms in the corridor came in with a ring of keys and a much-scarred baseball bat. Biff named him Goon One. The other inmates looked away and moved off.

Goon One unshackled Biff, cursing the odor. Biff sat on the bench. His head throbbed. He fought back puke while the orderly circled the room, slapping the bat in his left palm. Goon One departed, locking the doors behind him. Biff stood up gingerly and walked barefoot across the ward. He vomited next to an old man in a fetal ball so that the oldster would get blamed, knowing that the spew meant a beating from whoever had to clean it up.

He limped around the ward once, trying to size up what survival here meant. There were five cells off either side of the open room, ten total, four narrow cots crammed in each. He counted men, windows, chairs. Wretches hunched on the cots, babbling, screaming, chattering back at voices in their heads. *Me shut up? You shut up! You never gave me credit. No, you never did!* Men straitjacketed in the corner cried out that they were thirsty. Biff was in one of City & County's infamous open wards, the snake pits, reserved for violent offenders trying to fool the court shrinks, meantime preying on the chronics, who'd never get out.

A pretty kid was being butt-fucked over a cot by a tall sunburned man. The kid bared teeth as the sunburned man's shiny tool rode in and out. The kid turned his head, met Biff's gaze, and forced a thin, coquettish smile. Everyone eyed Biff. New meat.

The sunburned man came, braying and bucking, then drew his cock from the kid, lay on a cot, and began paging through a tattered magazine about boats. The kid was hitching up his pants and buckling his belt, walking like he just got off a horse.

"What're you looking at?" the kid sassed Biff, lower lip out, hands on slender hips.

"You," Biff said.

"Yeah?"

"Yeah. You got something I need."

"Take a number," the kid said. Biff's right knee came up into his crotch. The sunburned man got off the cot.

"This don't involve you," Biff said.

The man took a long look at Biff, and went back to his magazine as Biff ripped his shoes off the kid's feet, twisting the kid's ankles almost backward. Biff found an empty corner and sat down. He put his shoes back on, tied a knot in each, and looked around the room to make sure everybody got the message.

Biff figured Childs would have to come see him eventually if he kept saying he was Mears. When Childs came, he would recognize Biff from the Shecky Bliss shooting and, maybe, assume the worst—that Biff was undercover with official sanction, part of an investigation getting hotter and closer to Childs's LSD pipeline. Childs would panic, tell Mears, and let Mears do the dirty work in the Opens, Childs's home turf. Mears would come after him, dressed as an orderly or a patient. This would be Biff's chance. *Bait*, Biff thought. *I'm bait.*

"Mears!" Another orderly, an old guy pushing a cartful of meds in little cups. Goon One stood guard on the cart, bat slapping palm

Biff limped over. The orderly watched him swallow each pill: three blue, four gray. They felt wrong going down.

Ray dialed Vinnie the lawyer's office, still looking for Biff.

"He's supposed to be here right now," Vinnie said. "I wanted to go over his testimony at the fitness hearing. Coach him on looking zombielike, not that Biff needs any help in that department lately. What's going on, Ray?"

Ray wasn't sure how to answer. Vinnie couldn't know about the kidnapping of Bennie Anastasia.

"I was afraid of that," Vinnie said. "The hearing's in front of Judge Croft today at two. Biff's a basket case, so we're gonna win this thing. But Croft won't be giving us any more adjournments. If we dick around, maybe Croft hardens and does something rash, like finding Biff fit to stand trial. And if Biff doesn't show—well, you know Judge Croft."

"He'll issue an arrest warrant," Ray said.

"And because Croft doesn't trust the PD to find their own, he'll sic the troopers on Biff's ass. They'll tip the town upside down looking for him. It won't be jolly. Find him, kid."

Ray spent the rest of the morning cruising the blocks around the Skyway Motel, then on a hunch trolled Biffs boyhood haunts back in the Telegraph. Thinking Biff might be like the man who misplaces his keys and goes back to where he last saw them, Ray rode past the three towers of the Gibraltar Street projects. He walked through 10 Gibraltar, where Biff had met Joe Mears, found the derelict mill where Biff had lost Mears's trail on the morning of the doomed search warrant, and wound up at the bank of the Ship Channel where Biff and Sheck had run Mears down. Kids were out that morning, playing street hockey, skipping double-dutch, listening to AM radio, drinking beer.

When Biff's case was on in court that afternoon, Vinnie

Sullivan begged Judge Croft for a two-week continuance, and when Croft exploded, Vinnie said a week would do.

"Where is your client?" Judge Croft demanded of Vinnie, who stood beside a very empty chair.

"Your Honor, he is a man who has been diagnosed as delusional and severely depressed. He is a man sadly out of touch with his surroundings."

"He is a man," Judge Croft cut in, "who can't get to court to answer *murder* charges. Bailiff, get me the state police."

Two, three, four. Three times a day, four gray and three blue, then three gray and four blue, some whites, a yellow, Stelazine. Thorazine, lithium, the men in the ward said. It was raining. Later, it wasn't.

He was told all kinds of unbelievable things and asked repeatedly who he was.

Don't I know you?

Yes, well, it's possible, but, no. I don't think so.

Sure. You a cop. You bust me down Fort Point couple-five years ago. Drunk and drivin'.

No, no.

Five minutes later: *Don't I know you?*

Well, you know.

You sure?

The orderlies caught the pretty kid turning a cot trick for some chewing gum and took him away. He came back later, winking at the ward, new heavyweight champion of the world. A guy died in the middle of the night and nobody found him until at least one day later. The smell tipped them off. He asked a boy who said he ate acid what day it was, and it felt like it took an hour to get an answer of some kind.

Acid? somebody was saying. *Can't eat acid.*

The kid replied, *Windowpane.*

Can't eat windowpanes neither.

Stela, Thora, lith. He kept asking what day it was, and finally somebody said Thursday, and somebody said Wednesday, and somebody said Thursday, and somebody else agreed, so he decided it was probably that day.

Goon One came with the bat for every man except him until he thought he'd never see another room. He started to love the orderlies. Not like them. Love them. Especially Goon One.

They came for him, taking him out of the Opens, which made him grateful to these lovely men as they led him, slapping the bat, through corridors and up stairs and along catwalks, sticking him without a word in a little room before a two-way mirror. He waved hello at the mirror.

A young woman with intern written all over her stepped in. She had a clipboard and a caring gaze.

He waved at her.

"Joe Mears?"

"That's not my real name."

"Why did you say that was your name then?"

He looked at her.

"Why did you say that was your name?"

He could see how kind she was.

"Well, anyway, what should we call you today?"

"Biff. My real name is Harold, but I'm called Biff."

"That's fine, Biff," she said, writing "Harold Mears" on the top of her paper.

"I'm here to see Dr. Childs."

"Dr. Childs is very busy. I'm Miss Anthony. I'll do your intake interview, and then in a few days—"

"I need to see Dr. Childs right away. It's very important."

"Well, Mr. Mears—ah, Biff, we'll—"

"It's *very* important." He explained to her about the man in the back bedroom, the way the liquid felt in his eyes, the momentary blindness, and his friend Shecky, whom he had killed. He didn't want to kill his friend—didn't remember killing his friend—but everyone was saying he did. Gunshot wound to the face. Biff touched his own nose. He needed to find the man in the back bedroom. Dr. Childs would send the man to him.

Miss Anthony looked at him a long time and seemed sad. Then she nodded as if she understood. This surprised him, since he hadn't explained it very well. She left with his message for Dr. Childs. The orderlies took him back to the pills in the ward.

He was happy. It was a matter of time now—time to finish what he'd come here to do. Which was? He thought really hard. Find the man he'd chased out a bedroom window, the long fall, and had been chasing ever since: lost target, carrot-top, bloody murderer.

A trio of orderlies took him back to the Opens, one orderly a step behind, one at each elbow. He heard the baseball bat slap palm in a strolling rhythm: slap palm, slap palm, slap palm.

When he was locked back into the Opens, he knew the next time they came for him it would be to bring him to see Mears.

Two hours before dawn: big commotion in the ward. White men barking at the orderlies up and down the corridors. He saw flash-lights playing on the walls from the security desk, heard the boss orderly's big key ring jangling, rubber-soled hospital shoes quick-scraping the tile floors.

"Whas dat name agi'n, Cap'n?" the boss orderly was asking, putting on the phony shuffle-along accent.

"Dunn."

"Ain' no Dunn in dis ward, I tol' ya—"

"He's a bench warrant, you imbecile," the barker barked. "He'd be here under another name. Step aside."

The two plainclothes state troopers were from the Violent Felony Warrants Squad out of the South Weymouth Barracks.

They wore nickel-plated Charter Arms .44 Bulldogs, gargantuan sidearms favored by the unit because they fired the slowest, heaviest bullet commercially available, a body-stopping slug that plowed through guts and stuck, no clean hole, no ricochet.

The troopers were named Green and Jackson. They had been hunting Biff Dunn without pause for eighty straight hours, starting at Biff's mother's place in suburban Belmont, banging on that door and demanding to search her prim two-bedroom saltbox, busting up Ray Dunn's house in West Roxbury and Manny's deserted place on the water. The troopers grabbed a neighbor's son on the front lawn and checked his face against a photo of Patrolman Biff Dunn.

"Nope," Trooper Green told Trooper Jackson, who tossed the boy aside.

They hit Jay Scanlon's slutty sister's place because somebody told the troopers Biff used to mess around with her.

Ginger Scanlon was entertaining a gentleman caller at the time, but the troopers kept knocking, until she opened up wrapped in a towel.

"We have an arrest warrant for Patrolman Biff Dunn. Have you see him?"

"You kiddin' me? That punk hasn't so much as called me in a year."

Ginger Scanlon's gentleman caller was a sergeant from Auto Crime. He was married and naked and hiding behind the door, and when he heard the troopers demanding to come in he thought his wife had sent a private dick or, worse, Internal Affairs. He booked out the back, scooping up his pants along the way. The two troopers heard the philanderer scram and caught him in the alley.

"*Drop it!*" they roared, referring to the sergeant's trousers. He complied, hands up, penis swiftly shrinking from the April chill, flabby buttocks quaking. Trooper Green held the husband at cocked .44-point, while Trooper Jackson surveyed him head to foot, then slowly compared the sergeant's face to the photograph of Biff Dunn.

"Nope," said Jackson.

Biff was in the last bedroom at the end of the ward along with two catatonics and a sedated raver, who was diarrhetic and diapered. He heard Green and Jackson go from room to room, rousting every single man from bed, comparing each tortured, terrified face to the BPD photo. Old men, young men, black, white, blind geezers with milky eyes, amputees. Green yanked each head out of bed and tilted the flashlight, while Jackson held the photo, glancing at face, then at photo, bed to bed to bed, grunting, "Nope. Nope. Nope."

Biff had to make a move.

The troopers came to Biff's bedroom. Their flashlights raked the cots.

"We got an empty bed here," Trooper Jackson shouted. Orderlies came running.

"He was there at lights-out," the boss orderly explained, frantic that he might be blamed. He tore the cot apart, tipped it over.

"Well, he's not there now, is he?" Trooper Green said. "There any way out of here?"

"Windows all sealed up," the boss orderly said, Uncle Ben's Converted Rice accent disappearing. "Only ways out's past the security desk, and Moakey here, he been on since midnight."

The troopers pointed their flashlights into the face of the lumbering Irish cretin Moakey.

"You didn't happen to catch a *nap* tonight, did you, Moakey?" Trooper Green menaced.

"I, I, I—" Moakey stuttered, Adam's apple a yo-yo.

"What's past the security desk?" Jackson demanded. "Another ward? A low-security ward? Building exits?" Moakey and the boss orderly were nodding in unison, yes to all three questions.

"Christ, Dunn could be out of the building by now. What name's the missing man here under?" Jackson pointed at the tipped-over cot.

The boss orderly, flustered, consulted a clipboard. "Pugh," he said. "Clifford Pugh."

Biff lay facedown in his cot, sheets over his head, five feet from Trooper Jackson's leg, his body covering that of the diarrhetic raver Pugh. He waited for the troopers, brace of orderlies in tow, to hustle out of the ward in search of Biff Dunn a.k.a. Clifford Pugh. The stench of Pugh's runny stool under the sheets stung Biff's eyes. He didn't move for half an hour after the ward went quiet, then he dragged his savior across the tile floor to a janitorial closet and tucked him in under sour mops.

Joe Mears rode the city bus down Dorchester Ave for five miles. He knew it then went east on Q-Shore Drive, made a stop at the guardhouse at the mainland end of the City and County causeway, and continued south to points in Quincy.

Childs had been terrified on the phone that morning, reading to Mears from Miss Anthony's report.

"This guy says he's *you*," Childs stammered. "What the hell is going on?"

"Relax," Mears had told him.

"It's a cop. They're on to us—"

"Just relax. Look at the name: 'Joe Harold Biff Mears.' It's not a cop, it's an *ex*-cop. They aren't on to nothing."

"Then why send an undercover into my hospital?"

"Nobody sent him. He's all by himself. He came back to find me. Or maybe he's an elephant, he came back to die."

"Well, either way, I'm through. The deal's off."

"The deal's *on*. You were supposed to fix Biff Dunn. Looks like you didn't quite finish the job. Now I will. But the deal is on. Remember who I am."

Childs remembered. He made Mears promise: nobody dies at City & County.

"Okay, okay," Mears had told him that morning, "but you make sure you got my package."

"I'm working on it. I meet the party from New York tonight. I'll see you right after, like we said."

"Don't be late. I got one big thing to do, then I'm blowing Boston forever."

Now Mears scanned the block outside the causeway gate, letting five hospital workers off ahead of him. If he saw an odd car, an idle man reading a newspaper, anything out of place, he'd stay with the bus to Wollaston Beach. The block was clear. He jammed a foot in the closing door, and got off.

Mears wore the priest suit he had stolen from Sedgewick and carried Childs-supplied chaplain credentials. He was waved through the checkpoint, and caught a ride with some nurses. They let him off in front of the jail. Mears signed in, and waited for the elevator up to the electroshock department.

Biff marked time by pacing laps of the ward, five minutes a lap. He had counted ninety-nine laps when two guys jumped him looking to steal cigarettes. He smashed their faces together, then went back to pacing, but forgot the number he had counted to. This made him mad. He overheard the orderlies saying that the troopers thought Biff Dunn had skipped town. He was thinking about carrot-top, lost target, the bloody murderer.

Later, he saw two orderlies in the doorway.

"MEARS," they paged, looking at a white piece of paper.

"Upstairs," an orderly said, pointing out the door of the ward and down the corridor.

Biff went with them, ready.

26

After half a morning's fruitless search for Biff, Ray claimed his mail at the Suffolk County Courthouse. He opened an impressive-looking envelope and spread across his desk the Bank of Boston's response to his subpoena of Lemuel Childs's checking account.

Ray went over the records with care. This account had a pulse, a nice working hum. Childs took in $406 bi-weekly, his City & County paycheck, and irregular deposits in cash, five hundred here, a thousand there, which Ray read as Mears giving Childs the money to buy fentanyl or LSD, or both. Childs wrote checks for rent, utilities, and the usual miscellany, and a few things not so usual. Childs wrote checks to four different pharmaceutical houses, probably for fentanyl, and made healthy withdrawals to cash, which landed LSD in the underground network, or so Ray guessed. Ray nearly choked on the last transactions: a ten-thousand-dollar deposit in mid-March, followed by a ten-thousand-dollar withdrawal to cash, three days ago.

Ray remembered Caesar Raines: Mears was into something big, and cleaned Caesar out in early March, just before Childs made this big deposit. Mears gave the money to Childs, who sat on it awhile before withdrawing it last week. Ten thousand in cash, for what?

Ray remembered the kid chemist: everyone on the East Coast was scrambling to get a stockpile together before acid went criminal and Sandoz stopped shipping. And, Ray thought, before the price went through the roof. Childs was about to purchase one last big package for Mears, something like a pound of pure crystal

LSD. Ray did the math on the top of the bank records: ten thousand bucks buys five hundred grams times a million divided by seventy-five micrograms a hit. Ray put his pen down, awestruck. After this drug deal, Joe Mears would control something like six *million* doses of LSD. Jesus.

Ray knew that Childs would have to meet Joe Mears to give Mears the package. Childs might have the package already, or he might be waiting on it. They would not know for sure that the LSD was with Childs until Childs met Mears. If they let the package pass from Childs to Mears, Mears would control enough LSD to—to do what? Manny, watching Childs, was probably the single most important man in Massachusetts at that moment.

Manny pulled into a side street near the guardhouse at the foot of the causeway leading out to City & County and watched the back of Childs's car disappear onto the island. Manny had tailed Childs here three days straight, routine. To do a deal, Childs would have to leave through this gate, or Mears would have to arrive the same way. Manny bet himself five bucks that Childs would go to Mears, not the other way around. Childs would drive to his stash, probably his apartment, get the package, and rendezvous with Mears at some third location. They might meet at Childs's place, and do the handoff inside, but Manny doubted this. Too much risk for Childs. He was afraid of Mears. He'd want to see Mears in a parking lot or park, out in the open, someplace near a highway so he could get in and out fast, someplace Childs and Mears both knew so directions wouldn't be a problem.

Manny read the paper, smoked half a pack of Larks, and checked his watch: 4:12 P.M. In eight hours, the doc's package went criminal. Childs would need an hour to pick up his stash, then make the meeting. He'd leave himself a few hours leeway.

Childs had patient consultations scheduled until eight-fifteen, Manny learned by calling Childs's secretary posing as a tearful wacko who needed to see Childs that night. Childs would keep these appointments, wanting to appear absolutely normal. After eight-fifteen, Childs was unavailable, the secretary said. Manny bet himself another five-spot that Childs would leave the island between eight-thirty and eight forty-five. Settling in with a new cigarette, he immediately lost his wager when the doctor's gray Studebaker was waved through the guard gate and tore past Manny for the Quincy Shore Drive.

Four hours too early, Manny thought. *Something's haywire.*

Manny let the Stude pass, counted to five, and pulled into traffic, beginning the biggest tail of his life.

As Manny left the jail island in his rearview mirror, two orderlies were walking Biff through the hospital complex. They yanked him around a sharp corner. Goon One was waiting. "Hey, Sugar Ray," he grinned, producing a needle, which he stabbed at the inside of Biff's elbow. In it went.

Biff came to in a small room, strapped to a hard wooden table. The only other thing in the room was a control panel that looked like a motorboat dashboard. Had he been here before? He thought he had. *Do I know you?* he asked the dashboard. Yes: pain. This is a pain place.

He twisted in the straps. Somebody was putting what felt like mayonnaise on his temples. Light blinded him as he struggled to see the face that did this, and then he felt mini-telephones on his skull to talk through the bone right into the brain. He was squirming to see the face of whoever was in the room with him. He heard a man's voice: "Clear."

Biff's head went white with pain.

The second shock:

Pain was everything. The voice was at the motorboat controls. Straps bit Biffs chest, neck, cheek.

The third shock:

His knees convulsed up, down, up. His spine jerked. Then again, from his balls to his skull like a rope pulled taut, *jerk*. His jaw was open, shut, slammed. His teeth sought to shear his tongue. Spine: *jerk*.

The fourth shock:

Next he would be blind, so he corkscrewed himself in a last effort, and saw the face at the motorboat controls. *Red*. Red waved, *Hi*.

The fifth shock:

Biff went blind.

The sixth shock:

Mears had promised the doc that he wouldn't kill the cop with a heart attack. Mears had told him to get off the island if he didn't have the stomach. Mears jammed the volt button again.

The seventh shock:

Mears watched the cop flop like a rag doll, watched the volts romp. Here comes the grand mal seizure. Now the eerie stillness in the brain stem, a moment suspended. Then the tonic and clonic convulsions arrive, like your skull trying to ejaculate your brain. Want some more?

The eighth shock:

"Don't worry about me," Mears had told Childs. "Just get me my drugs—and watch for a tail, like I told you."

The ninth shock:

Pity Mears had had no time to rig the cop to an electroencephalogram, since the tonics and clonics, which now racked the cop, always produced the prettiest spike waves: first the six sharp dagger-stabs up and down, EEG pen scratching across the unrolling paper, great tonic storms settling into waves, then ripples of clonic voltage, asynchronous with the jerks and spasms that still twisted the cop, who now screamed and gulped his tongue. Mears loved to watch the EEG ride the crags and valleys of the brain blasted with three hundred volts. More?

The tenth shock:

Lungs and glottis spasm. Breathing stops. Blood floods the cerebellum. The heart stops cold, then stagger-pumps, all off-beat.

The eleventh shock:

Mears watched the cop *feel* his heart ejaculate his blood, his skull ejaculate brain, his lungs unstartable.

The twelfth shock:

Mears knew exactly what the cop was feeling. Your mouth's filling with saliva and snot, cop, and you're sucking fluids into frozen lungs. You could drown in snot. Work your mouth to spit out snot and your clamping teeth could bite off your tongue.

Mears called the orderlies in to stash the cop for an hour until the next session. The orderlies unstrapped Biff and began to free his head. Biff went for Mears behind the dashboard, electrodes still on his temples. Biff was a step away from Mears's hated face. Mears mashed down on the button and blew current through Biff's head. Goon One was on Biff, and Mears pounded his controls, volts and volts and volts from ear to ear. Biff was seeing white again, but felt the mini-telephones slip off his temples and into Goon One's grappling hands, and now Mears pushed a button and Goon One shrieked. Biff grabbed Mears's neck across the dashboard, but Mears was quick and powerful, and he had Biff's face in his hands. He meant to break Biff's neck, but Mears's left hand was stitched up the palm. Biff bit the stitches and Mears let go. Mears snatched the cord to the electrodes from the floor and looped it once, quickly, around Biff's throat, then yanked it strangle-tight. Biff fought to loosen the cord, finding the electrode ends, jamming them into Mears's mouth, and reached back for the controls, finding any button, pushing hard.

Mears screamed, eyes bugged, inadvertently swallowing. He rolled off Biff. Biff was pushing the button. Mears was screaming, and convulsing, trying to spit out the electrodes. Mears squirmed across the floor, jumping with each new shock, and pulled the electrodes out of his mouth.

Biff fell on him, but Mears again got his throat. Biff's neck would snap in a moment. Orderlies were rushing in the doorway with saps.

Biff grabbed Mears's neck as hard as he could and threw himself into the glass and out the window, falling unknown stories, pulling Mears behind him by the throat.

27

Manny stayed with Childs's Studebaker from the jail island, three winding miles past the Naval Air Station and the salt marshes. Childs made a few attempts to scope a tail, changing lanes, stopping short, amateur hour. Manny was more afraid that Childs would ram a bus or get pulled over for DWI than he was that the doc would make the tail. Manny knew that Childs led to Mears and Mears was the key to everything. Lose the Stude with the shitbum County shrink and lose the only line to Mears and to the load of LSD, probably forever.

Childs took the expressway north. Manny hung back, figuring Childs would go westbound on the turnpike to meet Mears and do the handoff somewhere on Childs's turf, Fens, Back Bay, maybe Cambridge. He nearly lost the Stude when Childs took the Park Square exit. It was close to eight o'clock, an off-the-harbor rain sprinkling, a raw April night. Manny put on his wipers and got up close, one car back, past Columbus, onto Stuart.

Childs was going downtown, driving straight for wherever he was headed, confident that he had shaken any tail. Manny, who had spent several thousand hours following people in cars, sensed as much from the way the Stude's brake lights went off and on, from the set of Childs's head in the front seat.

Childs pulled up on Stuart and parked. There were whores toward the pike. Childs sat in his car, looking every bit the up-tight cauc john here to hire a beating or a blowjob. Hookers strolled past the Stude in tight, loud skirts, thighs shivering. Manny, a half block up and across the street, could see them hawk Childs.

Wanna party, mister? Childs shook his head stiffly, definitely not, probably scared they'd snap off his car antenna. What the hell *else* could he be here for? Manny looked up Stuart. The Greyhound depot was lit like Vegas: runaways, college kids, winos, grifters. Manny eyed the Studebaker and then the terminal, Childs was meeting a bus.

A half hour passed. The Stude entered traffic and squared the block, pulling up in front of the depot. Childs left it parked under the neon, locking all doors, and went in. Manny slipped around to the side, where the buses pulled in, and caught Childs talking to a ticket-taker. He let Childs leave, then showed his tin to the ticket-taker and asked about the old bald guy.

"Him?" the ticket-taker said, pointing out the door.

Manny turned his back to Stuart and rasped, "Don't point, it's rude. What he wanna know?"

"New York bus. Due in at seven."

It was ten past.

"Heavy snow far down as Jersey," the ticket-taker jawed, "and it's coming our way. Channel Four says it's gonna get down to twenty tonight—"

"When's the goddam bus due?"

"Eight, they're saying. Got out of Port Authority late."

The Stude was gone. Manny cruised the neighborhood, mostly to keep warm, then set up across from Greyhound, knowing Childs would be back. He called Ray from a pay phone.

"Startin' to snow out here," he said.

"Where's Childs?"

"Around Greyhound someplace. He's meeting the New York bus at eight."

"The pickup," Ray said.

Ray told Manny about Childs's checking account, the big withdrawal a week before.

"So he paid up front and today's the delivery," Manny said.

"Yeah. He's getting a huge load, Manny—maybe six million hits of the shit. By street value, it's the biggest drug deal you ever staked out."

Manny yawned, unimpressed. He still thought LSD was for dips. Heroin, there was a man's drug. "Biff turn up?" he asked.

"No," Ray said. "The troopers are still on it."

"Them pricks, Jackson and Green. You hear they went to my house, nearly collared my neighbor's kid 'cause they couldn't find any of mine?" Manny coughed smoke into the phone. "What do I do when Childs meets his connect?"

"Nothing," Ray said. "Childs'll go from the depot straight to Mears with the LSD. We want the package *and* we want Mears."

"So I let Childs pick up his product and lead me to Mears. Good plan."

"Beats the alternatives, as if we had any," Ray said.

"Only thing, it's gotta be tonight. You know about Operation Clambake? I'm in a blue suit guarding the Archbishop bright and early tomorrow, no matter what. No excuses, no exceptions."

"Clambake?"

"Mass in English," Manny said. "Can you believe it?"

"Worry about tomorrow tomorrow. Childs will meet Mears before LSD goes criminal. Stay on Childs."

The Stude reappeared on Stuart at quarter to eight. Childs double-parked in the same spot under the neon, ducked in, ducked out, and pulled up a few car lengths to wait. The bus lumbered around the corner, coming from the pike, at ten past. Wet snow was falling fast. Manny watched Childs get out of his car. The Greyhound came up Stuart, diesel laboring in low gear, and pulled wide into the bays. Childs scampered into the depot. Manny skipped after him through traffic across Stuart, flicking his butt high into the air, unzipping his jacket, squeezing his gun in his armpit to keep it from jostling.

Inside the door, Manny scanned the busy terminal for Childs.

That was always the first thing, find your guy and get out of his line of sight. Then watch him meet the mule. Maybe they do the handoff here, maybe they take the package someplace private to purity-test. In a heroin deal, a test would be mandatory. Coke, probably not. LSD, Manny had no idea—he realized he didn't even know what the load would look like. How big is six million hits of LSD?

The New York crowd straggled into the depot. Childs stood to the side, fidgeting like a worried daddy from the suburbs, surveying the arrivals. Manny stepped behind a cement pillar. A waif type, female cauc, long dirty-brown hair, was last through the gate. Childs was on and off tiptoes, looking everybody over. The girl stopped, as if remembering something, and went into her shoulder bag, coming out with a shapeless denim cap. Childs saw the cap, and waded into the crowd, moving toward the girl, right hand out to part bodies. Manny felt suddenly lighthearted. He slid from behind the pillar. This was too easy.

"Freeze," said a quiet voice behind him. "You're packing a Smith .38 under your left shoulder, which makes you a rightie. Don't go for it."

Childs meets the girl, says five words. She nods. They head together for the door. Manny steps to follow, and feels a muzzle at the base of his spine.

"I'm Trooper Green," the voice said. "This is Trooper Jackson."

"*Christ almighty, you two!*" Manny half-wheeled but was stopped by a jab of muzzle.

"Don't. You're here to meet Biff Dunn. He lams for a few days, figures the heat's off, now he's sneaking back, right? Tell us which bus and we'll try not to waste him."

Manny watched Childs and the waif disappear through the Stuart Street doors.

"Excuse me, douchebags," he said, "but I'm staking out a couple of druggies just now. Them two. The ones getting ready to drive away. Do you see Biff Dunn in this bus station? Me neither. Now I'm gonna walk out the door to find my marks. Here I go. Do me in the back if you got the nuts."

Manny took a slow, careful step, then another, waiting to hear himself get shot. Then he ran across the depot and through the doors. He slid and stumbled in the slush. Big flakes swirled. Childs and the girl were gone.

Manny hustled back inside to stick his gun up Trooper Green's ass, but Green and Jackson were also gone. For a moment Manny stood alone. Passengers and baggage came and went.

He found a pay phone and called Ray. "They're gone, he said. "We lose."

28

Never before, not in the bin, not in the drug trade, had Mears ever met a man more single-minded than himself. But Biff Dunn, as they fell toward the unknown, *held Mears's throat* rather than protect himself against landing. Mears remembered this; his throat still burned. Mears knew that they had been five floors up and knew that the bay was below them and that they would both survive the drop. Even so, *he* had let go and balled up, feeling Dunn underneath him slap the surface and go limp, knocked out. Mears swam away fast, hoping Dunn would sink and die. This is what Mears was thinking Sunday at dawn, dressed in Father Sedgewick's priest suit and holding Dr. Lemuel Childs at gunpoint.

"You were supposed to meet me last night," the doctor was whimpering after Mears clocked him and took his gun, a pitiful one-bullet derringer.

"I got busy," Mears said. "Where's the package?"

At first Childs claimed he'd thrown the pound of pure crystal *d*-lysergic acid diethylamide in the Charles when Mears no-showed, but Mears yanked him close by the neck and inserted the derringer in the doc's mouth, serenely prepared to blow his skull off and toss Childs's apartment for the package, which was undoubtedly here. Childs broke and limped to the bookcase, finding a hollowed-out *Webster's Dictionary*, opening to the N's, and producing a plastic sandwich bag full of tan powder. *A hollow book*, Mears was thinking. *How corny.*

He made the doctor glove up and weigh out a gram of powder, then watched as Childs prepared a dilute solution, one part pure crystal LSD to one thousand parts Beantown tap water.

"Easy there," Mears taunted. "That shit's worth lots more than you are. I been wondering. You've handed out a few thousand acid trips in your day. Ever try it yourself?"

Childs shook his head at the awful thought.

Mears thought about Biff Dunn, who didn't care where he landed so long as he kept his hands on Mears's neck. He could like Dunn for that. They were kin now. Both had been through nuthouse jails, forced druggings, and punitive shock treatment, and come out the other side. He wondered if Biff Dunn had drowned last night or had somehow dragged himself out of the bay. If Dunn was alive, they would meet again. If Dunn was alive, Mears would someday kill him.

He took the dilute solution from Childs and made the doctor dry and iron the priest suit. He lifted Childs's wallet and demanded his wristwatch, then he did something he had been waiting years to do: he put on a rubber glove and licked his index finger, dipped the wet finger in the crystal dust, picking up a huge dose, slapped Childs to the carpet, and jammed the gloved finger in the old man's mouth.

"Suck," he ordered.

Childs held his jaws wide, squirming away from the finger.

"Suck!" shouted Mears, pistol hard between Childs's eyes.

Those eyes closed as Childs sucked Mears's finger. Mears stayed in that position until satisfied with his revenge, then yanked his hand out of Childs's face, empty glove tangling in Childs's teeth.

"The drug'll hit soon," Mears said, opening the door, pocketing the derringer. "If you stay here in the quiet room, you might not have a massive psychotic episode."

Childs curled up on the carpet and started weeping.

"Remember me," Mears said.

He flagged a taxi to West Dedham Street. His keys were lost in the bay, so he kicked open the door, and found the four thousand Eucharist under a loose board in the closet where he had hidden them after clearing out of Jamaica Plain. He dumped the bags on the unmade bed and ran his hand through the flesh of God. He put on rubber gloves and carefully applied the LSD from an eyedropper.

He looked at Childs's watch: ten-fifteen. He packed the Eucharist back into the plastic bags, rinsed the gloves in the toilet, then stripped them off. He put the Eucharist in a small black satchel.

Mears stepped through his own door and started down West Dedham Street. The priest collar pinched where Biff Dunn had wrung his neck.

It was like a reunion behind the Operation Clambake barricades. Guys Manny hadn't seen since the Academy, guys posted to the back beyond of Hyde Park or Wonderland, cops with inside jobs at Cartography or Personnel, thirty-year inspectors who hadn't buttoned a uniform in years—all mobilized to protect the Cardinal from a crowd of Catholics. Manny looked down Washington Street and saw unbroken blue.

A hearty, red-faced captain from Mounted briefed supervisors, sergeants and up, first thing. About eight thousand souls would attend the English mass, code-named "the Clambake" for the air, including Richard Cardinal Cushing himself, who would be called "Red Riding Hood," flanked by dozens of chancery grandees. About ten thousand people were expected in the streets around Holy Cross Cathedral—Washington, Union Park, Reynolds, and Harrison—either to heckle Red Riding Hood or to stop hecklers from heckling.

"Of the ten thousand, how many want to stop the mass, and

how many want to stop anybody from stopping it?" asked some wiseacre eager to impress this rare assemblage of downtown brass.

"We're ready for anything," the Mounted captain side-stepped.

Wiseacre again: "Do we have an idea of the tactics the pro-testers might use to stop the mass? I mean, are they talking about a sit-in or a rush on our barricades, or what?"

The captain shot him an annoyed frown, no doubt wondering what a "sit-in" was. Manny decided this cap was from the make-a-line-and-look-mean school of crowd control, which suited Manny fine.

The briefing broke up just past nine. Red Riding Hood would depart his official residence by slow motorcade at ten hundred hours—10:00 A.M.—arriving at Holy Cross Cathedral forty-five minutes later. Mass would begin at 11: 15 A.M.

Riot helmets and long batons were handed out. A rented truck pulled up in front of the cathedral. Men hopped from the cab and carried sealed boxes into the church.

"Shouldn't we check them?" Manny heard Wiseacre ask a lieu-tenant. "The boxes, I mean. You know, for bombs, or something."

"Nah," the lieutenant said. "It's been okayed. Those boxes have the new mass books, just printed yesterday."

"New mass books?"

"Yeah. In English."

The Little Sisters of Charity, Dover, under contract with the Cardinal and in strict adherence to canon law, baked all hosts used at mass throughout the Archdiocese of Boston. They beat the dough from unleavened wheat flour and rolled it flat. They had rolled manu-ally for sixty years, until the older sisters started dying off and the skilled hands dwindled and a salesman, nephew to one of the nuns, persuaded them to buy a machine made by a very nice com-pany called Hobart. The machine flattened the dough, and the sisters baked it quickly, at high heat, on wide steel tins. The dough came out an off-white crust. The sisters had a stamp, made years ago, which cut perfect, quarter-sized circles, imprinting a cross —+—in the middle of each wafer. The Sisters of Charity made five million hosts a year for use in the parishes. There were 1.1 million baptized Catholics in Greater Boston. About a third of these took communion each Sunday, on six annual Holy Days of Obligation, at a dozen other saints' feasts, when Catholics got married, when they died. The stamping, which was close work, took hours. But it was useful to God, and the sisters loved it. Finally, two old sisters with failing eyes inspected each host, checking for proper circular shape, identical +'s, wafer-thinness, off-white color flecked lightly with traces of grain. Canon law stressed uniformity, and the sisters took inspection seriously. Their wafers were trucked daily by a fine Italian man and his sons to the churches, where priests raised the wafers in mass, transforming them by miraculous sacrament from crusts to Eucharist, the literal flesh of God. The believers, 11 million, some perhaps weak of faith, couldn't see God or taste God. They had only these little white wafers to see and taste. God did not vary; neither could they.

The wafers for the first-ever English-language mass to be celebrated by the Cardinal at Holy Cross Cathedral that Sunday were baked, stamped, and inspected by midnight Friday, and delivered by the Italian man's sons to the chancery in Brighton Saturday midday, where the chancellor himself, Monsignor Martin Pasqua, signed for them. Pasqua carried the wafers to a storage room maintained for that purpose. Because they were mere hosts—not yet consecrated Eucharist—they could be touched by the hands of nonpriests and stored like anything else.

Pasqua rose Sunday morning and checked to be sure the new mass books, all in English, carefully proofread by fathers from the seminary, were en route from the printers to the cathedral. He opened the Cardinal's safe and removed the ciborium, an ornate brass box designated by canon law as the sole proper receptacle for already-consecrated Eucharist. Inside were something like four thousand white hosts. These were not, as the Cardinal and the *Boston Globe* believed, Eucharist consecrated by the hand of Pope Paul VI. George Sedgewick, rest his soul, had lost those hosts to a mugger at Logan on New Year's Eve. These were, instead, ordinary Eucharist rendered flesh of God by Pasqua himself at regular daily masses in the chancery chapel and skimmed, fifty at a time. Pasqua was running a small fraud on the Cardinal and on the believers who would gather at the cathedral to finally worship in English and take communion, mingled together, consecrated under the Latin rite in Rome and under the English rite in Boston. The mingled communion was itself a symbol of blended continuum, Latin to English, old to new, a wedding sealed by the Pope himself. The tabloids ate it up. Pasqua was a pragmatist. He couldn't reveal that his chosen courier, Father Sedgewick, had let four thousand fragments of God fall into the hands of hoodlums. What, besides the questionable virtue of honesty for its own sake, would this accomplish? It would sabotage the English mass, give the conservatives an excuse to condemn the entire reform, fill confused flocks with more confusion. No. The baffling Latin Church had been dying for years; declining Sunday numbers proved it. Pasqua believed in killing it off for the vital and exciting replacement: worship in English. He would not let a silly scandal over lost Eucharist endanger what they would do at the cathedral today.

Pasqua carried the brass ciborium containing the four thousand Eucharist from his own daily masses to his car and locked it in the trunk. He went to the chancery storeroom for the wafers that had been delivered from the sisters' bakery the previous day.

He placed the cardboard box on the backseat. He drove to the cathedral.

Ray was up early in his brother's empty apartment, keeping a vigil in case Biff turned up. Manny's last words from the pay phone the night before were echoing in Ray's head like a taunt: *They're gone. We lose.*

Ray made coffee and put it together. Mears learns from Childs that the priest will be alone at the airport on New Year's Eve. Mears goes to the airport to kill Sedgewick. Getting four thousand communion wafers and the priest's clothes in the bargain, well, that was just dumb luck. Mears keeps the priest suit and the flesh of God for some strange gig of his own.

Ray looked out the kitchen window down the hill toward the harbor. The snow of the night before was almost gone, melted to patches. The day had come up mild, mostly clear, tattered white clouds running out to the sea. Ray saw a lone figure struggling up the hill, an old man or a hurting drunk back from a brutal Saturday night. Ray watched the figure maybe five seconds before realizing that the man was wet, as if he'd just hauled himself out of the bay, and that the wet man was Biff. Ray ran down the stairs and down the hill, slipping on thawed ice, scraping his palms and tearing the right knee of his pants. Biff was dripping, smeared with mud, and racked with shivers. The brothers hugged quickly, awkwardly, then remembered themselves. Ray hung his arm over Biff's shoulders and helped him up to the flat, firing questions. Biff's teeth chattered.

Ray poured a quart of coffee into his brother and got him dry clothes. Biff stopped shaking, and said, "I went back to City & County. Mears was waiting. Dressed as a priest. They strapped me in to some kind of generator and then Mears tried to kill me, or drive me crazy. I broke out, got my hands on Mears." Biff held his hands before him, gesturing strangulation. "I remember falling, throttling Mears, him letting go of me. I kept both my hands on his fucking throat—I didn't care if we hit street or what. We fell, I don't know—seemed like it took a while. We hit water. Me first, big black *smack*—so goddam cold, the harbor, and so black."

He shook his head.

"I'm fighting for air, and I think it's because Mears is choking the life out of me. I'm hitting at him, kicking, fighting, then I realize it's just the ocean—I'm swallowing salt water and splashing around by myself. He's gone. There's a big hullabaloo on shore, but I know the troopers got a warrant for me. If I let them rescue me, I go to jail. I look across the bay and I see the lights of the city, so I swim for it. Real slow. The big tide's trying to drag me away. I'm fighting to get back to shore, swimming and floating and swimming, and I'm so tired. I coulda been swimming straight out into the open sea for all I know. Jesus, I nearly gave in fifty times. The only thing that kept me going was I got to live to kill Joe Mears, someday, someplace. Then the dawn starts coming up, and I'm a hundred yards from land. Jesus Christ. Thank you God for sparing me so I can kill that evil monster for you. I swim in, walk on the sand, throw up, and pass out. A dog wakes me up later, nosing at my balls like I'm dead."

He lit a cigarette, let out two ribbons of blue-gray smoke, one for each nostril.

"Fuck 'em all," he said. "I survived."

As Biff showered—this time for real—Ray sat alone at the kitchen table. The tabletop was white Formica with tiny gray-silver flecks. It had been sitting in the middle of this kitchen since his parents had moved into this flat. Ray traced the dips in the worn Formica and thought about Joe Mears.

Ray would never know exactly what had happened at the Portsmouth Naval Hospital, but he knew enough to understand

Mears's murderous rage. But the rest was a puzzle. Why wear a priest suit around Jamaica Plain? And the Bible next to the bed at Mears's place in Jamaica Plain—what was that for? The Bible was in Latin. Did Mears know Latin?

Caesar Raines said that Mears was up to something big. Mears hit Caesar up for money—ten grand, which Ray had traced to Childs through the doctor's bank account. Childs spent the money scoring Mears a huge package of acid just before acid went criminal. The acid was part of the puzzle—a big part.

A Bible, a priest suit, some wafers, and acid.

Any other dealer would have blown town right after the cops raided apartment 33, but not Mears: he stayed because he was up to something big.

Ray thought about his brother getting electroshock from Mears. Of all the ways to kill Biff at City & County, Mears—the shock treatment victim—chose shock treatment. It's an old story: a beaten child grows up to beat his children. Perhaps without knowing it, Mears was reenacting Portsmouth in Boston.

Which brought Ray back to the big thing Mears had stayed in town to pull off. But what was the big thing? What was Mears planning?

The Latin, the wafers, the acid, the shock.

He called the chancery and asked for Monsignor Martin Pasqua. He was told that Pasqua was out until the end of the day.

"This is Father Kelly. I must reach Monsignor Pasqua. Any idea where he is?"

"Sure, Father. He's gone to the Cardinal's mass at Holy Cross Cathedral."

The English mass. Ray thanked her and hung up.

Ray redialed. "Hi," he said. "Father Kelly again. What time's the Cardinal's mass getting started?"

The receptionist consulted some paper. "Eleven-fifteen," she said.

It was just before eleven. Ray was shouting in the bathroom, telling Biff to finish the shower. "We gotta get out of here. *Now.*"

Manny was posted to the southeast corner of Washington and Union Park, a dozen men under his command, with orders to keep the unwelcome from crossing Washington to the wide stone steps in front of the cathedral. He watched a car pull up and saw a priest take a cardboard box from the backseat and put it under his arm. The priest struggled with a second box, this one brass, which was in the trunk.

Mass was still an hour off, and a thin line of protesters were gathering, signs saying SAVE THE MASS and CATH'CS NOT COMMIES, stacked against a building. Manny sent a patrolman to help the priest. The cop shut the trunk for the priest and tried to take the heavy brass box, but the priest said no. He let the cop take the lighter cardboard box and follow him inside the cathedral.

Manny's radio talked. "All units, be advised: Red Riding Hood is in the forest, heading for the Clambake, ETA fifteen minutes. Over." Manny shook his head. Why not say "The motorcade's stuck in traffic—he'll be here in fifteen"? As if these people were here to kill him. The protesters were pipefitters and bricklayers and their wives, devout, hardworking whites who simply hated all the changes. Manny whaled on his seven daughters when they skipped mass, though he himself rarely went. Church was a woman's thing. Dot said the switch to English would lead to a breakdown of all morality. Manny had even been afraid that she would be among the protesters today.

"What next?" she asked. "Abolish confession? Sex outside wedlock? Condoms?" Manny personally couldn't give a shit.

More claptrap on the radio: "All units, be advised, Red Riding Hood still in forest, ETA six, repeat six, minutes. Footposts along Washington form up, move those bodies back. Over."

Manny called his platoon into line. The protesters, numbers

swelling fast, saw that something was going on with the riot cops, and figured the Cardinal, that back-stabbing SOB, was near. They, too, formed a line. A few called out heckles at random, as if practicing.

Manny, back to the cathedral, did not see the redheaded priest arrive on foot and go inside.

Workmen were finishing a jury-rigged dais as Joe Mears padded softly down the center aisle of the cathedral. The new rules. The altar, set by canon law sixteen hundred years ago in the sacristy wall, priest's back to the faithful, was now turned around. The Cardinal would celebrate mass facing his flock.

Mears figured the hosts would be kept in back while the priests suited up. There would be a gaggle of fathers in the sacristy, donning the garments special to the mass—alb, amice, chasuble, cincture, and stole—gabbing and dressing, like backstage at the vaudeville. The unconsecrated hosts would be loaded in gold chalices by a doughy altar boy or two, nobody paying much attention. Mears would send the altar boys on some errand, then finish their job, slipping his drugged Eucharist into the cups. He would stay as long as he could, watch beautiful *d*-lysergic steal over thousands of uptight a-holes, *in church*, then lam. He had 494 grams of pure Sandoz acid in his right jacket pocket and was bound for the West Coast, where he planned to be the most important man around. He'd catch a plane for California, get up Monday, and laugh at the morning papers. Even the Navy couldn't hush *this* up.

Mears in the sacristy saw exactly what he expected: backstage at the vaudeville. He realized the Cardinal himself was there. Mears had a gun in his pocket and could murder His Eminence right now. But this would fuck up the California plan. A gang of priests gathered around Cushing's old white head, kissing his ass. A few others sat to the side, studying the new English mass book in glum silence. Two altar boys were at the end of the room with three trays, twelve big gold cups per tray. The altar boys were opening a cardboard box containing wafers.

"Where you fellas from?" Mears inquired briskly. They were both about twelve, pale and gangly.

"'Maculate C'ception, W'bin."

"Well, there's a Father Biff says he needs to see you out front right now."

"But we gotta do this—"

"Get going. I'll finish for you."

Mears placed the black bag behind the cardboard box and began filling the chalices with acid-laced Eucharist. He risked a self-dosing, handling the wafers without gloves, but gloves would be too obvious, and he knew either way his head would be clear long enough to finish this and fly west.

Ray, Biff in tow, rushed the police lines along Washington Street. Ray was seeing nothing but strange faces, desk guys mobilized for Operation Clambake, and nobody would let him through.

He heard his name. It was Manny in riot gear. Manny fought his way to them through the crowd and hugged Biff. Ray was shouting that Mears was inside the cathedral right then, impersonating a priest, sticking drugs in the communion.

Manny took off his helmet to hear, letting go of Biff. Ray shouted it again.

"C'mon," Ray shouted over the heckles and chanting.

"C'mon where?" Manny shouted back.

"C'mon inside. I think Mears dosed the Eucharist. I brought Biff to identify Mears. If Mears is here, we know I'm right."

"And if you're right, then what? Stop the fucking mass and seize all the communion wafers we find?"

Ray hadn't thought of this, "Why not? It's *evidence*, isn't it?"

"You are nuts. Where the hell's *he* going?"

Biff crossed Washington flashing his shield in the direction of the last line of cops and disappeared inside the cathedral. He had heard Ray say that Mears was inside dosing the hosts, and he was going to find Mears and kill him.

Eight thousand were expected, but more came. They sang a hymn as the Cardinal's train entered grandly, "Holy God, We Praise Thy Name," in English, as on every other Sunday.

The crowd sat down, and Cushing stood up, new mass book with the unfamiliar words in the familiar language propped up discreetly before him. Could he do it? Could he break the spell of sixteen hundred years of Latin? *In nomine Patris, et Filii, et Spiritus Sancti,* that was how the mass began.

Cushing let them settle in their seats, then, almost casually, a revolution:

"In the name of the Father, and of the Son, and of the Holy Spirit. Amen."

And he was already ten or fifteen words beyond *Amen* before the faithful realized what they had heard.

There, Monsignor Pasqua thought, looking at ten thousand faces from the wings, *that didn't hurt now, did it?* His heart flapped in his chest, and for a moment he thought coronary. It didn't matter; he had lived to see today. He stopped and thanked God.

Biff ran up the center aisle. The Cardinal paused at the commotion before him and saw the raggedy man standing alone. Biff scanned the faces of the assembled Archdiocesan hierarchy—His Eminence himself, auxiliary bishops, fancy monsignors from all over—like a long robbery lineup. No Mears. He shook off the ushers again, showing ID.

He went out a side door, hurrying down a hallway that led to the back of the cathedral, figuring Mears was here somewhere. Biff tossed the sacristy, the stairwell, the street out the back door.

He threw open a broom closet, a toilet, another closet. Mears was gone, this time for real.

Biff calmly walked back through the sacristy and onto the spot-lit altar, bullying his way through bishops and monsignors, clumsy in their heavy vestments. Biff gathered up the trays of chalices in his arms, as much as he could hold, spilling and dropping many, then ran and stumbled through the sacristy and out the back door of the cathedral.

For a moment Biff Dunn stood alone, arms full of brass cups, and remembered this street—Union Park, he thought that was the name. He had been a cop here in another lifetime. Behind Biff, all hell broke loose, bishops and cops and everybody else tearing after him.

Biff simply released what he had. That was all. Just let it go. Gold cups clattered to the pavement as the first burly usher stopped short to watch in horror. Wafers tumbled everywhere, rolling like little wheels, blowing down the street, sticking in wet clumps to the shoes and pant legs of the arriving mob.

epilogue

1967

"THE HOSTS were dosed!" Ray had screamed, begging the mob not to shred his brother.

Nobody got it until His Eminence Richard Cardinal Cushing started acting funny. He had taken and eaten first, as was liturgical practice, the only person to sample the chalices. It was never confirmed that His Eminence took an acid trip, although when Monsignor Pasqua rushed him to a limousine, Cushing was studying his cufflinks with mounting awe.

The Cardinal was his old self soon enough. The next morning, he summoned the mayor and demanded Biff Dunn's head.

Ray and Vinnie Sullivan and Manny told everyone with ears to test the wafers for LSD—just *test* them—but nobody listened until Lem Childs came forward. He had survived a harrowing acid trip at Joe Mears's hands, and he had seen in his hallucinations the whole folly of his life. Childs was finally ready to talk about the Special Wing, the Navy's LSD experiments, and the deaths which followed: Poole, Zimquist, Garrett Hays, Father Sedgewick. He was ready to admit selling fentanyl and acid to Joe Mears to save his own skin.

Ray sent Lem Childs to Martin Pasqua at the chancery. Pasqua didn't want to believe Childs's story, since it implicated Father Wedgewick in the cruel experiments, but there remained the undeniable record of Sedgewick's scapular and self-scourging from the January autopsy. *Something* had happened in Portsmouth.

Pasqua was willing to test the wafers salvaged from the sidewalk. He saw a problem, however: only a priest could touch

Eucharist, but only a chemist could test them. Pasqua dug up an old Marquette Jesuit who taught organic chem. The Jesuit took the hosts into a lab and found that they were covered with *d*-lysergic acid diethylamide. Ray pounced on these results, insisting that the test cleared Biff of everything—proving both that Biff was drugged when he shot Shecky and that, by hijacking the chalices, Biff had saved thousands of people from a nightmare he himself had already endured.

Strangely, it was Martin Pasqua, Cushing's hatchet man, who pressed Johnny Cahill to do a package deal. Biff would retire from the Boston Police Department on one-quarter disability, sixty bucks a month; in return, Cahill would drop all charges forever. Pasqua got the Cardinal to weigh in on Biff's side, but Johnny Cahill hung tough until he got the prize he really wanted: Ray Dunn's signature on a letter of resignation in which he confessed to burglary, bribery, and abuse of prosecution. The letter went to Johnny Cahill's safe, silencing Ray and clearing the path for Eddie Cahill's run for DA that fall. As a threat of any kind to the emerging Cahill dynasty, Ray Dunn was finished—tainted, fairly or not, as a bag man's son and a madman's brother—and though Ray's letter of resignation never left Johnny's safe, word of its contents leaked out. Johnny and Eddie saw to that.

Eddie Cahill proved as weak a candidate as he was a man, and several challengers came forward, including an assistant DA who was very much like Ray Dunn, right down to his name, Ron Dolan. Both were respected lawyers from cop families. Both had three sons. Ray Dunn was thirty-four. Ron Dolan thirty-six. The two were so alike in looks and style and even in certain small mannerisms that it was a little spooky. It was as if the clean and promising half of Ray Dunn had been cut away and made into the perfect civil servant.

Ron Dolan beat Eddie Cahill two to one in the Democratic primary, then rolled to victory in the November general. He served quietly and well as Suffolk County DA until 1972, when he foolishly ran for governor. He was one of four candidates crushed by a little-known state senator from Brookline named Michael Dukakis.

Of course, a question remained: if Ron Dolan was everything clean and promising in Ray Dunn, what was left for Ray himself?

Ray Dunn became one of those ex-prosecutors who haunt the criminal courts, starving for work but ashamed to be seen in the courthouse canteen with the mugger or wife-beater he happened to represent that day. Ray had scorned such men until he joined their ranks.

Now he vowed that he would be different. He vowed he would be as devoted to defending as he had once been to prosecuting, and even made little rules to salve his conscience: no violent criminals, no sex offenders, no drug dealers. But this left almost nobody to defend, and by early 1967, Ray was facing eviction from his storefront office, foreclosure on his house, and personal bankruptcy, until deliverance came from an unlikely quarter.

Caesar Raines was paroled after serving a year for his part in the Gibraltar operation. Soon after his release, Narco busted him yet again. Caesar asked Ray to handle the defense and put a stack of fifties on Ray's desk.

"What is it this time?" Ray asked.

"Just good old dope," Caesar said. "I'm through messin' with the funky stuff."

"Haven't you learned your lesson?"

Caesar got all wry and grandfatherly. "Old dogs, old tricks. How 'bout it?"

"This drug money?" Ray asked, holding the cash retainer like one of Caesar's Chinese hand fans.

"No." Caesar smiled. "It's American money."

Manny Manning finished his tour in Narco and accepted a job teaching tactics at the Academy, where he was an awesome, battle-scarred figure to the cadets. He spent his free time on his motorboat, fighting the bluefish off Hull. Nat Butterman took over the team, becoming Sergeant Butterman, with Paddy Hicks as his Shecky Bliss.

Ray went to Manny's house for dinner and they argued bitterly about the Vietnam War.

"It's just another Operation Pressure Point," Ray said. "A half million troops, ten million bucks a day, for what? Bodycounts. Headlines. Clear the Vietcong out of the South End and move them into the Back Bay. Sound familiar, Manny?"

Manny's wife still complained about Sunday mass in English, the language of grocery shopping and police radio.

"It isn't right," she protested. "Mass should be in Latin. That's how it was for a thousand years. Why does everything have to *change*, Manny?"

Mary-Pat wasn't at that dinner. She and Ray had separated a few months before and were seeing a marriage counselor twice a week. Ray, being old school, hated paying a stranger by the hour to invade his privacy, but Mary-Pat said if he didn't like the marriage counselor, he could see a divorce lawyer. Ray moved in with Biff.

The first counselor they saw told them to scream.

Mary-Pat screamed right there in the man's office, long and loud, her tonsils vibrating. Then it was Ray's turn.

"Go ahead," the counselor coaxed. "Let it out."

Ray told Mary-Pat, "I'm sorry for whatever I did or didn't do. I'll be better in the future. Can we leave now, please?"

"*Scream*," she screamed at him, and opened her mouth to show him how.

But Ray couldn't scream, not in the marriage counselor's office, not in the elevator to the street with Mary-Pat, not even alone by the highway late that night when he pulled over at a rest stop and tried his hardest.

The next counselor hypnotized them. Mary-Pat, in a trance,

admitted that she loved Win Babcock. She wept. She told a long story about how she had thrown herself at Win for a year until she realized that he didn't love her back.

When Ray was hypnotized, the counselor asked him about his father and mother, and Ray, who didn't *feel* hypnotized, told the guy the plain truth: his father was a good man who fucked up a couple things and his mother was better than most. The man listened and took notes, then snapped his fingers sharply.

He asked Ray, "Do you remember what you just told me?"

Ray was desperate to please his wife, which meant pleasing this fucking clown, so he acted like a child just awakened. "No," he said. "Did I have a breakthrough?"

He didn't have a breakthrough—he didn't know what a breakthrough was. Instead, he had his sons every weekend at Biff's apartment, and he did all the dad things with them that he had been too busy to do when he was first assistant DA. He took them to ballgames, to playgrounds, and to the petting zoo—and when it rained he took them to museums, until they ran out of museums.

Ray Jr. was stoic, a Dunn. Timmy was more like Mary-Pat— dreamy and moody, easily excited and often disappointed. Stephen, who was just starting to talk, couldn't remember his parents together. He seemed the happiest of them all.

Biff spent his days pasting newspaper clippings into used photo albums he bought at the Salvation Army. One album was labeled *Precious Memories*, another *Our Daughter's Wedding*. Biff called the photo albums "books," a Narco term for surveillance files kept on long-term targets. There had once been books for Caesar Raines, for Bo Norman, and for the Cuban Angel. Ray figured Biff was carefully building a case against reality.

Biff had one book for clippings on the Kennedy assassination, another for applesauce recipes, a third for crossword puzzles he had "solved" by filling in the squares with careful, block-print

gibberish A three-letter word for "Santa pal"? Biff wrote NUD.
Seven letters, "Madagascar port"? Biff tried AXYLMOP. He sat in his
flat off Dorchester Bay listening to three radios. He spent hours
tuning the knobs down and up, trolling for a lost clue to everything that had happened.

In March 1967, Biff, at long last, detected the Clue. He snapped
two of his radios off and sat riveted to a song on the third radio:

> One pill makes you larger
> And one pill makes you small,
> But the ones that mother gives you
> Don't do anything at all.
> Go ask Alice
> When she's ten feet tall.

Biff took a trolley to Harvard Square and wound up in the
Discomat across Mass Ave from the Yard. He chatted up kids in
the record store. They told him about something totally new, The
Sound of San Francisco.

"What does The Sound of San Francisco sound like?" Biff
asked. He was twenty-nine, but looked forty-five. Everyone is
hitching out there for the Summer of Love, the kids said. It was
free space, be-ins, groovy music, great drugs.

"Acid?" Biff asked.

The most, the best, the purest, he was told.

Biff purchased the single "White Rabbit," by the Jefferson
Airplane, and listened to it in his ratty flat 102 times. During the
103rd listening, Biff made up what was left of his mind.

He cashed out his savings account and went up to Navy Avenue in the Heights. He saw a guy he once knew and paid him one
hundred dollars for a Marine-issue Colt .45 and two clips stolen
from a ship bound for Indochina.

That night, Ray came back from a desultory car ride with his sons and put them all to bed in his own room in the flat. Ray made up the couch and was ready to go to sleep on it when Biff dropped his bomb.

"I'm taking the bus to San Francisco," he said.

"What the hell for?" Ray asked.

"Make a new start," Biff bluffed. "Clean slate."

Ray slapped his pillow and threw it on the couch. "Forget about it," he said.

Biff dropped the pretense. "I got to go," he said. "Mears is out there. I heard him."

Biff played "White Rabbit" for his brother, volume low so as not to disturb Ray's sons in the back bedroom.

"That's a dumb song," Ray remarked when it was over.

The two brothers argued in hushed and bitter tones all night, finally settling down to beans and franks at midnight. They chewed in silence around the old kitchen table.

The next morning, Ray piled his sons in the car and drove Biff to Greyhound. Ray and Biff hugged goodbye alongside the bus. Ray felt the gun on Biff's hip.

Ray recoiled, "What the hell's that?"

Biff looked Ray in the eyes. "I'm gonna find Joe Mears in the Summer of Love. I'm gonna put this fat Colt in his face."

"Then?"

Biff said, "Etcetera."

The boys were whining for breakfast as Ray watched the Greyhound make the pike. Ray herded them back into the car and let them whine. He drove, without knowing why, to the Paulist Fathers' church on the Common. Ray dragged his sons inside and tucked five bucks—all he had—in the poor box for Biff. Ray had not been inside a church since his brother threw the hosts in the gutter.

Ray meant to go, but stayed. For the first time in his life, he heard mass in this language.